PILOT FOR THE KING
The Story of a Wayward Wing-Man

Table of Contents

PREFACE

At times we all battle with an inner voice not knowing its origin or objective. Those whispers to our inner being can come from God, the enemy, acquaintances, circumstance, or they can be generated as a result of our own carnal or temporal desires. Being able to tell the difference is probably one of life's greatest challenges as we tend to listen to and follow the influences upon our heart. I've been both a victim and guilty of situations that could have been altered for the better if they were acted on earlier.

Our present situation is a result of the choices we've made along the way. If we are given a choice between life and death, blessing and cursing, we have the ability and choice to be part of something wonderful. Even those born into seemingly hopeless situations are given a choice to accept a savior that is waiting with open and embracing arms.

We cannot anticipate all the trials we will face throughout our lives. We are incapable of avoiding every obstacle or the pain associated with our failures and frailties. Adversity in some form is a promise of life on this earth. Facing that, I make the conscious effort in choosing to be part of the blessing rather than succumbing to the temptations of the curse.

My experiences as a pilot are part of a journey that has taken me through many of my own trying times. Much like Billy Hawklyn, even when I chose the wrong path, a divine guidance always saw me through. I'm thankful that God is patient, for He has been, and continues to be, exceedingly patient with me.

I give Him the glory and honor for giving me life, and for that I am and will be eternally grateful.

—*W. G. Doscher*

INTRODUCTION

Prior to the establishment of the North American Free Trade Agreement (NAFTA), which became effective on January 1, 1994, duties and tariffs imposed on trade between the U.S. and Mexico created a rich environment for smuggling. The booming electronics industry created a new demand for the flow of contraband and the decade between 1975 and 1985 was its heyday. The technology of micro-electronics had arrived in the marketplace, prompting consumer desire for a portable class of personal devices throughout the world—including the developing countries of Latin America and Mexico. Portable televisions and cassette tape players were among the most popular items in those countries. With new orders at an all-time high, the open-minded entrepreneur could realize hefty gains.

The smuggling of electronics was an inherently risky proposition, and flying those products in an airplane even more so. The airstrips or *pistas* scattered around the Mexican countryside were short, rough and unmaintained. Activity was heavily reliant on favorable weather. Navigational aids were unreliable or nonexistent and in poor weather, flying under the cloud deck or, "scud-running" was a pilot's only option. Accidents occurred as pilots tried to sneak under low ceilings in low visibility to deliver their goods. And, of course, there was the risk of capture. The foreign governments assiduously pursued the smugglers, trying to stop the movement of all contraband across their borders.

The smuggling of guns and drugs was also present and the electronics carriers were sometimes confused with those higher-crime operators. To the foreign officials the difference was irrelevant, and shooting down an electronics smuggler was not considered a grievous act should one be mistaken for a gunrunner or a doper.

The authorities constantly patrolled the area, searching for newly built airstrips. A slight offset to the risk of capture was the widespread corruption among law enforcement. If a pilot was captured, ransom money was an attractive temptation to an unscrupulous *capitan* or police chief. It was dirty and corrupt, yet lucrative for the savvy *commandante*.

Surprisingly, the export of electronics from the States was a legitimate activity according to U.S. laws. The American authorities never harassed those hauling southbound contraband and turned a blind eye to the men who flew along the Rio Grande Valley.

PART I

The Mexican Connection

CHAPTER 1

FLYING KITES

I N JULY 1975 MY PARENTS went on a five-day business trip to Chicago. They left my older brother Mark and me, by ourselves, at home in our small Midwestern town.

It was a sunny Saturday and Mark and I were enjoying the second half of our summer vacation. In two months I would turn sixteen. Mark, who was nine years older than I, would be leaving for the weekend and return the following Monday. Until then I would spend the weekend with my grandparents at their home in town. Then Mark and I would spend the final three days at our house.

Mom and Dad figured Mark would take care of the place and keep me out of trouble. They assumed this college graduate would set a good example for me while ensuring that we did the household chores. At twenty-four years of age, Mark was responsible enough all right, but throughout my childhood he had occasionally recruited his naïve little brother to execute some kind of covert plan. More than once I was rescued from the edge of disaster.

Mark was a typical young man of the '60s who enjoyed cars and rock 'n' roll music. On this occasion he saw an opportunity to involve his little brother in yet another adventure.

On this beautiful late summer morning as the folks prepared to set off, I was outside and heard dad in the garage giving Mark some last-minute instructions. Then my parents climbed into the family car and as Mark and I stood waving good-bye, they backed out, turned around and were off. While I watched the car drive away, Mark went back into the house and reappeared with a large manila envelope in his hand. He handed it to me. I saw his name and our address on the front.

"This is what we are going to do," he grinned. "We can complete this project before Mom and Dad get back."

I opened the envelope and removed its contents, noticing the homespun fashion of the inserts. There was a typed letter explaining the details, a doctored black-and-white photo, a set of instructions and a set of blueprints. I suddenly realized what I was holding.

"These are the plans for a hang glider!" I said.

It was a hang glider, a real flying machine! Instantly, I could see myself soaring about the countryside. The design was a 25-foot span Rogallo or delta-wing glider called the "Soaring Hawk." It was an unpowered, homemade contraption where the pilot would hang, suspended by his armpits, in a cradle attached to the underside. These plans were somebody's get-rich-quick scheme you could buy for five dollars. The glider would be constructed of 4 MIL poly sheeting, 15-foot wooden clothes poles, some small-dimension lumber and an assortment of nails, carriage bolts, hose clamps, duct tape and Elmer's glue.

This was hardly your high-tech aerospace vehicle, but on the enclosed letters were black-and-white photos of some teenager actually flying the thing. Never mind trick photography and White-Out—he was flying and that was proof enough for me. Even better, Mark and I had the fifteen dollars that the letter stated our materials would cost.

Mark figured we could spend Monday and Tuesday building this thing in our family's two-car garage, and then fly it on Wednesday. Even if we suffered some setbacks we'd still be able to get in a test flight before the folks got back.

To build an aircraft from a set of mail-order plans and supplies from the local hardware store and lumber yard was about as preposterous as it gets. But to a fifteen-year-old boy the words "it can't be done" don't exist when you place something like this in front of him. And at that age the threat of bodily injury or death was irrelevant since the fifteen-year-old brain hasn't the capacity for such safety-like nonsense.

From that moment on the dream was alive. And in that dream was born all the desire, determination and fortitude I would need to reach the goal and grasp the prize. I didn't know it at the time but in the years to follow I would call upon those attributes to take me through the many challenges I would face.

After a trip to the local lumber yard and hardware store we had everything we needed. We spent Saturday morning inspecting the parts and arranging them on the floor of the garage. I was eager to tear into the project, but Mark had to leave and I lacked the confidence to tackle the build without him.

Mark was getting married in about three weeks and needed to finalize some of the arrangements. Early that afternoon, he dropped me off with my grandparents in town and told me that he'd return around noon on Monday. I spent the next two days dreaming of flight and trying to contain my enthusiasm. I didn't want my grandparents to get suspicious. I spent most of the time in my room at their home poring over the plans, studying every detail . . . and dreaming.

On Monday Mark arrived right on time and we drove back to our house. Everything was as we'd left it on the garage floor, neatly arranged and ready to go. We got to work, measuring and cutting, drilling and bolting, while we talked excitedly about flying and how cool it was that we could build this thing so fast. I was certain we would finish and test-fly the glider before Mom and Dad returned home. With all of the pieces cut and a few of the gussets in place we called it a day.

On Tuesday morning Mark had a couple of things to do in town. Since he was the master craftsman on the project, I decided to wait for him to get back. It was well into the afternoon when he got home, and soon we were building the frame of the glider. Next we suspended the kite upside down exactly twelve inches off the garage floor. The idea was to attach the poly sheeting to the clothes poles, allowing it to droop between each of the three poles at their trailing edges with the low points just touching the garage floor. This created a kind of dihedral that would form the sail and help stabilize the craft.

Soon it was dark outside. We figured we only had a couple of hours of work left to do, so we left the next step—the setting of the dihedral—for Wednesday.

On Wednesday I was up and out of bed and tinkering in the garage long before Mark got there. I decided to set the sail alone as I could no longer wait for my brother to show up. Besides, I was beginning to gain confidence in my aeronautical engineering skills and figured that this wasn't so difficult after all.

With the four blocks, each twelve inches high, the kite sat off the floor in a level position. I attached the poly sheet to each of the wing poles. It was exciting watching this thing being born—it was alive and the few remaining attachments were only moments from being completed. I was actually going to fly today! I attached one final bolt and gave each critical point a once-over. The glider was finished.

A flying machine in our garage! What a thought. So this is how the Wright brothers must have felt on that morning at Kitty Hawk. My heart raced.

I realized that I couldn't get this thing, with its 25-foot wingspan, out of the garage alone. But how could I wait for Mark to surface? It would take at least two sets of hands to maneuver the glider off the blocks, rotate it in order to get it out the garage door, and then flip it upright.

Mark must have sensed my excitement as he was up earlier than usual and appeared in the doorway in his underwear. He looked at the completed aircraft. I explained how easy it had been to attach the plastic. He looked satisfied.

"Good," he said. "We'll take it out this afternoon."

We thought it wise to leave the garage door closed. This would avoid damage should a gust of wind happen to flip the glider around.

Suddenly I felt hesitant. It hit me: I could go up and actually fall from this thing. I realized why Mark had inserted delays throughout our production schedule. He had also been feeling the nervousness that I was experiencing. This thing could kill us!

"Okay," I said. "Let's make sure everything is tight."

As Mark looked on I rechecked the wires and gussets. Then I followed Mark back into the house for a little breakfast and a lot of serious contemplation. I felt like a guinea pig and questioned the motives of my older brother. After all, he suggested that I be the test pilot. Originally I felt honored and fortunate. Now I wasn't so sure. *Hey, what kind of deal is this, anyway?* I thought to myself. I think he was the wiser.

Still, there was something inside me that felt confident. There was something strong that was pulling me in. There was something that even called to me and comforted me. I was ready, the kite was ready, and the day was here. Once again, thoughts of soaring overshadowed my fear and I fantasized about flying to school each day. I could float down and land right in the parking lot. Cool!

Mark still had second thoughts. But he knew how stubborn I could be. Mark could be a great encourager. His words bolstered my confidence in skills I didn't yet possess.

However, what I needed right then wasn't encouragement. What I needed was a good knock on the head, or my Dad giving me a swift kick in the pants and sending me out to the woodpile to split a cord of wood. Then maybe I'd think about my actions and yield to caution rather than run wildly into the unknown without considering the consequences.

Dad always told me, "Act with deliberation." Good advice. But what the hell, he wasn't home, and I was going to fly! I didn't think I was so stupid to go jumping off the barn or anything like that.

Mark and I talked about taking the glider out in the yard and running on flat ground to see how much lift the aircraft could create. Mark thought it best to stick with the gently sloping hills, at least for now.

Now our only obstacle was something that affects every aviator: the weather. A breeze had picked up. Learning to fly this thing required the best conditions a calm day could offer. I was attempting flight before I'd mastered the simple act of driving a car.

Mark and I decided to hold off until that evening after the wind had calmed down. The added time might give me a chance to reconsider our plans. Besides, I needed time to regain some of my courage.

Mark took me to the local drive-in restaurant for lunch. After we had a couple of burgers and a root beer float there were a few errands he wanted to run. Then we could spend the remainder of the day kicking back and waiting for the wind to die down.

When we got back home I immediately went to the garage and stared at the glider. I cleaned up the construction materials and put some of my dad's tools away. Cleaning up after myself was something I didn't normally do, but for this project I was more responsible and considerate of others.

This was new territory for me. Nothing I'd ever done inspired the exhilaration I was feeling. My thoughts raced and my imagination was on fire. The prize seemed within reach, looming before me, waiting to be claimed. I was going to fly and nothing was going to stop me. All I thought about was flying. I didn't even hear the car as it pulled into our driveway.

Suddenly the garage door began to roll upward. I panicked. Someone was about to discover our secret endeavor!

When the garage door had opened all the way I saw the front end of our car sitting in the driveway. My parents just sat there with the motor idling. They could see the glider inside the garage, but they had little idea what it was they were looking at. My mother turned to my father.

"What is that thing?" she asked.

I couldn't hear my father's response, but I didn't need to as I could clearly read his lips.

"It looks like a hang glider," he said.

My mother shook her head and got out of the car.

"No, no. Absolutely not!" she said.

She began to cry. She rushed past me and the kite and stomped into the house.

Dad walked toward me, one eye cast across the contraption sprawled across his garage floor.

"What is it?" he said.

"It's a hang glider!" I replied with a hopeful smile.

"It looks like you did a good job," he said, trying to sound encouraging. "Where's Mark?"

Mark appeared in the door as I pointed out some of the finer points of craftsmanship to my father.

"Who's going to fly this thing?" Dad said to Mark.

Mark shifted uneasily. "Nobody, Dad. I don't think this thing can fly anyway."

Wait a minute! I thought. What was this I was hearing? Wasn't this my older brother who had been so encouraging? Wasn't this the guy who gave me the confidence to go through with it? Hadn't he bought the plans?

No, this was my older and wiser twenty-four-year-old brother saying the words that his father wanted to hear.

Dad turned to me. The look on my face told a completely different story. I believed in this thing and believed in myself enough to risk my own life for it. And it was apparent I'd have to fight for this thing and the chance to experience all of its mysteries.

Dad peered at the kite.

"Where are you going to keep it?" he said.

I told him that it could be easily disassembled and stored. He nodded his head.

"How about you take it apart," he said, "and move it to the barn. We'll discuss the entire matter later."

Dad had a way of settling things down before they got out of hand. I'd like to think he instilled that quality in me, but from somewhere I inherited a gene that longed for adventure. Shortly after I returned from storing the glider in the barn he sat me down in the chair next to his desk.

"Do you know anything about flying?" he asked.

"No, but I can learn," I said.

"Do you know how to turn? Do you know what ailerons or elevators are?"

"No, but there are instructions that came with the plans."

It was obvious to my father that I intended to try this thing out. He and my mother were concerned, and rightly so. I had attempted to fly before. On a winter day with snow blowing into steep drifts around the property, I'd gotten on top of one of our barns with a plan to ride my toboggan off the roof. My parents were relaxing in the house, all warm and cozy, when they looked outside and saw me dragging the wooden sled up the steep pitch to the peak.

At first they were horrified knowing my intentions but then realized what I was doing. I'd loaded the toboggan with a bag of dog food and several cinder blocks for ballast. Instead of jumping onboard and merrily riding the toboggan off the roof, I was going to test it first.

Dad later told me how proud he was that I had the foresight to test my system. He also reminded me of the disastrous results of that test: I didn't want to end up like those broken chunks of cinder block or that busted bag of dog food scattered across the snow far below. He was glad I decided not to take the ride myself.

I never had a fear of high places. Often I'd scramble to the top of one of our barns or climb to the highest branches in one of the many pine trees on our property. One winter I climbed the tallest tree in our yard. It was an old western hemlock that'd been planted by a great uncle around 1900 or so. I wanted to celebrate the season by stringing a bunch of Christmas lights near the top of the tree.

Clutching a handful of lights and a hundred feet of extension cord, I climbed that tree and accomplished what I'd set out to do. The light pattern I made was in a conical shape—it looked like a smaller tree had been perched near the highest boughs. The lights were visible for many miles.

Dad understood my desire for adventure. He knew of that gene as he recalled his own youthful ambitions. He had taken flying lessons himself. I was just a small boy then, and that's when I was first introduced to airplanes. Dad flew out of a grass runway at a nearby airstrip in a Cessna 140 tail dragger. The instructor's name was Tony. Dad never finished the requirements for a private license, but he was able to fly solo cross-country and often practiced flying around the local area.

At one point Dad flew over the state capitol building while workers were applying new gold leaf to the exterior. Apparently Dad made a couple of passes that were a bit too low. When he landed an FAA agent and a very concerned highway patrolman were waiting for him with a few pressing questions.

Later, Dad got the urge to go flying shortly after a heavy snowfall. The countryside was blanketed with about fourteen inches of snow, and Dad wanted to take a look. He called his instructor and explained his plan.

"Sure," Tony laughed. "You can go flying if you can get that thing out of the hangar."

Tony was being sarcastic but Dad didn't catch on. He hung up the phone and headed for the airport. When he arrived at the snowbound airstrip he shoveled out an area in front of the hangar door and pulled the airplane out. He climbed in, started the engine, and taxied his way through the deep snow. The grass strip and all the markers were concealed in white so Dad had to guess where the runway was. (Dad said that it was a little tough finding it, but he knew that it was plenty wide, so he wasn't too worried.)

Satisfied that he'd taxied onto the center, Dad throttled up and accelerated down the runway. The little airplane chugged forward but had trouble burrowing through the deep layer of snow. Dad wasn't discouraged, though. He throttled back and drove a single path with his two main wheels down the length of the runway. At the far end he spun the little Cessna around and applied full power. The plane accelerated down the runway in the tracks he had made and soared into the sky. Victory!

Immediately after liftoff he realized he'd committed himself to a nearly impossible task. When landing he'd have to place the main wheels right back into the narrow furrows he'd just created. And since he'd made only one pass, those furrows were only one tire-width each.

Is there another place I can put down? He thought.

There was no suitable landing strip that had been plowed for many miles around. Dad could have chosen a road, or flown several miles to an alternate airport. Unfortunately he'd neglected to add fuel for a lengthy journey. The roads were not an option because the plows had only made one pass and the snow and ice made it too risky.

Dad flew around in circles for several minutes as he considered his options. If he attempted the snow-covered runway and missed he would plow into the snow and flip the airplane on its back. Eventually, he mustered up the confidence to give it a try. Even in the event of a mishap, a disabled airplane on a closed runway versus a public road was the better choice anyway.

Dad slowed the airplane down to its minimum speed and lined up with the two narrow furrows of the snow-covered landing strip. Slowly he crossed the runway boundary and cut the power. On his first attempt he plopped the plane precisely into the narrow tracks and quickly came to a halt. Fortunately he had kept the Cessna in the tracks and slowed just enough to keep it from flipping over. Dad plowed his way back toward the hangar.

Meanwhile, Tony, who'd heard the sound of an airplane in the skies near his home, arrived at the airport. He wanted to know what fool was out flying. As my father struggled to get the plane back in the hangar, his instructor gave him a good ass-chewing with some choice remarks about the future of his flying career.

Dad never finished his flight training because his lack of judgment and overexcitement could leave his wife a widow with two children. That was my father: able to put his ambitions in perspective. He always had a clear in that way.

Back at the farm I pleaded with my father to let me try out the hang glider. I assured him that I'd stay near small gradual slopes; high cliffs and barn roofs were off-limits. After we discussed my flying technique he agreed to the test flight. That afternoon I inspected the craft with the utmost care. That night I studied the instructions carefully and lay in my bed dreaming of flying.

The next morning I woke up early and carried my glider around the yard, giving it some dry runs. To feel the sail fill with air and the cradle lift in my arms was a thrill I had never imagined. The glider felt light in my arms. Just a little more speed and lift would carry me aloft.

Dad watched as I made a few passes in the front yard.

"Bill, I want to talk to you," he said.

I set the kite down and came up on the porch where he was sitting.

"I talked to your mom and we discussed your desire to fly," he said. "You've got a dream, and Mom and I don't want to get in the way of that. We talked about your future and decided to give you an opportunity to discover more about flying."

I appreciated what Dad was saying. He understood my excitement about flying.

"We set aside money that was intended for college," he continued. "I'm willing to let you use some of that money to take a few flying lessons over at the airport."

I'd never considered taking formal flying lessons. That was like taking the high road and doing this thing in a structured and well-thought-out manner. What a turn my life was taking. Just yesterday I'd thought of nothing more than soaring through the skies with this kite.

Now I might be taking flying lessons in a real airplane. Who could refuse?

The local airport was just a short walk across the cornfield and a mile-long bike ride the long way. That afternoon I rode my bicycle to the airport to get some information on flying lessons. The instructor told me I needed to be at least sixteen years old before I could start. Since my birthday was coming up, I was pretty sure I'd be flying real airplanes very soon.

I spent the rest of the summer cruising the rolling hills with my hang glider. Don't get the wrong impression: when I say "cruising," I actually mean "running." The first time I took that thing down a hill and my feet got light under me, I panicked, dropped the nose and planted myself firmly on the ground. I wasn't a true aviator yet; I was still part of the "firma terra tribe." That is, "The more *firma*, the less *terra*." I was terrified! As I ran around with the hang glider, my lack of skill and ignorance of flight slapped me hard in the face.

One day I finally mustered the nerve to lift my feet and glide a few yards at a time. Occasionally, a summer gust of wind would drive me nose-first into the ground but I was never hurt. Unfortunately the kite didn't fare as well, and soon patches of duct tape added to its look and overall weight.

One afternoon as I prepared to launch, a big gust came along and ripped the kite right out of my hands. It tumbled down a hill and through a ditch. I knew then that my hang-gliding days were over. It was time to abandon folly and move forward.

CHAPTER 2

INITIATION

I STARTED FLYING LESSONS in December of 1975. Because the Midwest winters could be quite harsh my pace was slow and sporadic. When the weather didn't cooperate, I kept busy with my ground school studies.

I first soloed on a Friday the thirteenth. It was February 1976. I'd received a bit more than seven hours of dual instruction when, on a cold but calm winter morning, I showed up at the airport for another flying lesson before I went to school. My instructor and I took off, circled around the pattern, and completed a couple of landings. After the second landing we taxied back to the end of the runway. Darin, my flight instructor, got out of the airplane.

"You've got it from here," he said.

After a brief chat he turned and walked to the concrete block building that housed the office and hangars. I'll never forget his smile and encouragement. I'll never forget his final instructions about following procedures and checklists. Darin showed confidence in me and instilled the confidence I needed to push the throttle forward for the first time alone. At sixteen years of age, I was trying my new wings.

Soloing an aircraft is a lonely feeling at first, yet it's also indescribably exhilarating. The simple mechanics of controlling an airplane under the best of conditions is no great feat. But having complete control over your own destiny—even for just a short time—gives you the confidence to achieve greater things. Anyone who has ever experienced his first solo flight understands that feeling of accomplishment.

I circled the pattern and made the required three takeoffs and landings. Then I taxied in. I'd done it. I'd made it to the first hurdle and cleared it with ease. This flying thing was in my blood. As far as I was concerned there was no turning back now.

After a few more hours in the local pattern Darin prepared me to fly solo again. The difference this time around? I'd be flying out of the local area and going cross-country. I needed several more hours of dual instruction so I could tackle my next hurdle, the private pilot's license. Now it was time for some one-on-one with my father and financier.

Back then the cost to rent an airplane with instructor was twenty-eight dollars an hour. If I paid in advance or in "block time" I could knock the rate down to twenty-four dollars. (The airplane was eighteen bucks and the instructor got six.) By the time I completed my first two solo cross-country flights my father had invested about five hundred dollars, including tax and ground school supplies. The minimum requirement for a private license was forty hours—half of them with an instructor and the other half by myself.

Dad and I talked about aviation careers and college. He wanted me to go to college and had set aside money strictly for that purpose. If I continued with my flying lessons we would need to dip into that college fund.

Private pilots are not able to fly for hire. However, they are able to carry passengers such as friends and family, but only when the weather conditions are good. Most pilots who earn their private license remain at that level. Some will then obtain an instrument rating, which allows them to fly in clouds or without visual reference to the ground. Other pilots choose to add a multi-engine or even a seaplane rating. If cost is not a limitation, adding ratings to a private license enables a pilot to stay current, proficient and enhance safety along with his skills.

If I wanted to pursue a career in aviation, I needed both the instrument rating and a commercial pilot's license. After that my only limitation would be a lack of experience. To fly for a charter company carrying passengers or cargo, a pilot needed a minimum of twelve hundred hours of total flight time. Pilots come up with creative ways of gaining that experience.

Dad didn't want me to make a decision right away. He would let me take a few more flying lessons but said that there would soon come a time I would have to commit, one way or the other. I flew a few more hours and completed all of my cross-country flight requirements. Dad suggested I take a short break from flying, and then make my decision. Even at sixteen I understood the gravity of that decision. I didn't schedule any flying lessons for the next few days and spent the time taking stock of my future.

After a week of soul searching I made my choice. I checked out a few other possible vocations such as forestry or broadcasting, but nothing stuck. Not like flying. Something had changed in me. I'd found something I could commit to—something that burned inside of me, enabling me to dedicate several years of my life to reach a goal. Sure, I'd succeeded with other interests before, but I had never experienced such abiding resolve. My future had opened before me and I was ready to run. And run hard I would.

I received my private license the day after my seventeenth birthday, with fifty hours in my logbook. Darin prepared me well for the practical exam. He was confident that I would pass without any problems. He knew Norm, my examiner, and had sent several other students to him in the past. Norm was a middle-aged man who was authorized to issue private and commercial licenses as well as instrument and multi-engine ratings.

"He's a great guy," said Darin. You'll like him."

"Is he tough?" I asked.

"You won't be able to pull anything over on him," said Darin. "He can tell right away whether you know how to fly or not. He'll be sittin' there gettin' all comfy and such, having you make turns and stalls . . . then he'll tell you to take him to Cheyenne, Wyoming, or somewhere with a stop for lunch."

Traveling to Cheyenne from Martin City, stuffed in a Cessna 150 at ninety knots, wasn't a comforting thought. The idea was to test the pilot's ability to flight plan. If I were to miscalculate things like fuel or high altitude limitations on the little Cessna, I'd bust the ride and have to get more training.

"That doesn't sound too bad," I said. "Then what?"

"He'll let you buy him lunch, and then you two will get back in the airplane and he'll ask you about your next leg to Wyoming. If you get it right he'll acknowledge your good judgment and ask you to take him back to Martin City. On the way back he might have you do a couple more maneuvers, or he'll just sit there quietly and watch you fly. With the sun beatin' in on his chest he'll get all warm and comfy and nod off to sleep."

I memorized what Darin had told me. On the day of my check ride, I had a burger and fries for lunch, while Norm had a chicken salad sandwich; and a little over an hour later when we touched down in Martin City, Norm woke up and said:

"That's good, you'll do just fine."

I could hardly believe I'd just crossed that hurdle. I shouted cheers of excitement the entire flight back to Watertown. Darin was waiting and congratulated me on the UNICOM radio after I touched down.

When I taxied to the ramp Darin walked out to greet me. I shut down and opened the door to a smile and a handshake.

"Norm called," he said. "Usually he only calls when the students I send him don't do so well."

Oh no. Maybe I screwed something up and hadn't realized it.

"What did he say?" I stammered.

"I was a little concerned when I heard him on the other end," said Darin. "But after the first few words I knew that it was good news."

"Yeah, great, but what did he *say*?"

Darin smiled. "He said that you're a natural."

I didn't *feel* like a natural. I'd worked hard and was sweating bullets the whole time. But I did perform well and I guess Norm took a liking to me. He was a good guy and I'd have the privilege of taking two more check rides with him in the future.

It's often said that the most dangerous new pilot is one who gets the first hundred hours under his belt. I had just crossed that mark. Most of my time-building flights consisted of taking friends and classmates up for joy rides. A few others were errands for Darin, flying to some nearby town for supplies or airplane parts. Darin had acquired a charter certificate and checked me out in the Skyhawk, Cherokee Six and Piper Archer. My job was to hang around and, when called, reposition an airplane on the ramp or fly out to fetch supplies.

Darin was a young man in his mid-twenties. He had a wife and, at the time, one daughter. Darin was what we would refer to as "a good feeler." He laughed often, enjoyed life and liked to chase women a lot. Darin would often drive to Westgate and hang out with acquaintances until late in the evening. When he overstayed his time and couldn't drive home he'd call me and have me fly down to pick him up. I felt like an accomplice to his behavior but it was a good way to build hours.

Darin soon realized that I was in this thing for the long haul, so he decided that I should pick up a few extra skills. One afternoon he asked me to accompany him on a cargo charter flight. We took samples of bovine blood to a university laboratory for analysis. The customer was a cattle exporter who needed blood samples transported on a regular basis. Darin put me in the left seat of the Cherokee Six. After he strapped himself into the right seat, he looked at me.

"I want you to take this trip as if I wasn't here," he said.

The weather was cloudy the entire trip and low ceilings forced me to make an instrument approach. I'd been taught about instrument approaches as a student pilot but had never executed one under actual conditions. Darin deliberately didn't help me. He sat in his seat and chatted about any number of topics except for flying. It was his version of throwing me out of the nest. It was fly-or-die, and I wondered how far he'd let me go if I got into trouble.

Fortunately the approach went smoothly and I made only minor technical errors. After we landed at our destination Darin gave me some pointers and helped me correct my mistakes. Once we were back in the airplane, she was all mine again and Darin could have been a shoe salesman for all the help he gave me. Again we talked about everything except flying.

We took another blood run the very next week. Once again Darin sat in the right seat talking about women, golf, and life in general—not a word about flying. The weather was no better than the previous week. Again, I shot an approach at our destination and one when we returned home.

A few weeks later I walked into the airport office. Darin had just hung up the phone with the cattle exporter.

"You wanna make a blood run?" he asked.

"Sure!" I said.

"You can take the Six or the Hawk, whichever you prefer."

"What do *you* want to take?" I asked.

"I can't go this time. I've got two students coming that I can't reschedule."

I told Darin I'd take the Skyhawk. I was more comfortable in that airplane, and since time wasn't a big issue, that was the better choice.

During the next few months I flew a half dozen more blood runs for Darin. I didn't realize it at the time, but I was flying charter. I had logged only about a hundred and fifty hours and already had nearly thirty as a charter pilot. I guess Darin figured that cattle blood was an exception.

It wasn't long and the blood runs would stop, but other charter opportunities came up. At first, Darin rode along with me when poor weather was a factor. Soon he felt confident enough in my instrument flying to let me take most trips alone. I only took cargo at first, but I eventually got to transport a passenger or two. I felt like a real charter pilot, yet I only had limited knowledge of instrument procedures and far too few hours to be legal. Darin had trained me on approach techniques and some en route procedures, but I was grossly ignorant of most of the rules and regulations involved in instrument flying.

Darin got his fingers into many different projects. He was a likable guy who promoted aviation heavily in our little town. At one point he had seventeen student pilots taking lessons simultaneously. Once I earned his confidence Darin included me in many of his business activities.

After I began my flight lessons I worked at the airport part-time. When I started flying blood my employment became more regular. I was still in school and involved in school activities, but I spent most of my free time at the airport. Sometimes Darin would have a schedule conflict and would require my services. I started to feel like a real professional pilot.

One afternoon Darin had to run an errand and asked if I'd take one of his students out for some dual instruction. Now, not only was I running the occasional illegal charter, but I also would be teaching others how to fly. He didn't pair me with any first-timers but had no problem letting me ride along and give pointers to higher-time students who'd soloed and had more experience. It was another way to build time and I appreciated every minute of it.

On another night Darin called me just as it was getting dark. He said he had another run in the Hawk and asked if I'd like to take it.

"Sure," I said. "Is it a freight run?"

"Not exactly," he said.

"People?"

"Just one, you pick him up in and take him to Huron."

"Sounds good, do I have to wait for him?"

"No, he won't be going anywhere," Darin chuckled. "He's dead."

By this time I was so immersed in gaining flight time I barely flinched when I heard that I'd be flying human remains. Darin told me to take the Cessna to a nearby town and meet a funeral director who would assist me in loading the body in the airplane. I met Darin at the airport and we removed the rear bench and the forward right passenger seat from the Cessna. This left just enough room for a stretcher.

When I arrived at the pickup point it was dark. I saw the lights of the hearse near the terminal so I taxied up and shut down. The driver stepped out and greeted me. I think he was a little surprised to see a kid taking on this somewhat unnerving task. It was the first real encounter I'd had with the deceased. The undertaker, who was experienced in remains transfer, took one look at the airplane and shook his head.

"Somehow we'll need to fit the stretcher in first," he said, "and then carry the linen-wrapped body and lay it out in the plane."

He'd expected me to arrive in the Cherokee Six, which had a rear door. In the Cherokee we could have simply loaded the body, still on the stretcher, through that door.

After a few minutes of struggling we finally got the stretcher in, and then loaded the body into the plane with its head toward the rear. I secured the body and stretcher with the seatbelts that were attached to the floor.

The rest of the trip was uneventful. It was a clear, moonless night and I arrived back home around eleven o'clock.

Darin was a natural salesman and opportunist. He contacted funeral homes around the area and offered special discounts to promote the use of small planes to transfer the deceased around the Midwest. Darin was able to do this because anytime I took the trip his pilot cost was zero. He sold several trips over the course of a few months.

All but two of the trips were solo flights with me at the controls. One was in the Cherokee Six. We took the Six for two reasons: it was a larger airplane and had better weather capability, and it had the extra room we needed to load a full-sized casket in the back.

One Saturday morning Darin asked if I'd like to make a body run to the state capitol. I was hanging out with a schoolmate that day and asked if he'd like to accompany me—warning him, of course, about the nature of our cargo. Tom was interested in the medical field so he jumped at the chance.

We removed the right front and right rear seat of the Cherokee, loaded the body on a stretcher in the back, and headed out. Tom sat in the back seat directly behind me. The weather was cloudy during the entire trip. On the way down Tom asked if he could examine the body. I didn't see any reason to discourage him.

"Why not?" I said.

Tom reached over and unzipped the vinyl bag. He peered at the gruesome evidence of embalming on what looked like a middle-aged male. This may have been the experience that convinced him to pursue a career in the healthcare industry. Tom finished his examination and was zipping up the bag when, looking for a laugh, I stuck a few navigation charts between the corpse's toes.

"Look," I said, "chart holders!"

I may have been disrespectful, but Tom and I had trouble stifling our laughter and maintaining our composure for the rest of the trip.

Soon the year ended and I had enough flight time to begin training for my commercial license. I hadn't acquired an instrument rating yet, but I could get my commercial license out of the way and add the instrument rating later. I signed up for commercial pilot training at another nearby airport. My instructor there was impressed by my confidence in handling the airplane, and I was ready for my check ride in the required minimum time. I was eighteen and fresh out of high school when I made the trip to Martin City to take another ride with Norm the test examiner. Everything went smoothly and I sailed into professional pilot status.

In late 1977 I tried to secure a job as a charter pilot for any of the local flying companies. I was unsuccessful because I lacked the minimum hours. I was a brand new commercial rated pilot but I lacked my instrument rating. Charter flying without that rating was possible but a pilot was extremely limited in what he could legally do. I was more of a liability than an asset to any of the charter operators hiring at that time.

By then Darin's aviation activities in Watertown had run their course, and he turned over his charter certificate to a partner he'd recently taken on. Charlie was a local pilot who'd eventually move the company to a more profitable market elsewhere. Meanwhile Darin and his family pulled up stakes and moved to Texas. Through contacts he made there he learned about flying opportunities across the Mexican border.

It wasn't long before I received a phone call from Darin.

"You've got to come down here, Bill," he said. "There's a lot of flying and the money is great!"

I reminded him that I still didn't have my instrument rating.

"That doesn't matter," he said. "None of the flying requires it, and as long as you have your written passed, this guy will hire you."

"How much flight time do I need?" I asked.

"Just tell him you have twelve hundred hours," Darin replied.

"But I don't have that yet!"

"You can handle this, Bill. You can handle an airplane good enough. You'll soon have those hours, and then it won't matter anyway."

"Who would I be working for?" I said.

"The guy I work for will soon need another pilot," said Darin. "If you get down here right away you can get a job working at the airport until that flying job opens up."

"How long will that be?"

"I'm not sure. But the turnover here is high. You could be flying in a couple of weeks. I don't think it will be more than a month before something opens up."

It sounded too good to be true. Here was a flying job that appeared to suit my needs. Because of the way the cargo was purchased, the flying was considered private transportation and not charter. Therefore, the FAA didn't require a charter certificate. The pilots flew under Part 91 of the federal regulations. It was a legitimate loophole in the rules—and I was about to fly straight through that loophole.

Without consulting my father I made the decision to take up Darin's offer and move to South Texas.

I packed up my Buick and pointed it toward the Texas border. Harlingen is a long way from the northern Midwest, and when I stopped in Paris, Texas, to visit relatives and check in with home, I was only halfway to my final destination. I had no reservations about my career choice and simply explained to my family that I'd be employed as a cargo pilot by a transportation company based in Kansas City, Kansas, with an outstation in Brownsville, Texas. For all I knew those facts were accurate. Even after I learned the truth, I never did fully explain that the trucking company was only a fence for the company's other activities.

When I arrived in Harlingen I looked up Darin, who offered to let me stay with him and his family until I found a place of my own. I soon got a job with Yates Flying Service, a local fixed base operator (FBO) at the airport. My position was a line technician, catering to the needs of fly-in customers and providing fuel services to the airlines.

One day Darin called me and gave me the address of a guy who needed a pilot.

"Go down there and meet with him," Darin said. "His name is Ray. If he likes you he'll put you to work in a Cessna 207, *(commonly pronounced 'two-oh-seven')*. Remember to tell him that you've got twelve hundred hours."

That afternoon I drove to Brownsville and found the address that Darin had given me. I pulled into the drive at one end of a steel building and saw a man standing in the opening of the large bay door.

Ray was a middle-aged man of about forty. At five foot eight he had a medium build, wore a Latin-style button-down shirt with the tails hanging out, and was chewing on an unlit cigar. I introduced myself and said that Darin had sent me. We stood on the concrete and talked about matters of aviation. Ray asked me how much flying experience I had.

"Not a huge amount," I answered. "How much do you need?"

"I prefer my guys to have at least twelve hundred hours," he said.

"Oh, I've got that," I said, lying through my teeth.

"Sure," said Ray.

I figured I'd blown the interview right there. Ray said that he'd be right back, turned and disappeared into his office. I stood there in his warehouse, a medium-sized building of about forty by eighty feet long. The walls were stacked with boxes crammed with electronics of all kinds. There were televisions of all sizes, portable tape recorders, boom boxes, stereos, radar detectors and several other small devices.

A young man about my age appeared from the office area and approached me.

"Hi, I'm Dave," he said. "My dad says you want to start flying?"

"Yeah, I was kind of looking to do that," I answered.

"Have you ever done any bush flying?"

"Do you mean like in Alaska?" I said.

"Yeah, something like that."

Ray reappeared and explained that he didn't need a pilot at the moment but that I should call him each week and check in. I was a little disappointed but agreed to do so. I got in my car and drove back to Harlingen.

The following Monday I called Ray's office and spoke with Trina, his secretary.

"Ray's not here," she said. "But he told me to let you know that there wasn't anything he needed this week."

"When will he be back?" I said.

"He's coming and going all the time. He'll tell me when he needs someone. Just give me a call next week."

I hung up the phone and, discouraged, went back to work as a line boy for Yates. I was beginning to think that I was being led on. Maybe they just wanted me to forget about it.

Nevertheless I diligently called each week, and each week I got the same answer: "Nothing this week, Bill. Thank you for calling."

It would be another month before I spoke directly with Ray again.

I was beginning to lose hope when, one day, Ray showed up at Yates Flying Service. He taxied onto the ramp in a brand new, all-white turbo charged Cessna 207, Stationair 8. She was a stretched-out version of the 206, which was a six-place high-wing airplane with fixed landing gear. The new 207 could hold up to eight passengers, but the aft-most seats were small and cramped. Still, like the 206 it had large double doors in the rear and was an excellent light-duty freighter. Both the 206 and 207 models could be fitted with a turbocharged Continental 520 cubic-inch engine that produced a maximum of 310 horsepower.

"How do you like it?" asked Ray as he stepped from underneath the wing of the Cessna.

"Is it new?" I said.

"It's brand new. I just picked her up in Wichita."

"It looks great, but where's the stripes?"

Ray smiled and shook his head.

"Stripes are frills," he said. "This thing is going to do some work for us. How'd you like to come out to the Cameron County airport and make some practice takeoffs and landings in one just like it?"

"Sure. When?"

"You can come out anytime. My mechanic will be out there. He'll explain the details."

Ray said he needed to take the new plane to Brownsville to get a wing tank extension, a cargo interior and an FM business band radio installed. It would be a couple more weeks before he needed a pilot for the new plane.

"You know what we do, don't you?" he said.

"Yeah," I said. "Cargo runs into Mexico, right?"

"You know the risks, don't you?"

"I think so."

Ray grinned and turned to get back in the Cessna.

"I'll see you at Cameron County," he said.

With that he departed for Brownsville. The tanks that he was having installed would give the airplane the range for flights deep into southern Mexico and parts of Central America.

I decided to venture out to Cameron County the next day to meet Wally, his mechanic. I drove up to the hangar and saw a young man with stringy black hair lying on his back on the hangar floor. He was working beneath a light-blue striped Cessna 207.

"Stripes are frills," I said as I approached him.

"You must be Bill," he said. "I'm Wally. Did you see the Spook?"

"The what?"

"The Spook," he repeated, "your new airplane."

Wally had given the airplane its nickname because of its all-white appearance. We would later joke that the only colors on the plane were the tires and exhaust stains on the belly. Wally named all the planes in the fleet; the one I would get to know best was The Spook.

I was excited to hear him call it my airplane. Apparently Ray had informed Wally that I might be the new pilot and that I'd be showing up for some test flights.

"Ray showed up in it a couple of days ago at Yates," I said.

"As soon as we get the tanks on I'll have it brought back here and rip the seats out," Wally said. "Are you ready to give it a try?"

"What do I need to do?"

He gestured at the 2-0-7 he was working on.

"First of all, help me load some sandbags in the back of Missy here," Wally said. "Then we'll see how short you can land one of these things."

It all sounded pretty exciting. If I succeeded, I'd probably get hired and would be on my way to Mexico in a matter of days. If not, I'd go back to Yates and reassess my career choices . . . or maybe return home and make a new start.

When Wally and I had finished loading sandbags, Ray walked into the hangar.

"I see you two have met," he said.

"Yep," said Wally. "We're about to see how he flies."

"I don't care how he flies," Ray said. "I want to know how he *stops*."

What I needed to do was land the aircraft and stop on the runway in less than six hundred feet. It wasn't impossible, but it was a little tricky and required some unconventional technique. The key was to land firmly at the very end of the runway and apply immediate and heavy braking.

I climbed into Missy, started the engine, and taxied to the end of the runway. The 207 felt like a big bulky Skyhawk, the little four-seater I was used to. The big Continental engine purred smoothly and I did a quick run-up. I could feel the power of all 520 cubic inches wanting to lunge ahead. The temperature was cool that day but the loaded 207 still flew like a sled. To get a feel for things, I circled around the airport and made a normal landing. Without coming to a stop I lifted off and flew the pattern again, but on the second approach I came in too high and too fast. On the third try I got lucky and hit the touchdown mark but rolled past the stopping point.

I paused on the runway for a minute and thought about my technique. For the next go-round I decided to try something different. Immediately after chopping the throttle I would try moving the flap selector to the full up position before actually hitting the runway. This allowed more weight on the wheels by taking the lift away from the wings. It also meant that the aircraft had less of a tendency to skid.

On my next attempt I dragged it in low, just over the trees, ready to chop the power and quickly move to the flaps. I waited for the exact moment. Just as the end of the runway was about to disappear beneath my nose I cut the throttle and flipped the lever up. The electric flap motor whined and the flaps began to retract. The plane settled firmly on the end of the runway and I stopped in half the distance than on the previous attempt.

I made a few more runs to get a better feel for what I was doing. Each time I was more successful and could stop even shorter.

That was it. I had the job!

It was a good day. Of course the brakes were cooked and the main tires had flat spots. But I guess that was to be expected.

I was excited but I couldn't start my new job just yet. First I had to return to my job at Yates to finish my time there as a line boy.

CHAPTER 3

MEXICANA 202

W HEN I GOT BACK to Yates Flying Service in Harlingen I put in my two weeks' notice. I'd be taking on a flying job soon, and that fact alone made working at Yates a little more tolerable. It wasn't a bad job but my heart just wasn't in it. I was about to launch my pilot career. But for now I would still do my best at Yates.

Yates, or Y.F.S., a.k.a. Yell-For-Service—was situated at the southwest side of the airport near the approach end of runway three-five left. Most of the commercial traffic used that runway because it was better suited for larger aircraft and was the closest runway to the terminal building.

Yates had been around for many years and was managed by a man named Terrance Wayne. We had several linemen on staff as we held the fuel contract for the airlines that serviced Harlingen. My supervisor's name was Henry. He was a middle-aged Hispanic guy who looked after the entire line department. I was the only Caucasian on the line crew and was often taunted by my fellow workers. Although I knew little Spanish, they had no idea that I did understand some of the comments they continuously hurled in my direction. I ignored their insults as a means of self-preservation but also because I knew that my situation was temporary. Things were busy most of the time. And hard work was my respite from the torments of the rest of the crew.

Our building was painted deep red. It was a steel and concrete structure that contained two large bay-style hangars and a lobby area on the southern end. Loudspeakers attached to the corners of the building were connected to a radio tuned to local air traffic frequencies. This way the line crew could monitor incoming aircraft and anticipate their arrival to provide better service. We could hear all communications between the control tower and the airplanes.

Despite the bullying I did enjoy my job there and got along with most of the staff. I even made friends with a couple of my fellow linemen; one whose name was Jorge, gave me the benefit of the doubt. Once he saw how hard I worked, he and I got along well. I would see him again many years later when I visited Harlingen. He now works at a fixed base operator across the field. (Yates Flying Service is long gone.)

Late one Saturday a Mexicana Boeing 727 was pushing away from its gate. I was sitting on a tug looking across the airfield. In a few minutes a Southwest 737 would be arriving from Dallas. I would take the fuel truck to the terminal and refuel the Southwest jet as it exchanged passengers and baggage for the next flight.

I had heard a few good stories about close calls and funny antics that took place at the airport. These things happen; we're human and will make mistakes from time to time. The vast majority of those mistakes go unnoticed by the passengers, and most of those miscalculations never placed anyone in danger anyway.

Mexicana seemed to be the subject of many of the fumbles and bumbles I had heard about recently. I'm not trying to belittle the Mexican airline or infer in any way that they are less than competent in their air carrier operations. But what I heard over the loudspeakers that day made me wonder about the communication barriers in the aviation industry. An isolated incident such as the one that happened that day occurs in all sectors of flying, from private to commercial. Fortunately, it is rare. And you can thank the skills, training, and professionalism of today's air traffic controllers for the safety and favorable outcome when communications do get bungled.

Mexicana 202 was beginning her taxi to the end of runway three-five left for departure. I grinned as I heard one of the pilots struggle to read back the clearance that the tower had given him. He had to repeat it two or three times before he got it right.

One thing I've learned about foreign pilots who struggle with English—which is the official language of international aviation —is this: if things don't go as expected, the first thing they forget is the limited amount of English they were required to learn when receiving their flight training.

Once the Mexicana crew recited the clearance back to the controller correctly, the taxi instructions proved to be just as difficult to understand. The pilot must have burned a couple thousand pounds of jet fuel just sitting on the taxiway.

Finally, the pilot apparently communicated with the tower correctly and taxied toward where I was sitting. As the 727 passed in front of YFS I heard the incoming Southwest flight contact the tower. The Southwest jet was making his final turns for the runway.

"Southwest 86," said the tower, "you are cleared to land, three five left."

"Roger," replied the Southwest pilot, "cleared to land, three-five left."

The Mexicana aircraft turned on the taxiway at the end of that runway and called the tower:

"Meheecana two-seero-two ready."

"Mexicana two-zero-two," replied the tower, "hold short of three-five left."

"Rahyer, two-seero-two cleared for takeoff."

The tower controller immediately jumped back on the mike:

"*Negative*, Mexicana two-zero-two, *hold short of the runway*! A Southwest seven-thirty-seven is on a short final for three-five left."

Unfortunately the Mexicana crew still didn't understand what the tower was saying.

"Rahyer, two-seero-two, rahway heading, cleared for takeoff."

"Two-zero-two, hold short, I say again, *hold short of the runway!*" shouted the tower.

The Mexicana 727 kept creeping past the hold-short boundaries that formed a runway safety zone. The tower tried again:

"Two-zero-two, do you copy the tower?"

"Rahyer, two-seero-two, here we go," came the reply.

The tower called to the Southwest flight, whose crew knew what was happening and was already aborting their landing.

"Southwest," said the tower, "go around, *go around*!"

As the the Southwest 737 powered up within a half-mile of the runway, the Mexicana was at full smoke and barreling down three-five left. Soon the aircraft were well separated and the Southwest jet simply peeled off to come around for another go at it.

The Southwest captain, obviously irritated by the whole communications breakdown, piped in again:

"*RAHYER*, Southwest going around!"

I didn't hear Mexicana make another radio call to the tower and assumed they got their act together sometime before reaching their destination . . . at least I hoped so.

CHAPTER 4
BRONCO BILLY

O N MY LAST DAY at Yates I called Ray. He said that I should head out to Cameron County about noon the next day and meet his other pilot, a guy named Rob. There was a trip scheduled for the following day, so I could ride with Rob to get more acquainted with what Ray's company did. After that, if I still wanted the job, I was expected to be ready for a flight on my own within a few days.

I couldn't wait to get out there. Following Ray's instructions I rushed to the Cameron County airport. I met up with Wally who was waiting for Rob to return. Wally and I sat next to the hangar in a couple of lawn chairs. We watched as Rob brought Missy in from Brownsville. Rob touched down and taxied onto the parking area. After he shut Missy down he stepped out and approached Wally and me.

"I'm Bill," I said. "Ray told me to show up and talk to you."

"I'm Rob. Are you going with me tomorrow?"

"That's what I am told."

41

"Great! You'll like the flying. We've got a trip in the morning. We'll leave from here around six."

"I'll be here," I said.

And with that Rob left Wally and I on the ramp, got in his car and drove home.

I discovered that Wally liked Budweiser, so I offered to make a beer run to the local Maverick Market for a twelve-pack. Wally and I sat on the ramp and polished off the beer and called it a day.

I returned home and could hardly believe what I was about to do. For some reason the thought of smuggling didn't affect me much. I was more excited that I had landed a flying job, and a good-paying one. I figured I could pull in nearly six figures during my first year. At the time I had no idea how much money that was.

With the recently acquired "Spook," Ray's company would be operating three Cessna 207s, a Rockwell Twin Commander model 680FL, a Piper Seneca II and a Cessna 340. The Commander, Piper and 340 were all light duty twin-engine airplanes. The Seneca and 340 were used only for pleasure flights and occasional business travel. I hadn't gotten my multi-engine rating yet so I wasn't expecting to fly any of the twin engine airplanes.

The next morning I showed up at Cameron County around 5 a.m. There was nobody around. I wandered around the airport, climbed in Missy and sat in the cockpit familiarizing myself with the new surroundings. Other than the few practice flights I'd taken a few days before, I had no experience in 207s. For single-engine airplanes they had plenty of power and performed well, even with a heavy load. I was impressed at how easily they handled.

I sat there in the dark wondering how I'd found my way into this job and whether I was cut out for it. I was nervous—less about the risk of capture than my own shortcomings and lack of skill. Had I bitten off more than I could chew? I worried that my lack of flight experience would surface in the coming days and what the repercussions might be. Could I be heading for that boundary and not even know it?

Still, I felt good about the flying and confident enough to take this next step. After all, Rob was going to be flying, and that gave me a sense of security about the whole matter.

Rob showed up about a quarter to six. After a quick preflight we climbed in and rode Missy to Brownsville to check through customs. Rob gave me some pointers and demonstrated the procedures of filing the DVFR flight plan and the paperwork at the customs office. It all seemed pretty straightforward. The DVFR, or Defense Visual Flight Rules flight plan, was required to avoid unauthorized crossing of the U.S. air defense identification zone and border. This flight plan would be activated on the way down, then a radio call ten minutes south of the U.S. border to announce re-entry on the way back. It was a simple procedure and an easy way to keep the U.S. military and the border patrol happy. It had nothing to do with the Mexican side of things.

Brownsville airport was a tower-controlled airport but was a non-radar environment. There was some radar coverage from the distant north, but any flying below two thousand feet above the ground was below coverage and invisible to radar. Once you got a few miles into Mexican airspace, radar was nonexistent until approaching Mexico City, more than four hundred miles farther south.

Our flight this morning was to *Pista Negra*, a cinder-chip landing strip about three thousand feet long, tucked in some trees just south of Tampico. The cinder chips gave the surface its black appearance and name: *pista* for runway, and *negra* for black. The airstrip was long and smooth and relatively close to Tampico, where the goods were usually transported and sold. *Pista Negra* was used when other landing sites were too wet. It was also used as an alternate if the Mexican army wandered too close to one of our other landing sites. On the way down Rob pointed out landmarks I needed to know in order to communicate my position to other smugglers who could be using the same airstrip. We flew two airplanes but there were other operators, creating possibly six or seven additional flights into and out of the country. Most of the time the pilots used other *pistas*, but on a rare occasion we would share. The *pistas* were usually too small to handle more than one or two airplanes at a time, so we had to coordinate with the other guys to avoid conflicts.

The smugglers looked out for one another, and at times the flights seemed almost a routine. But they weren't. Mexican officials were constantly trying to stop us. They were looking for smugglers whether the cargo was electronics, guns or dope. They didn't look kindly upon this infringement on their trade laws. In the eyes of the Mexican authorities, we were still *banditos,* but of a lower sort.

Fortunately bribery was sometimes an option, and a relatively inexpensive one. Still, you could go to jail, and the horror stories I'd heard emboldened my resolve to avoid capture.

My immediate challenge, however, was avoiding an accident on one of the unimproved landing strips. Some of the runways were incredibly short and had many obstacles to avoid.

Then there was Guerrero.

He was a bounty hunter hired by the Mexican government to locate and assist in the capture of smugglers. Guerrero used confiscated aircraft as his chase planes. His favorites were a modified Cessna 210 and a Piper Navajo. Either aircraft was capable of overtaking any 207 in the sky.

Guerrero was a pilot but would often leave the flying to someone else. He and his partner would carry semi-automatic rifles and were not afraid to use them should a smuggler insist on continuing illegal activity in their country. If Guerrero spotted you in flight, he would pull up behind you undetected to verify that you were hauling contraband. Then he'd pull alongside until he got your attention. He would then hold up a sign with a radio frequency written on it. Once you tuned in you would hear him repeating instructions to land immediately at the nearest airport. If he was unsuccessful in talking you down, he would wave his rifle in plain sight. If *that* didn't work he'd poke his rifle out of a modified window opening and point it directly at you. If you ignored this gesture he would open fire on your airplane.

You needed good situational awareness when you were flying. Some pilots didn't notice Guerrero flying alongside them until it was too late. If you missed him, it meant you had your head up and locked in the cockpit or some other anatomical cavity and were paying too little attention to your surroundings.

Guerrero was not predisposed to shoot you down but had the authority to do so. First he'd aim for your tail and plink holes along the fuselage, gradually moving toward the nose. If you hadn't seen him by then you'd hear strange popping noises as the rounds penetrated the freight.

Most pilots who saw Guerrero nearby took immediate evasive action to get away. If close enough, Guerrero and his pilot would give chase. A fully-loaded 207 has climb limits but is still quite maneuverable and can easily make abrupt turns and dives.

Guerrero's other tactic was to remain behind undetected then land behind you on the *pista*, where he would block your escape and capture you on the ground. This was actually his preferred approach but was risky as the receivers were often armed as well.

I hadn't heard of Guerrero actually bringing a plane down, but I did see a few aircraft that returned with bullet holes in their tails.

One pilot told me a story where Guerrero was flying in his Navajo, a light duty twin-engine airplane. He'd been looking for gunrunners for several weeks when he stumbled upon a suspicious-looking Piper Aztec heading south. The Aztec was a light duty six-place twin—very similar but smaller and slower than the Navajo.

Guerrero followed the flight from a high altitude and out of sight, watching as the Aztec flew deep into Mexico toward Central America. The Aztec landed at the Guatemala border and began offloading firearms. Guerrero called for help from another nearby patrol plane and then dived toward the airstrip. He had the pilot circle the airstrip while he crawled in the back, removed the emergency exit window, and began firing at the Aztec. The receiving crew scattered into the woods while the pilot, copilot, and one of the ground crew were pinned under the aircraft.

Within minutes a second aircraft arrived at the scene to assist Guerrero. Together the two planes circled and peppered the ill-fated Aztec on the ground.

The Aztec got shot up pretty badly. Guerrero blasted out all of the Plexiglas windows, and fuel poured from holes in the wings and spread across the ground.

When the gunfire finally subsided the two pilots made a break for a nearby thicket of trees. The lone Mexican who was hunkered beneath the airplane with them did not follow. He remained lying still under the bullet-riddled airplane.

Up above, Guerrero ceased fire and circled around to follow the second airplane that was about to land on the airstrip.

The pilot ran back to the Aztec and found that the Mexican had been shot and was laying face down and motionless in a pool of Avgas and blood. The pilot rolled him over. The young man had been hit in his upper body and was dead.

Realizing that there was nothing he could do, the pilot rushed back to his copilot, and the two of them dashed into the tropical bush and disappeared. It would take the two Americans nearly two weeks to get back to the United States.

After Guerrero and the other plane landed, they confiscated the weapons and burned the airplane.

From that one story I knew that I needed to stay alert while flying into Mexico. If not, I could end up dead.

Rob and I arrived at *Pista Negra* in the gray and misty morning hours. Rob gently touched down and rolled Missy out to the halfway point. When we came to a stop he pulled the mixture and shut the engine down. A truck at the far end of the airstrip rumbled to life and rolled up to our airplane. Four helpers jumped out of the back to unload our cargo.

Sitting in the front seat of the truck was a middle-aged man wearing a plaid shirt and cowboy hat. Rob looked at me.

"That's our receiver," he said. He got out of the airplane and shook hands with the man.

"*Qué pasa*, Cruz."

"*Qué pasa*, Rob," Cruz replied. "I see we have a new *piloto*." He gave me the once-over.

"I want you to meet Bill," Rob said.

"Are you a good pilot?" Cruz asked as he looked at me.

"*Sí*," I stammered.

I was nervous. Adrenaline pumping, I kept looking all around in the trees and up and down the airstrip. All I wanted was to unload our cargo and get out of there. I hadn't realized that my composure would waver once we were on the ground and vulnerable.

Cruz noticed how skittish I looked.

"It's okay," he said. "I take good care of Rob. And soon, you too, Bronco Billy."

I wasn't sure where he got that nickname for me, but it stuck. From that moment on I was Bronco Billy.

Cruz' reassuring words helped to ease my anxiety. Soon the plane was emptied and Rob and I were back in the air.

It was a good feeling being back in the security of the Cessna. As we climbed out I scanned the area for signs of soldiers approaching the *pista*. I didn't see any.

"Hey, relax," said Rob. "Cruz is a good receiver and he's really careful about keeping us safe."

The flight back to the States was uneventful. Rob and I got to know one another better as we passed each checkpoint on our way home. Among those checkpoints were Highway Number 1 and Highway Number 2. These were jetties built out from the beach. And then there was *Tiburon Uno* and *Tiburon Dos*—Spanish for "Shark 1" and "Shark 2." These were straight roadways that ran east and west, perpendicular to the beach.

There was also The Animal or Deer Head, a small lagoon south of *Laguna Madre* of the inland bay. As the name implied, the lagoon was shaped like the head of a deer.

Rob and I landed in Brownsville and I watched as he filled out the paperwork back at customs. We taxied over to Hal's Flight Line, the local fixed base operator, and met up with Ray, who was waiting in the pilot lounge.

"How'd everything go?" he said.

"Smooth," Rob replied.

"How'd you like it, Bill?"

"It was great!" I said. "I can't wait to go back."

Ray smiled. He knew he'd found another pilot who could handle the risk. However, he didn't know if I could handle the flying. So far he'd only seen me execute a few short landings on a smooth hard surface, with plenty of room for error. He knew that there were less forgiving *pistas* in Mexico, and he didn't know how I'd handle them.

"We're going back to *Pista Negra* tomorrow," Ray said, "This time Rob can ride with you, and you can get your feet wet flying in. After that there shouldn't be any more flying until next week. By then the new airplane will be ready."

Rob and I followed Ray to the shop. The wing extension tanks had been installed on The Spook. The Flint Aero tank modification added fourteen gallons to each wing, supplying the airplane with a total of one hundred and one gallons of usable fuel, or around six hours endurance. A fully loaded T207 flying at low altitude will burn an average of seventeen gallons of fuel per hour. I always figured eighteen to give me a little reserve. There were transfer pumps in each tank, and the wiring to the cockpit switches was nearly complete. Quantity gauges were attached at the wing root vents. The airplane was well equipped and a suitable vehicle for the upcoming flights. I was excited at the thought of flying a brand new airplane.

We left Missy in Brownsville and Ray gave us a ride to Cameron County. The next morning I met Rob at Hal's and he had me file the flight plan myself. Missy was loaded and waiting on the ramp, and after a quick walk-around we climbed in and were off.

Flying the 207 felt quite natural to me. After getting familiar with it during my sandbag flights it was an easy airplane to master. The weather was clear and sunny and our trip to the *pista* went smoothly. On the flight Rob told me all about his Air Force days flying the T-38, a supersonic jet training aircraft.

An hour and a half later I touched down on *Pista Negra* and rolled to a stop at the halfway point. Things appeared to be normal and soon the truck was positioning to receive the packages from the back end of the big Cessna.

Cruz got out of the front seat of the truck and approached us with a smile.

"*Buenos días*, Bronco Billy! *Buenos días*, Rob!"

I was less nervous on this trip, but I still scanned the trees for any activity up and down the airstrip. I tried to recall my Spanish for "hurry up" but I couldn't. Everything went as planned and I was in the cockpit and ready to fire up as Rob finished checking the back door. In a few minutes we were back in the air and on our way home.

Rob told me to fly toward some lakes west of Tampico. He wanted to show me another airstrip. We climbed to about five hundred feet and flew to the northwest until we came upon a short dirt-and-gravel landing strip. It was located far from any villages and there were few roads in the area.

"That's 'One of These Days,'" Rob said.

He pointed out the landmarks around the airstrip and explained the procedure for getting in. He also cautioned me about the gas well at the far end of the runway.

"It's hidden in the grass," he said, "but if you don't overshoot you won't hit it."

You could see the well head, but there was also a three-inch pipeline that ran across the end of the *pista* and was hidden from view. There was also a row of telephone poles to the north that ran parallel to the airstrip. The poles looked too close but Rob assured me that they were well beyond the wingtips of our airplane.

"Just don't get too far to the right," he said. "There's a ditch and it is way too rough."

We circled once, turned to the north and headed for home. Rob said that we could get two airplanes into most of the airstrips we used, and until I learned the location of all the *pistas*, I would follow him in for a while. Farther to the north Rob pointed out a few of the airstrips we used for Raúl, one of our other receivers.

When we landed in Brownsville we checked through customs and taxied over to Hal's, where Ray was once again waiting for us. He greeted us with a smile and an unlit cigar jammed between his teeth.

"How'd he do?" he asked Rob.

"He did fine. I think he'll get the hang of it right away."

Ray looked at me.

"Do you think you're ready to start making runs on your own?"

"You bet!" I said. "I can't wait."

"I'm going to pay you both now for today's trip. Rob will get a check and I'll just give you cash."

"Thanks," I said. "I could use it."

Ray reached into his pocket, pulled out four hundred-dollar bills, and handed them to me. He also gave me a small sales tablet.

"From now on you will keep track of your trips in this booklet. Put a week's worth on a single page and turn it in at the end of each week. I'll write you a check the following Monday. Do you want to pick up your check in person or should I mail it to you?"

"For now I'll just pick it up," I said.

"That'll be fine. If you have a trip on Monday, I can bring it to Hal's for you and give it to you when you get back."

"Okay."

"Stick around a few minutes," said Ray. "I want to discuss a couple more things with you."

Ray walked into Hal's while Rob and I went over to maintenance to check on the status of the tank installation on The Spook. It was nearly finished. It looked like a long-wing 207 painted all white, with the exception of gray primer tips that added about two feet to each wing.

I spotted a mechanic in the back of the shop and asked him when he thought the paint would be applied. He shook his head.

"We're not going to paint 'em," he said.

All he could tell me was that Ray wanted the plane ready by morning for the interior mod. That was going to happen at Cameron County. Evidently Ray wanted to put the airplane into service with its wingtips remaining a primer gray color.

"Who's taking it to Cameron?" I asked.

"You are," the mechanic replied.

Ray walked in and motioned for me to follow him to the pilot lounge. When we were alone he pulled the cigar from his mouth and looked at me.

"I just want to be sure you know what you're getting into," he said.

"I know, Ray. I've seen the system and I know what to do."

"It's not that. I want you to know all the risks that are involved with this job. You're aware that I do everything I can to make it as safe as possible for you guys?"

"I know," I said. "And I understand that there are some risks that just can't be avoided."

"You realize that capture and time in a Mexican jail is a real possibility, don't you?"

"I try not to think about it," I answered.

"I've been doing this for a long time. I myself used to take the trips and I've made a lot of friends down there. Unfortunately I've made a few enemies too. Cruz is a good friend of mine and he knows how I do business. He knows I do everything possible to protect my pilots first and take care of business second."

I was beginning to think that Ray was having second thoughts about hiring me for the job. Maybe he felt guilty for hiring such a young pilot for such dangerous and somewhat underhanded work. Ray made every attempt to provide safe and well-maintained equipment. He didn't want to deal with any problems from several hundred miles across an international border. He wanted to follow all of the FAA requirements. But Ray was a businessman and a pilot and he took advantage of every loophole in the system. He had his problems and shortcomings but for the most part he was a good and caring man.

Ray looked at me straight in the eyes. I felt he was truly concerned for my safety. I didn't know if his feelings were for my well-being or his own self-preservation. Whatever the case, I took comfort knowing he cared.

"I'll give you a shot at this, Bill," he said, "but I want you to promise me that if there is ever anything that bothers you, or if you are uncomfortable taking any of the flights, you'll let me know."

"Thanks, Ray," I said, "but I really want to do this. I thought about it and I know what I'm getting into."

"All right then. You'll start taking regular trips as soon as 921 gets her interior ripped out and cargo net installed."

"Yeah, I understand that you want me to take her over to Cameron."

"That's right. I'll have Rob follow you over in Missy, and you two can come back in the Seneca. I'm taking it on a trip in the morning."

I nodded and started to stand up.

"Just one more thing," Ray said. "It's about a little thing I have with some of the Mexican police."

I sat back down.

"I'm well known down there," Ray continued. "That's one of the reasons I no longer fly the trips myself. The receivers would rather I stay behind and make sure the supply of goods keeps coming. But if anything should ever happen and you get popped, I want you to stay calm. I want you to do whatever the *commandante* or police chief asks, but don't give them any information about the receivers. How much Spanish do you know?"

"Very little," I replied.

"Try to pick up as much as you can. If you do get caught, make sure you know who the leader is. You'll know him by the reactions of the others in the group. They will give him the highest respect. Shortly after you surrender at gunpoint he will come to you and begin asking you questions, first in Spanish and then in English, either directly or through an interpreter. He'll want to know a lot about you and who you're working for. Got all that?"

"Yes," I said.

Ray nodded and continued:

"Don't tell him anything about yourself and very little about me . . . except for one phrase. If he has any amount of experience, he will react in a favorable way and either keep you on the airfield and wait for one of us to arrive with ransom money, or simply let you go. I can't guarantee it, but it is your only chance at avoiding Mexican jail."

"Why don't we just carry ransom money with us?" I said.

"There are American laws about carrying large amounts of cash across the border. I'd have to send as much as fifty thousand dollars with you every day you fly. And if you ever got caught at customs with that amount, we'd both go to jail."

"I understand," I said. "So what should I tell the Mexicans if I get caught down there?"

"*Piloto para el Rey*," Ray said. "Hopefully with that they'll know you work for me."

"*Piloto para el Rey*," I repeated.

"Good."

"What does that translate to?" I said.

Ray smiled and made a royal gesture with his hands.

"What else?" he said, "Pilot for the King."

CHAPTER 5

THE CANE FIELD

I SPENT A COUPLE OF DAYS moving into a new one-bedroom apartment in a different part of town. When I originally arrived I stayed in a low-rent, twelve story high-rise in a small twelve-by-fifteen-foot room. It had a bathroom with a three-stall shower that was shared with the other occupants on the floor. The elevator had no buttons, just a single-three position control that you selected up, down, and stop. I rented that room for twenty-eight dollars a week.

Once I landed the flying job I could quickly afford to move into an apartment of my own. I found a nice one-bedroom in a more affluent neighborhood. With my new income I could afford new furniture and even an almost-new Datsun 280Z sports car. It was a limited edition and one of the last straight 280Zs off the line. It was a 1978 model but had only four hundred fifty miles on the odometer. It had been owned by an attorney who, unbeknownst to his wife, kept it in a garage at his office. When she discovered it she suspected that the car belonged to a mistress. One thing led to another and she filed for divorce.

The court judgment was leaning toward awarding the car to the estranged wife, so the husband decided to return the car to the dealer. I walked into that dealership and bought the car the day after he returned it. For several months afterward I kept an eye out for an angry divorcée out for revenge. Fortunately nothing ever happened. It was an awesome car and I owned it for many years after that.

My first true solo trip into Mexico came within a few days when Ray called and said he'd like Rob and me, in separate aircraft, to make a run into One of These Days. It was the shortest *pista* but probably the most secure. Ray felt I could handle the challenge and we decided that Rob would go in first and I would follow.

When we arrived at the *pista,* Rob landed to the east and I popped over the hill, hit the end and rolled to a stop alongside him. He met me at the door of my airplane with his hand extended.

"Welcome to Mexico," he said. "You did that nicely."

I was a little shaky but soon regained my composure. Cruz approached us as we stood under the wing of The Spook.

"Bronco, I know some English," said Cruz. "I teach you Spanish."

"*Sí, bueno,*" I said.

Cruz laughed and patted Rob on the back as he turned and made his way back to the truck.

"You want some breakfast?" Rob asked me.

"Sure," I said.

"You'll like it," he said.

Cruz reappeared carrying a box that held a special kind of tamale. They were large and square and wrapped in banana leaves. These tamales were quite popular in El Salvador. Each was wrapped in plain brown paper that helped soak up the grease. The tamales were hot but not too spicy and tasted wonderful in the cool Mexican morning.

At One of These Days, Cruz always had at least two tamales for each pilot; I never refused either of them. I usually ate one on the field and took one home, but eventually I couldn't resist the smell of the freshly cooked delight and would down the second one on the return trip.

Rob and I finished our tamales as the crew emptied both airplanes. When they were done, Rob gave me the thumbs-up. We thanked Cruz and climbed in our 207s. I launched first as Rob waited off to the side to avoid any rocks I might kick up. Soon we were in the air and on our way back to the States.

I wanted to do something to commemorate my first solo flight across the border but couldn't think of anything extraordinary. I thought about taking something insignificant from the airplane as a token—an unused knob, maybe—but I didn't like the idea of defiling the new bird. So I decided on something simple. For each flight the pilot carried a small bundle of paperwork that included the load manifest and customs documents. These were held together with a paper clip. That seemed to be a suitable token, so I removed it and fastened it to the visor above my head. As I flew more missions the visor collected more paper clips.

The rest of the flight went smoothly. Rob and I had only a few exchanges on the radio. We arrived back in Brownsville, parked at the customs ramp, and checked through. This time the customs officer recognized that I was new and unfamiliar. In an authoritative manner he thoroughly inspected both me and my airplane as Rob casually taxied back to Hal's without so much as a second look.

The inspector was quite interested in my airplane, maybe because it also was new. He looked under the instrument panel and behind the aft bulkhead. He looked over the airplane as if he was preparing to buy it. He asked questions regarding my whereabouts and itinerary while I was in Mexico. I began to get nervous and hoped I'd answer his questions correctly.

With much chin-rubbing and reluctance, the customs officer finally handed me the document along with his clearance signature. I breathed a little easier and counted it as just another part of my initiation into this new world of flying.

Rob and Ray were waiting when I finally brought The Spook to a stop on Hal's ramp. They were privy to the intense scrutiny I endured at the customs ramp and seemed to delight in my ordeal. I always suspected that they'd set the whole thing up.

Ray asked me how I liked One of These Days.

"If Rob hadn't gone in first, I might not have found it," I said. "When's the next trip?"

"Tomorrow, and were going to the same place," said Ray. "Have the airplanes here by 7 a.m. and we'll load them here."

Rob and I got back in our airplanes and flew back to Cameron County. When we arrived Wally was waiting for us.

"You didn't break my new airplane, did you?" he said.

"I don't think so," I replied.

"How'd she run?"

"Great. I really like the way she handles."

"Well," laughed Wally, "I suppose I'd better order some tires and brakes if *you're* going to fly her."

Wally was a good-hearted man and truly cared about our safety. We seemed to understand one another and would have fun in hurling jokes between us.

The next morning Rob and I showed up at Cameron County and took our airplanes on the short flight to Brownsville to be loaded. When we arrived Rob led me around the ramp and introduced me to a few of the other pilots who also made regular runs into Mexico. There were about ten of us that flew similar airplanes. The Hispanics outnumbered the Caucasians. The *gringos* were Rob, me, Buddy, and Darin, my flight instructor. Darin only flew the 207s on occasion; he usually flew in a Piper Aztec or Beech 18. There was Xavier, a short tubby Hispanic pilot of about forty. He owned three airplanes and flew one himself. His two pilots were Juan and Emilio, who spoke just enough English to get by. There was Alberto and Sal. Those guys flew 207s painted in green camouflage. They rarely hooked up with us and usually used *pistas* much farther north than ours.

Then there was Cam. He flew a 207 that was owned by a local car dealer. He flew part-time alongside Xavier and his group. Cam was very quiet and hardly ever joined in the conversations on the ramp or at our usual breakfast gathering at the terminal restaurant. I discovered later that he understood even less English than Juan or Emilio, and probably lacked a U.S. pilot's license as well.

Unlicensed pilots were not uncommon. But it was only a matter of time before either customs or the FAA would check up on us. I was legitimately licensed, but who knows how many bandits had come and gone before me?

On rare occasions we would join up with the others on missions. When we did, Buddy, Xavier, Juan and Emilio were the regulars, and Cam would sometimes tag along. Imagine one small landing strip receiving six or seven airplanes at the same time. It was a flurry of activity that sometimes lasted nearly an hour.

We could fly together only once in awhile because it always drew the attention of the Mexican authorities. Still, I remember flying an entire week with the whole crew and using only one or possibly two *pistas*. After a week like that we got some time off or broke up and used other *pistas* of our own. Payoffs and bribes were only good for so long. After that, we weren't sure who would be chasing us next.

One day Buddy came across the ramp to speak with Rob and me.

"Hey Bronco, how you gettin' along?" he said.

"Good," I said. "I'm figuring out more every day."

"I was thinking about flying down to check out the new *pista* after we drop our load," he said. "You wanna join me?"

Buddy was talking about a *pista* several miles southwest of Tampico. It was in an agricultural area not far from a small mountain range. Ray had told us that we'd be using the new airstrip soon. Other than its general location I didn't know much about the new *pista*.

By this time I'd seen three of the strips where Cruz offloaded his cargo. In addition to *Pista Negra* and One of These Days, there was the Barn Yard. But this new strip was supposed to be in the middle of a sugar cane field. We'd heard that it was very secure and difficult to find by road.

Before a new airstrip was put into service one (or preferably two) pilots would volunteer to make a dry run in and out of it. This was done to evaluate a new airstrip for the other pilots and learn of its secrets or hazards. We always liked going in pairs in case one of us dinged his airplane and needed a ride home.

Xavier had made arrangements with Cruz to build and use the new airstrip and had asked Buddy if he'd like to give it a try before we started using it.

I told Buddy that I'd like to join him. On that morning Buddy, Rob and I were going to use One of These Days while Xavier, Juan and Emilio would fly into another airstrip. We decided to let Rob go in first and drop his load; then Buddy and I could go in at the same time. That way we could also leave together and hook up and buzz down to the new strip. We dropped our loads at One of These Days and, as Rob headed north, Buddy and I took off and pointed our airplanes south.

I would fly quite a bit with Buddy; we often flew in formation or low-level so we could chase each other through the Mexican treetops.

One morning I decided to play a practical joke on him. I emptied my Styrofoam coffee cup and placed it upside down on the anti-collision light on the top of his vertical fin. The eight-ounce cup covered the beacon and held snug on the retaining ring at the base.

The cup stayed in place throughout the mission. Later at the *pista* I had a lot of fun teasing Buddy about the oddity he was carrying around on the tail of his airplane. He tried returning the gesture the next morning but I caught him in the act. Instead I slipped another cup on his tail as he was climbing in for departure. When we hooked up later in the flight I pulled up behind him and began teasing him over the radio.

"Bronco," he said, "you need to get that thing off my tail."

"No problem," I replied. "Hold still."

With a little tricky maneuvering I closed in behind him and, with the precision of a surgeon, successfully knocked the cup off Buddy's tail with my left main wheel. Unfortunately I also smashed the glass lens of the beacon. Buddy and I laughed about it the rest of the morning. We would continue to jam coffee cups on each other's tails from time to time but I no longer attempted the in-flight removal.

Xavier had done a good job describing to us the location of the new *pista*. We knew the landmarks and headed straight for the airstrip. I came upon the cane field first and circled, but I couldn't pick out a landing area. Buddy also made a pass and found nothing. I raised him on the radio.

"Are you sure this is the right field?" I said.

"I think so," Buddy replied. "That's the mountain Xavier was talking about. I'm sure of it."

There were numerous cane fields in the area but only this one matched Xavier's description. We didn't want to draw too much attention, so after a quick look at some of the other fields we decided to head back.

The whole matter was quickly resolved when Buddy called Xavier on the radio while flying home.

"Hey, Xavier, we couldn't find the *pista*," Buddy said.

"Oh, it's not there yet," Xavier replied.

"What? I thought you told me to go check it out!"

"I saw one of Cruz's boys at our *pista* and he told me they hadn't built it yet. Until then I thought it was ready."

"Well, there's nothing there," said Buddy.

"He wanted to know the wingspan of our airplanes. I guess they are going to plow out the *pista* later today."

Evidently there was a communication breakdown and Buddy and I were a day early. It wouldn't take Cruz and his men long to build the airstrip. They'd simply drive a truck through the field, knocking down the sugar cane, and then clean up the debris, making a suitable place to land. It was a large cane field. Even if they plowed only half its length we would easily have about eighteen hundred feet to stop in.

Back in Brownsville Ray was a little agitated when I explained that the *pista* hadn't been built yet.

"Those sons-o-bitches never do anything except for the last minute," Ray growled.

"Xavier said they were going to build it this afternoon," said Rob.

"Well, I hope so. I talked with Cruz a little while ago and he thought the new airstrip was ready and wanted us to use it tomorrow morning."

Rob shrugged "So much for a dry run."

Ray called Cruz and told him we wouldn't leave Brownsville until Cruz had inspected the new *pista* himself. After a quick hop back to Cameron, Rob and I decided to call it a day.

The next morning Ray called me and said that Cruz had been on the strip himself and that it was ready. I drove to Cameron and joined up with Rob and together we repositioned to Brownsville to be loaded for the trip.

Buddy's airplane had been loaded in the hangar and towed out. It was sitting patiently on the ramp. Rob and I taxied in and parked next to it. We walked over to the restaurant, met up with Buddy and had some breakfast. Soon Ray strolled in, handed us our paperwork, spun a chair around and sat down. We talked about the new *pista* and decided to call it "The Cane Field." Duh!

"I guess it'll be easy to pick out," Ray said. "It is smack dab in the middle of the largest field on the north side of that mountain."

"We'll find it, Ray," Buddy replied. "Bronco and I have already been there."

"Well, I'm leaving it up to you guys to let me know how it is," said Ray. "I wish we could have made a dry run but, it should be okay."

After breakfast we walked over to the ramp where our heavily loaded 207s were sitting. We decided to take off together in a formation of three aircraft. It was a good way of breaking up the routine.

Once we were south of the border Rob peeled off and Buddy and I took the lead and headed due south. I was first in line. When we got within ten miles of the strip, Buddy called me on the radio.

"Looks like you're going to get the cherry on this one, Bronco."

"Yeah, looks that way," I replied. "I think I can see it now."

"Okay. I'll hang back and Rob and I will wait 'til you're on the ground."

As I came upon the large field I picked out the long, narrow *pista* that Cruz's men had carved out with their trucks. It looked more like a gap in the rows of sugar cane than a landing strip. I throttled back and slowed down before flying a pattern to line up. It was an easy pattern with flatlands all around except for one small extinct volcano to the south. That hill made for a great landmark.

The plan was to land to the north and roll out into a large clearing on the far end. There was supposed to be enough room for all three airplanes to park there at the same time.

I saw the clearing and it was quite large. A couple of pickup trucks and the receiver's truck were parked there.

I made a tight left-hand pattern and rolled out on about a half-mile final. I picked up the microphone.

"That sucker's pretty narrow!"

"Go for it Bronco," Buddy replied. "You'll be fine."

I had to concentrate especially hard on keeping the airplane in the center of the *pista* and nervously, I committed to land. I wasn't that concerned with the length, but the width of the strip was frighteningly narrow. It looked like I had to drive this thing into a crack on a sidewalk, it was so narrow. I was about to call Buddy or Rob and ask if they knew anything about the width, but it was too late. I crossed the fence at the south end and began to settle into the sugar cane.

Suddenly I heard a terrible flapping noise and I hit the ground hard. The airplane decelerated on its own—and quickly. It was obvious that the opening was too narrow and my wingtips were dragging in the tall sugar cane.

The rate of deceleration was incredible and I figured that the airplane was sustaining damage. I lost control and the aircraft veered sharply to the left and nosed into the standing cane. I really don't remember but something must have prompted me to pull the mixture and shut down the engine because the prop was nearly stopped when it struck the fibrous tall cane.

During the rapid deceleration all of the packages to my right jammed against the instrument panel. The entire load behind me broke through the broom handle that supported the cargo net and the load slid forward against my seat. My body was jammed forward and my face was almost against the glare shield above the instruments.

I could barely move but was able to reach my door latch and pop the door open. As the receiving crew rushed to my aid there was nothing I could do but wait until they removed the packages that were pinning me in my seat. While I sat there I saw Cruz approach in a pickup truck behind the box truck, and soon heard Buddy and Rob closing in from the north. Cruz informed them of my situation. Soon I heard the 207s fading to the west.

Cruz asked me if I was all right.

"I'm okay," I replied as I wedged myself from the cockpit.

"Ah, Bronco, you have long wings."

Cruz and his men tried to blame the accident on my airplane's extended wingtips. The real problem was that the strip was built too narrow and offered no margins. Someone had miscalculated the numbers and nobody ever checked it out. I placed the blame on Cruz, as he was responsible for the *pistas* we used. But at that point it didn't matter; we needed to get the airplane off the *pista*.

Cruz's men unloaded my plane as I walked around and inspected for damage. The wingtips were stained from the impacting cane and there were a few dents in the aluminum lower surface inboard of the fiberglass extensions. The nose wheel was jammed with cut cane as it had ground sideways when I lost control, but the wheel looked like it could be cleaned out with some effort. The propeller was unscathed.

I breathed a sigh of relief. If we could get this thing free of the sugar cane I could still take it home.

A pickup truck was frantically driving up and down the field, knocking down the standing cane and widening the landing area. As long as Buddy and Rob stayed in the cleared-off middle their wingtips would be well clear of the standing cane. Cruz had plenty of time to clean up the mess later.

With The Spook emptied out, Cruz's men and I maneuvered the airplane out of the cane and dislodged the stalks from the nose gear. I started her up and taxied to the north end of the strip. Cruz was waiting for me there and signaled that it was okay for me to leave.

I hesitated for a moment. Should I take a closer look for more damage? According to my gauges everything was running normally. I heard Cruz on my FM talking to Buddy and Rob. He was speaking with Buddy in Spanish but I could tell that he was giving them the all clear. I flipped on my avionics master switch and called Rob on the VHF radio.

"Do you need a ride home?" he asked.

"No," I said. "I'm about to take off."

"Buddy told me that you plowed into the cane."

"I did, but my plane isn't hurt."

"Are you sure?"

Suddenly Buddy piped in:

"Then get the hell out of there. Bronco. I'm comin' in!"

"I'm about to roll," I said. "Where are you at?"

"On a mile final," he replied.

I could have waited for Buddy and Rob to land. There was plenty of room in the clearing for the three of us. My engine was running and I was pointed back down the *pista* in a position to take off.

People and vehicles were still milling around in the clearing where I could park my airplane. Cruz, on the other hand, expected me to leave. My best choice was to get out of there.

I saw Buddy flash his landing light as he drew closer from the south. I couldn't resist temptation: I throttled up and launched to the south, headed straight for him. He was fully loaded and not as maneuverable as I. With an aggressive roll to the left I passed in front of him and peeled out of the way at the last moment. (I caught hell from him later on, but it was all part of the fun.)

Buddy and Rob made it in and out without incident. Cruz continued to blame Ray for not informing him of the extended wings. We knew better.

Back in Brownsville I met up with Ray and we looked over my airplane. Other than some green and brown stains where the sugar cane impacted the wings, there was some cracked fiberglass and minor dents in the aluminum. All of it could be repaired easily.

After Buddy and Rob cleared customs they joined us in inspecting my airplane. Everyone—including me—was amazed that there wasn't more damage. Ray decided to give Wally a couple of days to work on the aircraft.

We chuckled about the incident and vowed never to let Cruz design our *pistas* again. Someone (not Cruz) had mistakenly specified the *standard* wingspan of a 207 as the width to carve out of the cane field. Obviously there had been an error in the translation. It was a simple mistake.

Ray just smiled as he chewed on his cigar.

"I guess it's a good thing I didn't have those tips painted," he said.

CHAPTER 6

COLLEGE BRAVADO

O N SLOW DAYS I'd sometimes take The Spook over to South Padre Island to fly along the beach and scope out the sunbathers. It was March, the beginning of Spring Break for college students and I could count on large groups of girls lying about or walking along the shoreline. They were all kids my age enjoying the party atmosphere and letting off steam.

South Padre Island was one of the many locations that attracted its fair share of youths willing to strip down and soak up the sun as they paraded their stuff along the shoreline. Alcohol was ever present, and the party atmosphere was certainly an attraction.

One beautiful sunny afternoon I arrived at the Cameron County Airport and spotted Wally in the hangar changing a tire on Rob's airplane, Missy.

"What's up, Wally?" I yelled through my open car window.

Wally looked at me and went back to work on the tire. I pulled into the hangar and parked my 280Z next to where he was working. I hopped out to shoot the breeze while Wally greased the wheel bearings.

"Not much going on today, eh, Bill?" he said.

"I was thinking about doing a little sightseeing along the beach," I said

Wally told me about a friend who worked on the island, and that I should pick him up and bring him back for a beer.

"Maybe toss in a couple of college girls while you're at it," he added. "I'll just wait here and see what you bring back." He turned his attention back to the tire change.

After a quick preflight and check of the fuel I climbed into The Spook, started the engine and taxied to the end of the runway. As soon as I lifted off I banked the airplane around and headed across the bay. The beaches were only a couple of miles from the airport and there was no need to climb to more than a few feet above the water of the inland bay.

Approaching the island I passed over the dunes that ran next to the beach. I flew out over the water and checked out the population as I gained some altitude. Then I throttled back and slowed down.

I saw several groups of people lying about and walking along the shore. On my first pass I spotted a group of six girls wearing brightly colored pink and yellow bikinis. This deserved a closer look. As I approached, a few of the girls sat up and pointed at the airplane that was headed right for them. Slipping to the right I made a nice slow turn above them. I got a good look at them as they all turned to get a better a look at me. I was curious about their lack of sun protection, and they were curious about who was disrupting their afternoon. One or two of them clutched their towels to their breasts, which was a sure sign that their tops were undone or missing entirely.

Oh, Wally would love this! I thought.

I made another slow pass from the south, wagged my wings and proceeded to look for more sunbathers.

Along the west side of the beach there was a road that'd been abandoned after the last storm washed out big sections of it. Occasionally you could find a portion of the road that was just long enough to set down and park on. It was practically on the water—just a few steps over the sand dunes to the beach. I had used this road before with both the 207 and the Citabria. My girlfriend Kara and I used to have picnics on the beach. Kara was a beautiful young girl of eighteen, not quite a year younger than I. She had long sandy blonde hair, a soft and pleasing body and deep sparkling brown eyes that looked like smooth precious stones moistened by the glistening sea. We'd met while I was working at Yates and had quickly become very fond of one another.

Today, if there weren't too many bystanders, I could set down, park safely, and walk out to the beach and mingle. Perhaps offer some joy rides to the cute ones. Unfortunately there were just too many people around for me to land safely. So with that idea gone, I decided to continue flying up and down the beach and check out the scenery.

I flew to the north end where the crowd dwindled and the sand was less attractive, and then turned around to make a pass right on the water line. If I could find a level spot I could set down right on the beach. Unfortunately, the undulations in the sand made landing anywhere along that stretch of beach a risky proposition.

Somehow I justified a few low passes overhead with my wings passing just a few feet from the helpless vacationers. On that day I had to be satisfied just looking. I could always drive over later and make a few new friends.

As I approached the north end of the group of hotels and resorts I noticed a large gathering of young men near the water's edge. They didn't notice that I was approaching, so I slipped a bit to the left, flew out over the water, and passed them by. As I did I saw that they were each carrying what looked like homemade spears about seven feet in length.

The guys shouted at the airplane and shook their spears, as if challenging me to come back and fight. I'm not sure what sparked such reaction. Maybe I threatened their male pride by taking the girls' attention off them for a moment. Or maybe they were feeling invincible from the effects of too many margaritas. In any case I was amused at their bravado.

I turned the airplane around, lined up along the water's edge, and headed back toward them.

I counted twelve guys in all. They were young men in fairly lean shape, wearing only bathing suits or some sort of loincloth. I understood the youthful male pride and I joined right in. Better judgment be damned I decided to play chicken with the lot of them.

Half a mile away, I pointed directly at them and drove on at full speed with the throttle nearly wide open. I must have been doing a hundred and seventy miles per hour.

The first ones to scatter went for the water. A few made tracks toward the beach. The closer I got to them, the more of them realized how lopsided this battle was, and bailed out.

As I bore down on the few who remained I thought how incredibly stupid they were to think they could take on two tons of aluminum coming at them with such vigor. I was close enough to pick out the designs on their swimwear and could see the expressions on their faces as all but one dove for the sand. The remaining guy stood there, staring at my airplane.

What kind of idiot would stand in front of an oncoming airplane? I thought.

Bearing down on my target, I contemplated driving right through and waiting for him to flinch first. I was young and bold, and pride can certainly cloud your judgment.

He shouted in rage, both hands clenching his spear above his head. At the last moment as his silhouette was about to disappear beneath my propeller I saw him crouch down. I panicked and a thousand images zipped through my mind. I pulled up violently to avoid buzz-sawing through the guy.

A loud BANG came from the tail of my plane.

Oh my God, I've hit him!

When I pulled up, my tail was within a foot or two of the sand. He certainly hadn't been able to get low enough to avoid being struck.

I took off his head! I killed him! I thought.

I dipped over the dunes and headed back across the bay. I didn't have the guts to look behind me.

What am I going to do?

The only thing I could do was to race back to Cameron County and avoid the whole thing. Maybe it would just go away.

Maybe he was only injured, I thought. But I knew very well that being struck by anything going that fast would certainly be fatal.

When I reached Cameron County I landed at nearly cruise speed. When I touched down I stood on the brakes. I got to the ramp, bailed out of the plane, and barely glanced at the tail before jumping in my Datsun and fleeing the whole scene.

The incident kept playing through my mind and all I wanted to do was run. Certainly the authorities would soon be looking around the local airports for a bloodstained airplane with a damaged tail section.

As I made for home I considered fleeing the state to avoid capture. But this was manslaughter at the very least. My only option was to flee the country and live out my life as a fugitive, providing mercenary flying services in some third-world jungle. Yeah, my life as I knew it was over. But it seemed fitting after what I'd done on the beach.

When I rushed into my apartment my phone was ringing. I stood and stared at it until it stopped. Moments later it started ringing again. It was all I could do to keep my sanity, knowing it was the police wanting to talk to me.

I threw some clothes into a suitcase and thought about what I could bring with me and what I should leave behind. There were many things in my apartment that I wanted, and many things I didn't want anyone else to find. Although I was a fairly clean housekeeper, my lifestyle was certainly not exemplary, and much of what I had hidden in drawers and cupboards wouldn't reflect well on me. I was a smuggler and a drug user, after all—not some college student who was living out his rite of passage into manhood at a spring break party. I was a professional dodger and manipulator—and, now, a killer.

Again my phone rang. This time I thought about making up a story that could serve as my alibi, and talk my way out of this. So I picked up the phone.

"Hello?" I stammered.

"Hey, Bill."

It was Wally! I was relieved to hear his voice on the other end of the phone line. He'd noticed something strange about The Spook and wanted me to come out to the airport and take a look.

"Why?" I said.

"Just come out and tell me what happened," he said.

"Who's all there?"

"Nobody, just me."

"I'll be out in a bit," I replied and hung up the phone.

There was something refreshing about Wally's tone that made me feel a little better about going back to the scene. Maybe it was nothing after all. Maybe I'd hit something on the ground. Maybe I wasn't as close as I thought, and simply got hit by a beer bottle or a rock or something.

I replayed the incident in my mind: the thud and how it felt in my seat cushion, the feel of the controls as I pulled up violently. It sure didn't *feel* like a beer bottle. No, it was a solid thud. Much heavier than any beer bottle. It felt more like a human head.

If the airplane was damaged, I could instruct Wally to fix it quickly and cover up any evidence.

As I drove back to Cameron County my conscience started to bother me. How could I avoid responsibility for what I had done? There was an eerie calm around the airport as I approached from the service road. I scanned the area and looked for police vehicles. All I saw was Wally's Grand Torino, parked in its usual spot. An old fuel truck and a couple of junkers sat behind the hangar.

Wally was standing at the hangar doors, leaning against the steel structure, drinking a Bud and smoking a Winston. I didn't see anything out of the ordinary about The Spook. If it were spattered with blood I would certainly see it against the all-white paint job.

I looked at the underside of the tail control surface hanging down and didn't notice anything there either. There was no evidence of a strike on the leading edge of the horizontal stabilizer. Everything appeared to be normal.

Relieved at the sight of an apparently undamaged airplane, I pulled my car up to the hangar door next to Wally. Something was definitely up. Wally had a big grin on his face. I put the car in park, shut off the engine and stepped out.

"C'mere," Wally said. He turned and walked toward The Spook.

As we got close to the airplane I looked for signs of the horror that lingered in my mind. I couldn't find any. Wally strolled to the back of the airplane and knelt down under the left horizontal stabilizer.

"What happened here?" he said.

I leaned over and looked at the area he was pointing at. I didn't see anything

"What?" I said.

"Just forward of the elevator attach point."

I got down on all fours and looked up at the stabilizer. There was a hole in the aluminum skin. It was a teardrop-shaped puncture about an inch in diameter and three inches in length.

Wally stood up and pointed at a similar but smaller hole on top of the stabilizer.

"Now tell me what happened," he said.

"I hit something," I mumbled.

"No kidding!"

He got up and walked toward the shop.

"Where're you going?"

"Just c'mere," he said.

When we got inside the shop he went right to his toolbox.

"Bill, it would have been awhile before I discovered that hole if it weren't for this."

He pulled an object from his toolbox. It was a two-foot broken section of what appeared to be some sort of homemade spear.

"Now tell me what happened," he chuckled.

I laughed out loud. As I replayed the whole incident back in my mind I thought, *He speared me! That son-of-a-bitch speared me!*

I described the whole thing to Wally. He then understood my hasty departure after I had returned from the beach.

We talked about the big *cojones* on that college kid, who displayed such bravado when, on a sunny afternoon, he stared down the whirling teeth of a flying dragon and lunged, striking the beast in the tail and causing it to retreat.

CHAPTER 7
POPPED

I T HAD BEEN RAINING across central Mexico for over a week and I was enjoying a few consecutive days of rest and relaxation. Although it was common to have a week or more with no activity, rain like this meant our normal *pistas* would be soaked.

Even when the weather became favorable to fly we couldn't use many of our normal airstrips until they had several days to dry out. We had a few alternates. *Pista Negra*, the cinder-covered strip close to the city of Tampico, was one of them. There was *Pista Sierra*, much farther to the west, situated in a small mountain range in western Tamaulipas. It was part of a rock-covered road at the base of an extinct volcano. *Pista Sierra* was in mountainous terrain but considered very secure. It was also very narrow, rolling and crooked.

There was *Pista Numero Uno* and The Ranch. These were two of the three airstrips we used to visit Raúl. He was one of our other customers. *Numero Uno* was all dirt and seldom used as it was located far from Raúl's other two airstrips. The Ranch was actually located on Raúl's homestead property and was heavily watched by the *federales*, Mexico's national police force.

Then there was *Numero Dos* on the flats north of Tampico. It was the third of Raúl's landing strips and was built out of a chalky limestone material called *caliza*. Numero Dos was approximately fifteen hundred feet long, oriented north and south, and was situated in a cornfield just south of a dense jungle. The northern end came to within thirty yards of the trees. I had flown into *Numero Dos* a few times before and I kind of liked it. It offered a nice, open approach and was well graded. Plus, landing on *caliza* was a soft and smooth experience, and you didn't need to brake heavily like you did on some of the other *pistas*.

Toward the end of a week of heavy rains, Raúl called and asked us to make a delivery. Ray told me that if the weather cleared in Mexico we'd use *Numero Dos* the next morning. The plane would be loaded and ready at Cameron County, and all of the customs documents would be completed and placed on the pilot's seat.

"Plan on getting to *Numero Dos* around dawn," Ray said. "I don't know for sure how secure it is, but Raúl says that the weather has kept the soldiers away for several days."

Raúl was a different sort of receiver. He operated on a smaller scale than Cruz, and we knew that he wasn't inclined to pay off the police. The shell game of switching *pistas* was not as advantageous for Raúl because he normally had only three airstrips to choose from.

The airplane was at the Cameron County airport, just as Ray had said, fully loaded with the proper customs documents on my seat. I had filed my DVFR flight plan from home and was ready to launch after a quick pre-flight.

I climbed in and broke ground into the dark morning hours. The weather in the valley was patchy, with a few scattered low-level clouds. After a half hour of flying I could see a few lingering rain clouds en route to my destination. I also noticed there wasn't any radio chatter. I was probably alone since the heavy rains had also stopped the others from flying as well. I looked forward to an early return for breakfast at the terminal in Brownsville.

After flying through a couple of rain showers I broke into a clearing as dawn approached. A few minutes later I dropped to the deck and began my approach to land. Flying right above the lush terrain, the fragrant, pungent tropical air filled my airplane. It was a beautiful and peaceful morning with clouds mixed with early morning sunlight and muted earthy tones.

I throttled back and circled around for my final approach. There was no radio contact with Raúl prior to landing as we usually had with Cruz, nor was there a guarantee that he or any of his help would be waiting. It was a shot in the dark, but that's what I got paid to do.

As I came around and lined up to land, I spotted a truck parked in a wooded area just beyond the north end of the strip. I didn't see any people but Raúl and his helpers usually remained in their truck until I touched down. They had added more *caliza* to the southern two-thirds of the landing strip. The surface appeared fresh and relatively smooth. Unfortunately, the north end looked muddy and unusable.

I glanced at the surrounding croplands. The young corn stood about eight inches high and puddles of standing water were heavily scattered throughout the fields. Raúl flashed the lights on the truck, signaling that it was okay to land.

When I touched down it felt like someone had thrown an anchor out of the airplane. The drag was incredible as the airplane plowed into the fresh layer of *caliza*. Rather than applying brakes I found myself *adding* power in order to get to the other end. The huge amount of rain, combined with the added *caliza*, made the surface very soft and spongy. It was like landing without wheels.

Once I slowed down, directional control became tricky. At the slower speed the rudder was less effective and I kept adding power in order to steer the airplane. At nearly full power I was able to keep The Spook on the *caliza* and not wander off into the muddy cornfield.

As I drew near the north end I kept the airplane on the fresh *caliza* to avoid getting stuck in the deeper mud. Even with full power applied I couldn't spin completely around at the end, so I came to a stop pointed at an angle to the *caliza*. Although I wasn't aimed perfectly to take off again, once the plane was unloaded, with the help of several Mexicans we could push it around by hand and I could then depart.

I looked out and saw that my main wheels were buried halfway in the *caliza*. The nose wheel floated on top because of the excess weight in the tail. This didn't bother me much—I would be nearly a ton lighter once the airplane was emptied.

I pulled the mixture to kill the engine, popped open the door and stepped out into the soggy muck. I had stopped several hundred feet from where the receivers were waiting. I stood beneath the left wing and watched as the crew struggled to drive their truck through the mud. Nobody had thought about laying down *caliza* all the way to the tree line. I'd made deep tracks in the *pista* and dug huge furrows when I'd tried to turn around. Taking off might be tricky.

The truck got stuck about a hundred feet from the airplane. Raúl decided that was close enough. He and his helpers unloaded my airplane, bucket-brigade style. The cargo was all boom box tape players that weren't very large. Unloading went smoothly. Raúl spoke almost no English so there was little if any communication between us. The simple *hello*, *goodbye* and *thank you* were about it.

The airplane was a mess. The tail, empennage and underside of the wings were covered with mud and *caliza*. The crew was tracking mud into the back of the airplane and door opening so badly that I wondered if I could close the door without giving the threshold a good scraping first.

The crew was about three-quarters done when I spotted something moving beyond the distant trees. I peered across the tail but didn't see anything more.

As the work continued I inspected the plane and thought about how to get this thing out of the muck. After the back doors were closed I could be airborne in less than a minute. A 207 has a small baggage area forward of the cockpit, with a door on the right side that hinges at the top and is not accessible from inside the airplane. Although the airplane will fly with this door unlatched it is not recommended because the door could be damaged or ripped off entirely in flight.

The main cargo area has two large cargo doors that close and latch in the center. Either or both can be unlatched and not hinder the airplane from flying. The forward door trails to a nearly closed position from the slipstream, and the aft door lies flat against the fuselage in the fully opened position. It is a bit noisy but still airworthy. In fact, skydivers usually fly with both doors removed entirely. Normally there's a small chain that prevents the doors from opening all the way and damaging the side of the plane.

Raúl's crew finished emptying the forward baggage and closed the door. We were about a minute away from securing the back doors when it happened.

I was standing on the *caliza* next to my open door when I heard someone shouting from the distant trees. Suddenly all of Raúl's men began shouting and running toward their truck. Before I could figure out what was happening I heard a single *pop* from the tree line.

A dozen men dressed in olive drab clothing and wearing matching caps appeared from the woods. It was the Mexican army! Three of the soldiers were pointing their rifles directly at me. They were a good distance away but I was still within range. There was a lot of commotion and shouting. Of course it was all in Spanish, but I assumed that one of the soldiers was shouting, "Throw down your weapons and put your hands up!"

Three of Raúl's men stopped and stood with their hands in the air. The other two were hiding behind the truck. Raúl was in the driver's seat, waving frantically in my direction. I couldn't understand a word he said, but I was able to interpret his hand signals loud and clear:

Get the hell out of here!

I turned in the doorway of my airplane and leapt into the pilot's seat. I heard at least three more *pops* of rifle fire. I hadn't closed the door but I ducked down, slammed the mixture and prop levers forward, and engaged the starter. The 310 horse Continental engine roared to life.

Now relieved of her heavy cargo, the little 207 popped right out of the *caliza* and plowed right into the muddy cornfield. I glanced back over my shoulder and saw that Raúl and his men had all dived for the ground. The soldiers continued firing at me—*POP! POP! POP!* I wasn't sure if I was still hearing gunfire or actual rifle rounds hitting the airplane.

Could I gain enough speed for takeoff? I considered just plowing my way to the other side of the field—a good half-mile away—and making a getaway on foot.

NO DISPARAR! NO DISPARAR! I kept thinking. *Don't shoot!*

My airplane had very little directional control and I found myself zigzagging back and forth through the cornfield. It took full power just to keep the airplane moving. I finally gained some speed and was now heading in a straight line. I didn't dare make any turns.

Directly in front of me though was the south end of the *pista*. I was headed right for the mound of *caliza* and couldn't avoid hitting it at this point. Because of the added layers there was quite a hump of gravel at least a foot high. If I tried to turn I might stike the *caliza* at an angle and flip the airplane over. In my haste I hadn't closed my door or fastened my seatbelt, so flipping an airplane at sixty knots would probably result in some serious injuries as well.

At full throttle I took direct aim, hit the flap handle to the approach position, and braced myself against the rudder pedals. I tugged on the controls one more time, and to my amazement the nose wheel broke free of the mud at the instant the hump of *caliza* passed underneath my propeller. My main wheels hit the hump and the aircraft lunged into the air.

I was just inches off the ground but I was flying. Now free to accelerate, the empty Cessna did so quickly. In no time at all I was streaking through an opening in the trees, well out of range of the Mexican soldiers who wanted to end my career that day.

Raúl and his men were in trouble, but there was nothing I could do for them now. Besides, it was high time that Raúl coughed up some pesos to satisfy the local authorities. They were sure to arrest Raúl and all of his helpers. Although the Mexican government frowned on the smuggling of contraband, it was the American supply chain they were especially interested in—and I represented the last link of that chain. They wanted to capture the pilot and hold him and his airplane, hoping for a large reward in ransom.

If I had flipped over in the field and survived, I would have been beaten up a little but kept alive for several hours awaiting rescue. When my rescuer arrived, if he did not have enough American dollars, gold or other valuables—sometimes even automobiles—the authorities would arrest the both of us and cart us off to jail.

I always carried a few hundred-dollar bills in case I needed to buy a ride back to the U.S. or appease an angry farmer should I need to use his field for an unplanned stop. I also carried a Buck knife in my pocket. I'd given several knives to the receivers and their helpers as a sign of goodwill and camaraderie.

I came up out of the trees and turned north. I laughed out loud and shouted my victory over the close call.

"Hooah! Yes!"

All of my senses came back to me now. You know the phrase "you've lost your senses"? During all the commotion I must have lost my senses of smell and taste because I was now experiencing a flood of both: the smell of the paper used to wrap the cargo, the wood of the cargo floor, the mud that was left from the offloading. It seemed I could smell everything that made up the interior of that airplane. I also noticed a strong bitter taste in my mouth. My brain must have been on overload.

With these aromas were the sounds of the racing engine and the wind pounding through the interior from all the open doors. With little effort I was able to get my entry door closed and latched. I throttled back the engine and twisted the prop lever to a comfortable climb. There wasn't much else to do except head north and keep an eye out for chase planes. Once I was sure that I wasn't being followed I'd attend to the doors in the back. I didn't really need to close them, but I didn't want to arrive at customs in Brownsville in a muddy airplane with its cargo doors hanging open. That could draw unwanted attention. To be muddied up was not that uncommon, but open cargo doors were a sure sign that you'd left in a hurry.

I heard a story of one bold pilot who dropped his cargo loads just across the border, close to Matamoros. This was risky since border towns had a constant military or police presence.

The pilot flew in and out of a dirt strip just southeast of town. When it rained the strip became very muddy and practically unusable. You couldn't tell him that though. He continued to thumb his nose at the Mexican authorities . . . until the day they stormed his airstrip.

It had been raining and the pilot took a load just across the river. He landed at the airstrip and got stuck in a mud hole at the turnaround point. Several workers sat on the tail, trying to raise the nose wheel out of the mud. The pilot tried to power out of the mud hole; as soon as the airplane moved, the workers were to jump off.

During this fiasco the police showed up yet the pilot was able to escape in his airplane. But there was such a commotion that one of the helpers didn't let go of the tail and ended up taking an airplane ride to visit the United States. Too frightened to detach himself from the moving airplane, he sat facing forward on the tail with a tight grip on the vertical fin. Fortunately for that worker the flight to Brownsville took only five minutes. I heard that the guys in Brownsville had to peel one terrified Mexican off the tail of that airplane. His face and teeth were compacted with mud.

My airplane had an autopilot but did not have altitude hold. So when the time came to head back and close the doors I had to roll in a couple increments of forward elevator trim.

I estimated how much nose down trim I needed to compensate for my weight being shifted to the aft part of the airplane. As soon as I was in cruise at a safe altitude I set the autopilot, adjusted the trim, and went for the doors. I noticed that one piece of cargo hadn't been unloaded. I'd dispose of it before landing in Brownsville, probably by throwing it out over the open countryside or into the Gulf.

As I carefully approached the open doors I thought to myself, *What would the accident investigators do if I fell out somewhere over Mexico and my airplane continued into the U.S. before running out of fuel and crashing in the middle of South Texas?*

The forward door was closed but not latched, and the aft door was fully open and trailing against the side of the airplane. I would have to position myself in a safe place, reach outside and grab the door, and attempt to pull it against the 150 mile-an-hour wind. Then I'd push the forward door out enough to get the aft door closed first.

Pulling the aft door closed proved to be too difficult . . . unless I could slow the airplane down first. And that's exactly what I did. I shuffled back to the cockpit and pulled the throttle to nearly idle and lowered the flaps to full. With the plane wallowing pilotless through the air I reached out, grabbed the door and pulled with all my might. Finally I got both doors closed.

The stall warning horn had started blaring while I was still in the back. The airplane was in a nose-high attitude and on the brink of a stall. I lunged at the throttle and advanced it. What a close call!

It was much quieter in the airplane now and all I had to do was ride this bird back home and think about the conversation I was going to have with Ray.

I had about an hour to go and I began to think. *Was it all worth it? Or have I gotten carried away by the money and excitement?* When I hired on to do this I told myself that I would only do it until I made ten grand. I passed that goal awhile back. I thought about my career and how I'd lost sight of the goals I had set just a couple of years before.

I also thought about how fortunate I was that Raúl's men hadn't laid the *caliza* down all the way to the trees. If they had, I would have parked the airplane much closer to the tree line . . . and would have been captured by the Mexican soldiers.

After landing in Brownsville I taxied to customs and parked the muddy airplane. As I entered the U.S. Customs building I saw Ray standing by the door, arms crossed and cigar between his teeth.

"Glad to see you back," he said.

"It was pretty rough," I replied. "Raúl got popped."

"I know," he said. "I'm also glad to see that you're alright,"

He then turned and walked out the door.

Raúl had been arrested but his brother had called Ray and explained to him what had happened. He wanted Ray to send cash to pay for Raúl's release.

I turned toward the customs official.

"Bad day at work?" he said.

All I could do was laugh and shake my head.

Once I had finished the customs paperwork I walked onto the ramp and took a close look at my airplane. I didn't find any evidence that I'd been hit by the gunfire. I was lucky. The airplane had been parked several hundred feet away from the soldiers with its lowest profile exposed.

A sense of closure came upon me. The whole incident was now over and I felt like I was at a crossroads of an important decision. But, all too quickly my foolish attitude rendered me indifferent to the gravity of this recent experience. Much too soon pride regained its foothold and wisdom vanished. Again, my ego took charge of my rationale. It was a close call and one that should have shaken me into a clearer reality.

I suppose I should have been scared, but I was still very young and foolish. I'd live to fly another day, and that was good enough for me.

CHAPTER 8

THE STUDENTS

O NE EARLY WEDNESDAY evening my phone rang. It was
Buddy. He was taking his boat out on the nearby river and
wanted to know if I'd like to join him.

"Do you water ski, Bronco?" he asked.

"Yeah, I grew up close to a lake," I said.

"I like to ski up and down the Arroyo Colorado. It's narrow, but
deep enough with plenty of turns."

"Sounds like a good time," I said.

"Meet me at the hangar at nine on Friday morning. You bring the
beer."

"I'll be there," I replied and hung up.

Buddy was a local pilot who'd spent much of his boyhood in South
Texas. He was a few years older than I was and had also started flying
when he was sixteen years old. His father was a retired airport
maintenance manager and was now the caretaker of the Cameron
County airport.

Buddy was also a contraband pilot working on his own. Although we used different *pistas*, Buddy and most of the other operators flew on the same days as we did. This policy put the Mexican army at a disadvantage because they couldn't know all of the operators' whereabouts. This may have given us a false sense of security, but with numerous flights going on simultaneously, I was betting that it'd be the other guy and not me.

We'd contact each other on the VHF if anyone ran into trouble. Occasionally someone would spot the authorities and warn the rest of us. This allowed us to adjust our plans and destinations for the next day's flight.

I had a morning departure for One of These Days, so I called it a night. It had only been a week since Raúl had gotten popped on *Numero Dos*. I lay in bed thinking about Raúl and the close call that almost got me in trouble. I played the whole thing over in my mind. My heart began to race as I could still hear the unmistakable sound of gunfire. Raúl got bailed out the next day and paid off the *commandante* to make things right. I was quickly learning how corrupt the Mexican authorities were, and how little they could be trusted.

After Raúl's incident all flying had stopped. But it wasn't long and we were all eager for life to return to normal. The Mexican cops had been paid off and we felt there might be a reprieve from our pursuers. Everyone knew that it couldn't last forever and sooner or later, someone was headed for jail.

The next morning Ray met us on the ramp in Brownsville and we talked about the busy schedule ahead. We were happy to start making money again. Ours was the first flight since the close call on the *caliza*. We felt confident that enough money had changed hands and the Mexican authorities would leave us alone for a while. But there was still a lot of risk involved. To his credit, Ray always informed us of any additional risk and left the final decision in our hands. Within a day or two the skies would be busy as the smugglers resumed practicing their craft.

Rob and I were raring to go, and soon we were back in the air. The flight went smoothly and we made the round trip to Tampico with no interference. When we landed in Brownsville, Ray was waiting on the ramp with news that Cruz had called and asked for a second load.

Evidently he wanted to catch up on some deliveries he'd promised his customers.

"Are you two up for it?" Ray asked.

"Yeah," I said. "What airstrip are we using?"

"The Students."

As I've mentioned, every trip was optional, with no consequences should we choose to stay home. I don't recall ever turning one down, though. The adrenaline rush associated with the high risk was too much to resist. I was already addicted and would have done anything for my next fix. Airplanes are a rush under normal circumstances. Throw in low-level flying, makeshift airstrips and the chance to get chased by the Mexican police, and you have a potent cocktail.

To be fair, there were a few times on missions when the weather was so bad I wished I was somewhere else. I had a pretty good mental picture of the local terrain and would fly down the beach until I reached a checkpoint before I ventured inland. Southeastern Mexico was underdeveloped and radio towers were few and far between. The swiftly rising terrain was our biggest threat. But the challenge of flying at a hundred and thirty knots a few feet under the deck and a few feet above the trees in poor visibility was a real thrill. It was nearly an overdose of that stuff that makes your heart pound. Scud running the Mexican bush was a unique experience that a few did not survive.

While we waited for our takeoff time, Rob and I hit the airport restaurant and had some coffee. Ray strolled in around 11 a.m., gave us our paperwork.

"We'll see you two when you get back," he said.

"You can buy us a late lunch," Rob replied.

Ray grinned. "You guys are the ones making all the money today."

It was a good day. Anytime we got a double or triple haul, we collected that much more cash. The only thing better than adrenaline was money; and like adrenaline, the more of it the better.

Rob and I looked through the restaurant window and saw a truck pull up to Missy. Ray's son Dave and a friend got out and began stuffing boom boxes and portable TVs into our two airplanes. The goods were all wrapped in plain brown paper.

First Dave stacked the cargo from floor to ceiling into the area where the copilot seat was usually mounted. Then, from front to back, Dave and his friend filled nearly every square inch of the aircraft with packages. Dave was good at what he did and could stuff an airplane like no one I'd ever seen. Of course, I'd never seen anything remotely resembling this anyway.

After stuffing Missy, Dave and his friend did the same with The Spook. If need be, Dave could slide the pilot's seat to the forward limit to accommodate more packages. I usually complained about this as it made the ride quite uncomfortable for me. Dave would smile and say, "That's too bad," and, "You'll have to make do."

The pilots got paid by the trip, but Dave got paid by the piece. They wanted to maximize their profit.

Rob and I watched as Dave and his friend continued loading both airplanes in front of Hal's. A young man in a line suit showed up at our table and asked what kind of fuel load we needed.

"Top the inboards and leave the tips," Rob answered.

The line boy quickly left to fill the order. Thanks to him we were fueled and ready to go in a matter of minutes.

Rob and I left the restaurant and walked over to the FBO to file our flight plans and call Ray with our departure time. We decided to leave as a flight of two, and Rob agreed to lead and make all the radio calls.

We got into our aircraft and Rob headed out. I taxied right behind him and monitored the radio. With a push on the throttles we were in Mexican airspace in about a minute. I contacted flight service and activated our DVFR flight plans. Then I broke formation to give us some maneuvering room between the two airplanes. We headed south.

Because of the recent rain, The Students *pista* was very wet on one end and Cruz asked that only one airplane be on the ground at a time. To accommodate this request, Rob and I put about ten minutes between us. A little later I called Rob on the radio and verified that I was now about thirteen minutes behind him. That was good enough, and I set my power to maintain speed until it was time to land. Soon, I heard Rob on the FM as he was approaching to land.

The Students was a twenty-five-hundred-foot foot dirt strip just west of Tampico. It was on the edge of an inland lake and was open on three sides, with trees at the south end. The strip was long, flat and smooth. It got its name because Mexican student pilots used it to practice their soft field landings. The Students was an easy airstrip to use, but its proximity to Tampico meant less security for our operations. We normally used The Students when we had confirmation of the whereabouts of the local soldiers or when the top brass had been paid to look the other way.

I was still about five miles north of the airstrip when Rob called me. He was back in the air, and it was my turn to land. I saw him skirting at low altitude to the north and northwest of the *pista*.

"I got you in sight," I called.

"Where are you?" said Rob.

"I'm at your nine o'clock and above you. I'm setting up on a five-mile final now," I said.

"I won't see you out there," he replied. "Everything is good. I'll talk to you on your way out."

I dropped down and came in low over the lake, approaching the *pista* and thinking about how I could catch up with Rob on the way home.

I touched down gently at the end of the *pista* and rolled to an easy stop at the south end. As soon as I pulled the mixture the doors opened and our familiar offloading routine was underway.

As I climbed out from under the wing I saw Cruz standing in front of his truck. I greeted him but he did not acknowledge me. While I was landing he'd heard another airplane and was watching the skies to the north. I got out and looked but didn't see anything. My airplane was almost unloaded when I noticed that Cruz was again focused on something north of the *pista*. It was an airplane, and it was setting up to land on the *pista* and cut in on our little party.

Cruz instructed his men to get out of my plane and run for their truck. I jumped back in my seat, hit the master switch and pushed the mixture lever forward.

We had no way of knowing if the approaching aircraft—a single engine Cessna 182 Skylane—was a threat. I knew that Guerrero had one of those in his fleet, so it could be Guerrero or someone working for him.

As the Skylane touched down I could make out two figures sitting in the front seats. Guerrero always flew with someone else. Or this could be an instructor with his student, out practicing takeoffs and landings.

I looked back and waved my hands at the young Mexican who was still kicking portable TVs out the back door. I opened the throttle and hit the starter. The Continental immediately fired, and I throttled up and began to roll. The helper in back of my plane now understood clearly that I was leaving with or without him and quickly bailed out.

The approaching plane landed and stopped at the halfway point of the airstrip. It didn't shut down or move out of the way, even though I was obviously about to launch. I still didn't know if they were friend or foe, but I was beginning to think the latter, as any other pilot would have seen me and avoided using the *pista*.

As soon as I began my takeoff roll I saw the two occupants exiting their plane. They still hadn't shut down but each was brandishing what looked like assault rifles.

It was Guerrero!

I was barreling toward two men who, for all I knew, were about to open fire on me. I was more concerned about my cargo, however. Neither of the two doors in the back had been closed properly, and the aft door was wide open and lying flat against the side of the plane. The nose baggage was closed and still loaded with packages. Several pieces of cargo flew out the back when I wheeled around and starting my takeoff roll.

I was at full power and I accelerated toward the intruders as they pointed their weapons directly at me. I had plenty of room to take off. If they were trying to stop me they had made a big mistake: they left me a good twelve hundred feet of *pista* to use as runway. I had my airplane flying several hundred feet before reaching the guys with the rifles.

I stayed on the deck and accelerated directly toward them. I wanted to fly over their heads and make myself a fast-moving target so they'd have little opportunity to fire at me.

Just as I pulled back on the controls they disappeared beneath my propeller. I saw them following me with the barrels of their guns. I gripped the control yoke in anticipation of taking a few rounds as I roared overhead.

As soon as I cleared them I peeled off to the west and headed for the trees. After a few seconds I was safe behind of a row of small scrub trees. I headed across an open field. I'd made it!

I gave myself a couple hundred feet of altitude, turned due north, and began looking for bullet holes. I didn't see any but would go over every inch of the aircraft once I was safely back in Brownsville.

I made a couple of sharp turns to see if anyone was following me. I didn't see anyone and continued to climb out to the north, still looking for signs of a chase plane.

As soon as I calmed down I reached for the microphone and called to Rob.

"What happened?" Rob said.

"Guerrero followed me into the *pista*."

"What, in his airplane?"

"Yeah," I said, and explained what had happened.

"Are you alright?" he asked.

"Yeah, I'm fine and I'm pretty sure no one is following me now," I said. "Where're you at?"

"I'm about ten south of *Tiburon Dos*. Do you think they got Cruz?"

"I'm not sure. Everybody was scrambling for the truck."

I headed out over the Gulf, set the autopilot and climbed in the back. I kicked out the remaining pieces of cargo into the water below. The only thing left was the nose baggage. Since I couldn't reach it from the cockpit, there was nothing I could do about that. Returning with your freight increased the possibility of a customs inspection and could result in delays. I couldn't completely close the aft door and had to live with it until I was parked on the ramp at home.

Rob arrived in Brownsville first and met with Ray. When I touched down a few minutes later I taxied and tried not to expose my open door. I parked with the cargo doors facing away from the customs terminal. I got out, ran around to the back and closed them both.

When I entered the customs office the only person there was a single agent, and he didn't seem aware of anything out of the ordinary. I filed my paperwork as I'd done dozens of times before. The customs agent barely said a word—just took my signature, thanked me and threw my inbound declaration in a basket on the table behind him.

I walked out the door and back to my airplane. Everything felt so anticlimactic! I got back into the airplane and realized I hadn't claimed the unopened nose baggage. I wasn't about to raise any questions now, so I started the engine and taxied to Hal's to meet up with Ray.

As I climbed out of my airplane on the ramp, Ray and Rob walked out to meet me. As Ray looked over my airplane, I told them I still had cargo in the nose.

"Did you take any hits?" said Ray.

"I don't know. I'm not even sure they fired at me."

"Oh, they fired," said Ray. "Cruz called and said that they were trying hard to bring you down."

"How did Cruz make out?"

"Nobody got popped."

"That's good."

"While they were focused on you," said Ray, "Cruz and his guys got away in the trucks. I guess Guerrero thought that if he could drop you they could easily get the load."

Cruz told Ray that Guerrero may have been patrolling the skies somewhere, saw my plane, and started to track me. He was probably flying high overhead and picked out my white airplane against the deep green background of the terrain below. Once he confirmed I was flying a 207 he knew I was probably a smuggler. He likely followed high and behind until he saw me descend, then dropped in behind and followed me to the *pista*.

As we looked over my airplane we counted three bullet holes in the right flap, two in the belly just aft of the main gear, and two in each of the horizontal stabilizers. The exit wounds from the belly came out the roof. One of my VHF antennas had been hit and had shattered the mounting base.

I felt a chill rush through my veins. The flap and tail strikes were benign compared to the rounds that had pierced the belly of the aircraft. The VHF antennae were situated directly above the two front seats. The bullet that killed the one antenna had first passed within inches of my head.

Guerrero and his pilot weren't trying to send warning shots. They weren't trying to frighten me. They took aim at the center of the airframe and were trying to kill me and bring me down.

I hadn't seen bullet holes inside the airplane but looking at everything on the ramp I noticed that the plywood floor was splintered in two places, with two matching wounds in the headliner above. The holes may have been concealed by the packages being shuffled around as I kicked them out over the water.

Apparently my decision to drive directly towards Guerrero and his sidekick and race directly over their heads prevented them from zeroing in and causing more damage. I had a funny feeling that my survival had nothing to do with my flying skill. I'd been lucky. Really, really lucky.

It had only been a little over a week since the last time I was shot at. I thought about my actions and their potential consequences. It seemed my luck was running out? I felt like I was a target being followed everywhere. I literally dodged the bullet twice in almost as many flights. I had a strong sense that it wasn't a coincidence. Something was going on and I worried that I was set up to be the next victim. It wasn't a simple capture and incarceration anymore. It was a "dead or alive" personal attack. Maybe I should make some changes. Other than being targeted my biggest fears were allowing distractions to interfere with my piloting abilities. If I couldn't overcome my anxieties I would need to walk away from this lifestyle entirely. It should have been an easy decision. But I was past a point of reality. I was in the grips of fantasy and faced with a decision that demanded more rationale than I was capable of at the time.

Yes, I had been shot at before, but now I'd actually taken rounds. Bronco Billy had become a full-fledged *bandito* in the eyes of the Mexican authorities. I wondered if they had discovered my real name yet. Up to this point I'd felt safe back in the States. Would I have to start looking over my shoulder? Was I still protected by the border and international laws? Maybe I was a target. Maybe every Mexican soldier or policeman had a photo of me or The Spook in his pocket.

We completed our inspection of the airplane and found no more damage. We laughed at the ogre that had tried his best to get me that day. Except for the pieces I kicked out over the Gulf all the packages were recovered. The delivery mission was considered a success.

Ray didn't expect more activity until the following week and told me to take the damaged airplane to Wally for some patchwork.

When Rob and I arrived at Cameron, Wally met us on the ramp. He performed a thorough inspection and determined that no critical structures or cables had been hit.

It was time to celebrate. We sat on the ramp next to the hangar and had enough Budweiser to settle the dust in South Texas. It was well after 2 a.m. when I finally put myself to bed.

The next morning I was awakened by my phone ringing. It was Buddy.

"Hey Bronco, where you at?" he said.

"I got in late last night," I mumbled.

"Well, get it together, bud! After we get our fill of waterskiing we can take some target practice with my new AK-47. Do you like machine guns, Bronco?"

I had forgotten about the plans I'd made with Buddy. That afternoon we spent the day having fun. It was just another day and soon Buddy and I were enjoying the lives we often filled with our own versions of distorted reality.

Little did I know that there would be more encounters that would bring me back to the point where I'd reassess the direction in which my life had gone. I would soon be taken much farther than I ever planned to go.

CHAPTER 9

THE CHANDELLE

S INCE MY DAYS in the Mexican bush country I've often wondered how I survived the whole thing but, more importantly, why. I had a free spirit and had disregarded my father's concerns. I liked feeling close to the edge but cared little about the fact that there was no barrier between life and death. I assumed that I had been automatically granted a full life and that my actions would have no mortal consequences whatsoever.

But now my situation had taken an ominous turn. The long-running civil war in Guatemala was escalating, and gunrunners could profit by supplying certain groups with weapons. We heard through our receivers that Bronco Billy was spotted in Guatemala in an airplane loaded with firearms. It was also rumored that he was backhauling narcotics and bringing them into the U.S.

Someone had assumed my nickname, and the name "Bronco Billy" was now associated with both gunrunning and drug operations. It didn't matter that the person they saw wasn't me. I was now a marked man.

I wondered if I was becoming too much of a liability to my employer. I paid much closer attention to the people I talked to, and I constantly watched my back. I felt cursed.

Ray offered me a run for Raúl. It had been awhile since the incident at the *caliza* strip *Numero Dos*. We had even taken a couple trips into The Ranch for Raúl with no mishaps or glitches, and things seemed to be getting back to normal for him.

"Where are we going?" I said to Ray.

"*Pista Sierra*," he answered.

"But that's not one of his airstrips," I said.

Raúl's truck was in the area of *Pista Sierra* so it made sense to use that airstrip as the pickup point. Evidently he was paid up with the landowner in order to get permission to use it.

I was scheduled to depart directly from Cameron County about an hour before sunrise. My paperwork would be waiting on the pilot's seat. If all went as planned I'd see Ray when I returned in time for breakfast.

I got to Cameron County a little before 6 a.m. and found the airplane loaded and fueled. There was still some patchy fog and mist around the area but I could see through it to a canopy of stars overhead.

There was a hint of first light in the east when I rolled off the runway and headed south. The fog was more widespread than I had realized. I looked around and picked out the glow from the lights of South Padre Island and Brownsville. I could see breaks in the fog toward Harlingen and San Benito.

I continued climbing out. It was a routine departure. I felt good with the cool breeze from the overhead vent on my face, the calm air and smooth drone of the Continental pulling me along. The familiar smells of cargo—brown paper wrapper and plastic—added to the familiarity and bolstered my confidence.

As the sky brightened in the east I flew deeper into Mexico and found some breaks in the fog beneath me. I saw the shoreline as I passed over The Animal, a familiar checkpoint. The weather wasn't looking much better to the south.

Of all the flights I'd taken into Mexico, about a third had been solo. I'd spent many hours droning along in radio silence, checking my progress, staring at the stars or the early morning light. Often I would just stare off into space, picking out constellations from my single-engine observatory. I had little to worry about except for making the *pista* and getting in and out without mishap. Since I was flying in the

94

twilight of the early morning, there was little chance that Guerrero would pull up behind me.

I looked down and double-checked my navigation lights and beacon. They were off. It was as though the entire world aloft was mine and everyone else was either sleeping or just getting up, awakened by the distant drone of an overflying aircraft. I felt secluded in my little space, yet I was never alone. It seemed as if God was guiding me. But why would He guide me to do something like this?

Because of the low ceilings I had to descend visually and follow the beach to a checkpoint north of La Pesca. Then, flying beneath the overcast, I'd turn and pick my way to higher elevations to the distant west. I would follow roads and winding rivers that grew harder to identify further inland.

The fog gave way to an overcast layer at about nine hundred feet. I saw a few breaks in the clouds that I could drop through and continue flying below.

Things needed to improve quickly if I was to make it over the ridge and drop into *Pista Sierra*. With low ceilings there was only one way in: I had to follow a river until I was pointed at a 3,200-foot ridge with rising terrain all around and a steep upslope just beyond. On the other side of the ridge I would drop back down and set up to land, committing to the airstrip about a mile ahead.

Locating *Pista Sierra* in bad weather was a matter of finding the easiest rather than the shortest route. There was a shorter way in, but it brought you over the airstrip at nearly a ninety-degree angle, leaving no room for circling around to land. This was my third flight into *Pista Sierra*, but I had never done it in bad weather.

The visibility was still about three miles and the ceiling at four hundred feet above the ground. Although I couldn't see it yet, the first of three mountains was up ahead. From there I'd make a series of turns through some valleys, leading me around the second mountain. I was at fifteen hundred feet above sea level with my tail dragging in the soup above and the terrain rising below. I turned and flew up the valley. I never saw the first mountain but knew it was rising off my left wingtip. As the elevation rose beneath me the cloud layer above me wasn't improving.

I was only a couple hundred feet above the trees, but I still had a mile visibility, so I continued. Very soon I'd have to see more of the terrain in order to avoid it.

Leaning forward in my seat with one hand on the yoke and the other on the throttle, I peered out the front windshield and tried to find the next landmark, after which I'd make a sharp turn to the left to avoid a tall rock face.

With the second mountain coming up on my left I continued to follow the valley toward my next turn. I was now about two hundred feet above the ground, and visibility was getting worse. If I didn't see the next mountain I'd have to abort and turn around before I got trapped by steep cliffs on three sides.

Just as I came upon my point of no return I saw the rising terrain of the second mountain. After the next mile I banked hard to the left and picked up the valley, which led me around it. Then I saw the terrain rising on both sides of me and hoped I was flying through the correct valley. This would take me along a winding river and point me over the ridge.

I was getting close and I was getting nervous. I throttled back to slow down and added a few degrees of flaps. For some reason I still assumed I would see the airstrip in time to land. It should be a few miles in front of me. With only a couple hundred feet underneath me, I banked and side-slipped, attempting to stay in the valley.

Now I was committed. With one mountain to my left and another to my right, the ridge I had to clear was a mile directly in front of me. Once I cleared that ridge the *pista* was only about a mile farther.

I saw a stream below me that did not look familiar. I was looking for the stream that marked the southern boundary of the valley where the *pista* lay. But I shouldn't have seen a stream until I'd crossed over the ridge.

I got panicky. I squeezed the controls hard and jerked them around. I felt confused about my choice of valleys. I wished more than ever that I had aborted the mission. If I had pulled up just a minute before, I could have climbed out of the terrain and popped up on top of the cloud layer.

I hoped that once I crossed the ridge there would be a few more feet of ceiling above me. Beyond that ridge the terrain would drop a little. But, would it drop enough to reveal the landing strip?

The terrain rose steeply around me. If I wasn't careful I would meet one of those rock faces in a very personal way. If there had been a few hundred more feet of ceiling I could have easily identified the ridge and flown into the open valley where *Pista Sierra* was waiting for me.

Suddenly everything went white. I was surrounded by thick clouds. I was dragging through the treetops between fifty and a hundred feet up . . . when the clouds ahead of me dropped and blended with the rocky forest below. It was as if the earth suddenly lunged skyward into the clouds.

I was now totally disoriented and probably headed toward a mountain. The rush of adrenaline was so intense I felt as though I was going to pass out.

Then something erupted from inside me. From deep within I heard an inner voice coming forth.

I couldn't hold it in and shouted, "GET OUT!"

I slammed the mixture, prop and throttle levers to full forward and pulled upward. I tried to imagine the surrounding hills but I was flying completely blind. My airplane was barely climbing and all I could think about were the mountains all around me.

I had to turn around. I decided to execute a chandelle.

A chandelle is a maneuver learned in commercial pilot training where, by making a sharp climb and a steep bank at the same time, an airplane is forced to reverse course. After the pilot initiates the climb, he then rolls the airplane into a steep bank to a point just above a stall.

The chandelle is considered a precision maneuver. It's not difficult, but it's definitely much easier in a light, unloaded airplane . . . and under good weather conditions. I had neither.

I began a bank to the left and heard the blare of the stall warning horn. Then I realized that in my panic I had just made a terrible mistake. It was very likely that one of the taller mountains was directly on my left. I had involuntarily banked in that direction, since a left turn is a natural maneuver for both plane and pilot. This is because the pilot is sitting on the left side of the airplane and because the torque produced by the rotation of the engine and propeller tends to roll the airplane to the left. In any case, it was a bad decision on my part but there was nothing I could do about it now. I was committed.

I looked to my right and left. The clouds were so dense that I could barely see the wingtips of my plane. I had the aircraft at full power, pointed sharply upward and rolled into a dangerously steep bank. The engine was roaring, the stall warning horn was screaming, my knees were shaking, and I tensed in anticipation of hitting the hill.

I jerked at the controls, hoping to avoid a stall. If I stalled the aircraft would spin and plummet to the ground. The plane was loaded too heavily, and the center of gravity was too far aft, to expect anything other than a total loss of control.

There it was: the barrier between life and death. I was in the clouds, unable to see the mountain I was about to hit. Yet that barrier was clearly visible and I was crossing it. Maybe I would luck out and somehow survive the impact. Maybe I could plow through the trees and vegetation and come to a stop. But at the angle I was flying, I was sure that the aircraft would break apart on impact. Any thought of surviving this crash was pure foolishness. I was moving at nearly a hundred miles per hour in a fully loaded 207 with a makeshift cargo restraint system. Even if I were to impact and remain upright, the sudden deceleration would cause fifteen hundred pounds of electronics to come forward and crush me against the instrument panel. I didn't have a chance.

I thought about the moment of impact and if there would be pain. I wondered if there would be fire. I waited for the jolt. It was going to happen, and I sat there, waiting. In my peripheral vision I could see out the side window. My surroundings began to darken as I neared the terrain. I thought I might catch a glimpse of the mountain as I plowed into it.

The Cessna continued its turn. I glanced at the gyro compass as it slowly slipped its way around. Just a second or two more, and it would be over. I was shaking violently and could barely keep the airplane under control.

Just then I thought about the consequences of my life choices, and I felt instant and overwhelming remorse. I was sorry I had tempted fate and sorry that I'd failed so many friends and family. *Oh please, just get this over with*, I thought to myself.

The gyro continued its roll . . . and then . . .

The clouds disappeared and I emerged into clear air and blue sky.

I quickly rolled level and pushed forward to avoid stalling. I was headed out!

I could see another mountain poking up through the cloud layer to my north. I leaned forward, straining to see to my right, but the stacked-up cargo blocked my view. I looked at the altimeter. Somehow I was now at an altitude of nearly nine thousand feet and clear of the peaks around me.

I was alive. Somehow I had turned this heavy sled around and missed colliding with the mountain. I didn't know how. I wanted to think that I'd just performed the perfect chandelle maneuver, but something inside me kept saying, "Impossible!"

I shuddered as I thought about how close I had come to dying. I must have been only inches away from that mountain.

As I climbed out to the north I replayed that maneuver over and over in my mind. I had started my climb much too slowly to have gained the maximum effect. I probably could have done a better job at it and should never have turned in that direction in the first place. That was a stupid mistake, but I was already stupid for being there.

I had the sensation that I'd just received a second chance at life, but I felt undeserving of it at the same time.

For some strange reason I began to cry. I'd played foolishly with my life, and yet, there I was, given another chance. It was as if all the wrong I'd done built up against a dam, and the dam had just broken. Everything rushed past me in a torrent. I was truly sorry for all the hurt I'd caused anyone. Now thanking the God who had just spared me, I was overwhelmed by His presence.

Eventually I stopped crying. I felt peaceful and calm. I felt better about the whole incident. Back in those mountains I had left something behind. I wasn't sure what it was. Maybe it was my pride or my sense of immortality. Maybe it was both.

I landed in Brownsville and checked through customs with the full load that I'd been unable to deliver. My declaration indicated that I'd returned without ever landing on foreign soil. The inspector seemed to understand that, and only casually glanced at the loaded 207 through his window in the customs office.

I taxied back to Hal's and met Ray in the lobby. Raúl had called him to report that I hadn't shown up at the *pista*. Ray was only a little concerned; he told me that for some reason he knew I was okay and was on my way back. I told him the weather had gotten too bad to make it in and I turned around. I didn't elaborate on the close call I'd just been through. In fact it would be many years before I spoke about that incident to anyone. I was ashamed of my poor judgment.

It wouldn't be long that I'd be on my way back down into Mexico with another load. I still wasn't prepared to give up this life. During the next several flights the weather was clear. Things were normal and routine. All too quickly I buried the fear and pain, replacing it once again with that same pride and false sense of security.

I knew that neither luck nor skill had spared my life on that fateful morning. I had experienced some kind of intervention. Yet I quickly resumed living my life with little regard for the consequences of my actions. But, in some small but significant way, I was changed.

CHAPTER 10

ROB

R OB WAS A GENTLE and soft-spoken man. I always liked flying with him and admired his caution and calm demeanor. I was the young, anxious and haughty one, and Rob was a good counterbalance. He introduced me to Mexico and most of the *pistas* we used. He had a wife and two young children that I had met only once and never got the chance to get to know them better.

Missy was also equipped with the long-range fuel tanks and Rob and I had taken her on a few scouting trips deep into the Mexican state of Veracruz. We were flying for a new customer that had several potential landing areas that he wanted us to check out. His name was Renaldo and he imported a wide variety of products from the U.S. In addition to the usual electronics like televisions, stereos and boom boxes, Renaldo hired us to transport washers and dryers, motorcycles, cigarettes, oil well equipment and toys of all kinds, especially during the Christmas holiday. The normal schedule for Renaldo was to leave Cameron County at about 4 a.m. and arrive at the *pista* shortly after sunrise.

I'll never forget packing a load of baby dolls for delivery to Renaldo. When we loaded the airplane we discovered that we could fit in more dolls if we removed them from the bulk packed boxes and placed them separately in the plane. Each doll was wrapped in its individual cellophane bag.

These baby dolls were the type that cried "momma" when they were turned upside down. You can imagine what loading them was like: doll after doll crying "momma" as we squeezed them into every nook and cranny.

In order to maximize our cargo we loaded the back end of the plane as best we could, then closed the back doors and filled any remaining space by dumping the boxes of dolls. Forward of the cargo net, next to the pilot, we stacked the unopened boxes. The baggage area in the nose held a couple boxes and about forty loose dolls.

With the aircraft packed to the gills, the only space that remained was a narrow little area for me to sit and fly. I could barely reach the mixture lever and had to turn my arm upside down and snake my hand in front of the boxes to reach it. My seat was shoved forward and the only thing visible out the right side was the leading edge of my right wing.

So, squished into my little space, I taxied out and took off for Mexico.

About three hours later we landed at our destination in Veracruz. Everything proceeded as usual until one of the loaders opened the back cargo door and was buried by an avalanche of baby dolls all crying "momma." The receiving team busted up in laughter. We all had a good time that morning.

The Highway was about four hundred nautical miles from Cameron County and about one hundred fifty miles east of Mexico City. It was a smooth, hard-surfaced portion of roadway situated on a small plateau amidst the volcanic mountains of southern Mexico. There were beautiful green-covered hills all around and deep, dense forests, deep valleys and waterfalls. The soil was rocky with a beautiful amber volcanic hue.

The Highway was about a thousand feet long at an elevation of around sixteen hundred feet. Mountain peaks in the immediate area rose all around. There was a two-hundred-foot knoll just off the approach end of the strip, and a steep two-hundred-foot drop on the far end. This meant that the pilots had to fly directly over the knoll and drop quickly onto the airstrip.

The landing strip was a leftover from a paving project that had failed. What remained was a straight paved section of a gravel road that wound its way through the countryside.

The only downside to this *pista* was the fact that it was so narrow—only about fourteen feet wide with a six-inch drop-off on both sides. The main gear on the 207 is just over ten feet, leaving only two feet on either side. There was no shoulder and the drop-off presented the greatest hazard.

The airstrip was situated at the boundary of a high flat meadow, and the land sloped away sharply along the west side. If you dropped off that edge there was little hope of keeping the airplane under control and avoid driving into the ravine.

There was a sharp turn in the gravel area at the southern end, leaving just enough room to turn around. We always flew down there in flights of two and were able to park both airplanes on the gravel portion so we could unload. The first plane would land on the paved surface and taxi onto the gravel, and then go as far as he could and spin around. Then the second plane would land and taxi up close to the first one. Both airplanes were then pointed back down the *pista*, ready for takeoff. The loaders could unload both airplanes at the same time while Rob and I would enjoy an egg-and-chili burrito that Renaldo would occasionally bring for us.

Because of the distance to The Highway, the receiving team always had four jugs of Avgas waiting for us. Rob and I would take two each and pour them into our wing tanks. This gave us a comfortable margin for the trip home. There was always some discussion about whether we could round-trip it without taking on the additional fuel at the *pista*. If we were empty we would probably make it. But if for some reason we couldn't land, unload and get the extra fuel, we'd have to make it back to Brownsville with a full load of cargo. The higher consumption rate of a loaded airplane made getting back successfully without running dry uncertain.

The weather at Cameron was clear with light winds as we headed south into the darkness of northern Mexico. Our conversations on the radio were minimal; it was a quiet morning flight.

Up ahead we saw some cloud cover illuminated by the early morning moonlight.

"I hope the *pista* is clear," Rob called.

"Yeah, me too," I answered.

As we continued we started picking up some turbulence. Nothing serious, just some gentle rocking—a telltale sign that weather conditions were changing. We were flying into a different weather system but had no idea of what lay ahead.

I hadn't slept well the night before; I spent the evening with my friends Jake and Kara. We were up late watching TV, having drinks and smoking a little weed. I knew I would have an early morning so I knocked off before my friends did, but I still hung around until just before midnight. I got a couple hours of sleep and woke up about 3 a.m. and had to rush to get to Cameron in time for departure.

An hour into the flight I was beginning to feel the effects of the previous night. Whenever I partook in alcohol or drugs I always gave myself a little time to sober up or clear my head before takeoff. I may not have been completely legal to fly, but I was usually alert enough for the challenging flights that often awaited me. At twenty years old I recovered quickly. After all, the difficulty wasn't in taxiing and taking off; rather, it was all about the landings.

A few of my fellow pilots imbibed and pushed their luck the next day, and some lost that contest. Fortunately, most of the guys were mature enough to know better. I was the youngest and probably the most reckless of them all. I did have my limits, though, and I knew that I had to be on my game in order to survive.

But this morning I lacked sleep more than anything. I was getting drowsy, and the monotonous drone of the propeller in the darkness made it all the more difficult to stay awake.

I was leading this morning and made a couple of checkpoint calls to Rob. Shortly after passing *Tiburon Uno* I spaced out and missed *Tiburon Dos*.

"I'm at *Tiburon Dos*," called Rob. "Where are you?"

"I'm passed it," I said, "but can't see since I'm in the soup right now."

If you're groggy, flying in the clouds only adds to the problem. With nothing to look at, boredom fogs your head. It's only a matter of time before you're struggling to keep your eyes open. I was nodding off frequently. I had some time before the next checkpoint, and it was unlikely we would see it anyway because of the clouds.

I was thankful for the autopilot but using it only encouraged me to doze off. I was now scooting down in my seat to get more comfortable, a sure sign that things were about to go dreamy. The gentle rocking of the turbulence wasn't helping matters.

Suddenly, I jerked awake, looked ahead and saw the sunrise coming up in my windshield. I was breaking out from the cloud cover but something was very wrong.

Seeing the sun in my windshield meant that I was headed east. That wouldn't normally be an issue. But heading east from my normal flight path meant that I was over the Gulf of Mexico somewhere! With the early morning light reflecting off the waves below, I saw nothing but water all around.

I was confused and disoriented. *Did I sleep through the whole mission? Did Rob leave me behind? Maybe he had gone ahead, dropped his load, and headed home without me.* I didn't have a clue how long I'd been asleep. My first reaction was to turn back to the west and get back on course.

After a few minutes I saw the coastline to my southwest, so I aimed for it and looked for familiar landmarks. I tuned in the Tampico VOR to get a bearing and found out that I was somewhere off the 120-degree radial. (VOR stands for "Very high frequency Omni-directional Range." It is a ground based navigational transmitter.)

Through the occasional breaks in the clouds I could see "The Wolf"—Lobos Island—so I took a heading straight for it.

My head began to clear. By my calculations I'd been sixty miles off the coast southeast of Tampico when I awoke. I couldn't figure out why my wing leveler caused me to turn ninety degrees off course. The autopilot was still working and engaged, but I was heading in the wrong direction. Somehow the heading hold function of the autopilot became disengaged and the aircraft turned slowly to the left.

There was still a lot of cloudiness in the area. Below me the waves were breaking well off shore. The wind was picking up directly out of the east.

I picked up the VHF microphone and called, "You there, Rob?"

"Yeah, right here," he replied.

What a relief! I hadn't flown off the edge of the earth. It can get pretty lonely, flying deep into a country where you're not welcome. But hearing Rob's voice my feeling of isolation vanished.

"Are you in the clear?" Rob said.

"Not anymore," I said. "Where are you?"

"I'm just coming up on The Wolf."

"I'm behind you now," I replied.

Rob was surprised.

"How did that happen?" he said.

"I fell asleep and found myself out over the water."

"Good thing you woke up when you did! I guess I'll be going in first."

"Yeah, it looks like I'm about ten minutes behind you now," I said. "Call me when you're getting ready to land."

I didn't hear from Rob for another forty-five minutes. The weather hadn't improved much and I was in the clouds more than not.

Our final checkpoint was a small peak just a few miles inland. We would steer to the west of the hill and call Renaldo on the FM radio. Renaldo didn't always answer right away; in fact, we usually had to call him twice.

I was still in the clouds when I heard Rob call Renaldo on the FM. Shortly after that Rob called me on the VHF.

"It's pretty windy down here," he said. "I don't know if we're going to be able to land."

"Be careful," I said. "If we don't land, I'll have to get some fuel somewhere."

The radios were silent from that time on. I tried calling Rob a couple times after that just to see if he'd turned around for some reason. But there was nothing. I took that as a sign that he was on the ground and in the process of offloading the airplane and dumping fuel in the wings. I kept on course and hoped for the best.

Five minutes later I broke out of the clouds just north of the small peak. In the direction of the *pista* I noticed a plume of smoke coming from beyond the hill and streaking across the landscape to the west. Maybe Renaldo had built a signal fire to help us locate the airstrip. I couldn't actually see the strip as it was obscured by the hill on its north end. There was no need to continue calling Rob as he was certainly on the ground by now and would have told me if he'd decided to turn around. I continued towards the *pista*.

I followed our normal procedure and dropped to a low altitude, getting ready to land.

The plume of smoke was getting bigger and much darker.

I picked up the FM and called Renaldo but got no response. I called him several more times with the same result. I tried to raise Rob but he didn't answer either.

About the time I was supposed to set up for landing I could see just over the hill, about halfway down the landing area. I saw flames rising up through billowing smoke that was now very thick and black.

I added power and flew over the hill. When I looked down my worst fears were realized.

Rob's airplane was on its back, lying sideways on the airstrip at the halfway point. His right main landing gear had dug into the gravel off the right side of the hard surface. I could see the skid marks where the airplane weathervaned in the strong crosswind and where his propeller had struck the pavement just before flipping over.

I didn't see Rob anywhere. Renaldo and several of his men were running in all directions. They were frantically waving their hands, gesturing for me to go back.

I made a turn around the scene and realigned myself with the *pista* to attempt a landing short of where Rob's plane had come to rest. It was the only open area where a landing was even remotely possible. As I topped the hill at the north end the turbulence was severe, and controlling the airplane became difficult. There was no way of landing from either direction and stopping before colliding with Rob's burning airplane. As I've mentioned, The Highway at Veracruz was only fourteen feet wide. On top of that, I had just a little over five hundred feet to touch down and bring the aircraft to a stop. And did I mention the strong and gusty crosswinds?

I estimated the winds to be directly across the *pista* at thirty knots, with gusts to over forty. On a normal hard-surfaced runway of sixty feet wide, even an experienced pilot would have difficulty keeping the nose wheel on the centerline.

A little voice inside my head asked me a question:

How do you feel about two accidents today?

I had to make one of the most agonizing decisions of my life. Renaldo's ground crew continued running about and frantically waving their hands. They knew I couldn't land and didn't want me to try; they didn't want to deal with another tragedy. My chance of making it in successfully was zero. I had no choice but to abort the mission.

I wanted to help Rob but there was no place to go—no other roads or landing strips. The only *pista* was over a hundred miles away, and even if I landed there, I wouldn't be able to communicate with anyone. The unused pistas are remote and usually unoccupied. And landing at a local airport would have been futile and only caused confusion.

All I could do was hope that the Mexicans would take care of Rob until I could get back to the United States and help with the rescue from there. That assumed, of course, that Rob was still alive. From what I saw of the crash site, I had my doubts. I was relatively certain that if Rob had survived the crash, the ensuing fire would have killed him. And nobody on the ground had firefighting equipment.

I could be in Brownsville in three hours and provide information so that someone could coordinate everything from there. This seemed like the best option. I made up my mind and turned around . . . leaving the chaos, and Rob, behind.

All I could think about was Rob and his family. I replayed the events in my mind, over and over again. *Was there anything else I could have done?* Right or wrong, I made the call . . . and I'd have to live with it.

Because I had fallen asleep and turned off course, I lost my place in line and Rob ended up ahead of me. If I had been first and had attempted the landing, would the outcome have been different? I felt guilty flying away from the scene.

I made many attempts to reach someone on both the FM and VHF radios. I even tried to contact a Mexican ground facility. Nothing worked. So I continued north into the early morning, racing back to Brownsville as fast as I could.

I realized I had another problem. My time aloft was now beyond three and a half hours, and I had three more to go. I hadn't been able to add fuel at the *pista*, and my jaunt over the Gulf burned even more precious gas. I throttled back for maximum range and adjusted the mixture to the leanest setting possible. Any leaner and the engine would have run rough and lost too much power. I started calculating speed, distance and fuel burn on the plain brown wrapped packages beside me. The results were not good. The added time over the Gulf, circling at the accident site, and the fact that I hadn't conserved fuel on the way down, meant that I'd run out of fuel several miles south of Brownsville. Over and over I jotted calculations on the brown wrappers, and over and over I arrived at the same answer.

I was going to come up short.

I needed an alternate plan. For the most part it was simple: when the engine quit, I would land. At this point I didn't care too much about what happened to my airplane; I just wanted to get back and send help to Rob.

What I would land on was almost as simple. There was a beach that stretched for nearly five hundred miles ahead of me. I could dead-stick the airplane onto the sand.

Problem was, by my calculations I would run out of fuel about forty miles south of Brownsville. How would I find help from there?

As I continued on, I kept checking my mixture and power setting to get maximum range. As I passed north of Tampico I entered the clouds again and encountered some light rain. I could tell by the occasional breaks in the clouds that the weather was deteriorating in the area. I hoped that by the time the tanks ran dry I'd be far enough north to be in fair weather again. I wanted to be in the clear when the time came to glide this thing in.

Now I had to make plans for a forced landing.

Once the fuel tanks were empty I'd have to dead-stick it onto the sand. I wondered if it would be better to land under power rather than chance a dead-stick landing on an unfamiliar beach. I'd probably damage the airplane either way, yet I couldn't bear the thought of landing with fuel remaining only to discover I had enough to get ten miles closer to the border. Even though my calculations kept coming up about forty miles short, I could have made some math errors. I could actually have less fuel than I'd figured, and would be forced down sooner than expected. Regardless, I decided to press on.

I wanted to be sure that the wing tanks were completely empty. I planned to run one dry and as soon as the engine surged I could switch to a fuller tank. The tip extension tanks were already empty. I knew that I had about twenty minutes of fuel in the left wing tank, so I decided to run the right one dry first. Then, with the last twenty minutes in the left I could descend below the clouds and fly along the beach until all the fuel was gone.

The weather was crappy and I was solid in the soup. I figured I was within a mile or two of the beach but with the strong northeasterly winds, I couldn't be sure.

I tuned in the Tampico VOR to get a fix and verify that I was east of the mountains. With just over an hour to go I made a course correction and dead-reckoned it in the clouds for about twenty minutes.

I avoided descending because the engine burned more fuel at lower altitudes. At five thousand feet I could squeak her back to about fourteen and a half gallons per hour. At sea level the best I could do was sixteen, and that might have made the critical difference. I continued on in the soup until I was sure to recognize the landmarks once I broke out underneath.

I wanted to be sure I had a running engine when I was forced to descend to clear air below. If I didn't plan properly and exhausted my fuel while I was still in the clouds, I'd be gliding into the unknown. If I broke out under a five-hundred-foot ceiling with a dead engine I wouldn't have time to make corrections to reach a good stretch of the beach. My descent rate at my current weight would have been close to a thousand feet per minute with no power.

At that time there were few radio aids in Mexico and no radar whatsoever in that area. Even if I could have established radio contact, there would have been no guidance. The norm here was strictly dead-reckoning.

Still in the soup, I watched the right fuel gauge drop until it no longer bounced against the empty peg. I tuned in the Brownsville VOR and looked at my DME (Distance Measuring Equipment) and saw that I was only making a hundred twenty knots over the ground. The DME also informed me that I was ninety-six miles and forty-eight minutes away from Brownsville. *It would have been nice to have an hour's worth of fuel,* I thought. With even fifty minutes I could make it home. I wasn't looking forward to ditching on the beach.

Fifteen minutes later the engine surged and I reached down and rotated the fuel selector to the left. Almost immediately the engine caught again, and with just a few surges from the propeller I was running steady again.

Now I had to descend below the clouds and find the beach. I adjusted my heading a little to the east and started down. At two thousand feet above sea level I broke out underneath the clouds. I was finally able to navigate visually.

I was about 2 miles inland from the beach. I set a heading to intercept it within a few minutes. I was over *Laguna Madre.* That was good news. I was only about sixty-five miles from home.

Soon I was flying along the east shoreline of Mexico. I looked at the waves below and noticed the streaks in the water signaled a shift in the wind direction.

Wind speed and direction usually changes with altitude. Sometimes this works in your favor and sometimes it doesn't. Fortunately, the lower I'd descended the more the wind shifted towards the south. At this altitude I was able to pick up the Brownsville VOR from about sixty miles away. I tuned in the nav radio and received the signal. It indicated that I was now only twenty eight minutes out, doing a hundred and twenty-five knots.

Maybe a lower altitude would give me even better ground speed, I thought. I brought the airplane down to a thousand feet and verified that I'd gained another five knots. I wondered how much better this could get.

I was getting closer to the deck and wanted to have some altitude available to make adjustments before I hit the beach with a dead engine. Altitude equates to time, and I would need that little bit of extra time to give me a better chance at walking away from the forced landing.

I looked again at the streak pattern across the waves: the surface winds had now shifted to the southeast. I decided to drop to the deck. Again, because I was too low, I lost the Brownsville VOR signal; but just before I did, I noticed my speed had increased to around a hundred thirty knots. I could only assume I was doing better than that down here, fifty feet above the sand. If my groundspeed had increased to a hundred thirty-five knots as I'd hoped, there was a slight chance I'd make it. That thought made me anxious.

One more thing: I was beginning to suffer a problem I'd known about for the last couple of hours: my bladder wasn't happy.

I'd been flying this thing for over six hours, and the last time I pissed was before we left Cameron County. The pain was growing intense but wasn't yet unbearable. I only had to make it another twenty minutes.

I laughed. If the engine decided to quit before I reached Brownsville, I'd probably piss my pants anyway. Come to think of it, if by some miracle I made it to the United States, I would still probably piss my pants out of pure amazement.

I had to make another hard decision. Brownsville International Airport is not located on the beach. I had to cross some rough ground pockmarked with ditches and ponds. Inland of the beach there wasn't a suitable landing area for several miles. I was flying no more than a hundred feet above the deck with zero gliding distance. The cargo net between me and the twelve hundred pounds in the back wasn't designed to restrain the freight from slamming forward in a crash. But staying over the sand meant I was accepting more delays in helping Rob. I had to go for it.

It was time to turn inland. My heart was pounding hard and my bladder was about to burst. I tuned the VHF radio and called the Brownsville tower. I gave them a position report and declared I was inbound for landing. I also informed him that I was unable to reactivate my flight plan for coming back across the border and the tower controller offered to relay that for me. It was good to hear the American over the radio speaker.

The tower informed me of the weather and said the winds were blowing from a hundred and twenty degrees at eighteen knots. The controller asked me to execute a right-hand pattern to runway one-three. I didn't have the fuel to fly the pattern to the northwest of the airport so I asked for a straight-in approach to runway three-one; I needed to land as soon as possible. The tower repeated the wind direction and stated that it favored one-three.

I glanced at my ground speed, and sure enough, I was now skimming over the landscape at a hundred fifty knots. It was almost too good to be true. But I was still worried that the engine would starve itself of fuel before I touched down. I called the tower again:

"I really need three-one," I said.

"Roger, understand," said the tower. "Report crossing the river for three-one."

I was just a few miles from the border and coming upon Mexican farmland east of Matamoros. Now if I had to force it down, I might be able to land in a cornfield and walk away.

My fuel gauges showed no sign of life. All needles were dead on "E"—empty.

As I crossed the Rio Grande I called the tower again. The controller cleared me to land on three-one. It was time to slow down for landing so I raised the nose a bit and traded some of my airspeed for altitude.

I then realized that I would make it.

I was only a mile from the airport and just high enough to glide to the runway should the engine stop. Because I was landing with the strong wind at my back I was coming in fast. Fortunately the runway was plenty long, and even at around ninety knots touchdown speed I'd have plenty of room to stop.

As my wheels hit the runway I thought about Rob. I wondered if he was alive.

I turned left off three-one, and shortly thereafter the engine surged but kept running. I was low on fuel all right!

I taxied directly to customs. When I spun around to the right to park, the engine stopped. I was out of fuel. My ordeal was over, and now maybe I could provide some information to help Rob.

Customs rules didn't allow anyone near the airplane until an agent had inspected it. I knew Ray was inside, anxiously awaiting news of the accident. I shut down the electrical power and rolled my stiff and aching body out of the airplane. The pain in my abdomen had me hunched over as I ran for the door to the customs office. As I approached the building the door swung open. It was Ray.

"How you doing?" he said.

"Not so good," I said. "I don't think Rob made it."

I ran into the building and painfully grimaced at the customs agent.

"My bladder's about to burst," I said. "I'll be right with you."

"Go ahead," he said.

Later, as I filled out my customs paperwork, Ray told me that Renaldo had called and said that Rob had survived the crash. Unfortunately, he was badly burned and wasn't expected to live much longer.

"I'm making arrangements to have him picked up in Veracruz," said Ray. "I don't suppose you want to ride along?"

"Do you need me to go?" I said.

"Not really. They've already taken him into town and a doctor is supposedly looking after him. Happy Boy is on his way here from Cameron County and will go get him in the 340."

"I tried, but there was no way I could land," I said.

"I know. Renaldo didn't want to deal with two accidents. You made the right decision. Rob got medical care sooner than if you had loaded him in your airplane and flown him back."

"When's Happy leaving?"

"He's coming here first and then will be leaving right away."

Happy Boy had come along about a month earlier and was beginning to make occasional trips with Rob and me. He was a native to South Texas, in his early thirties and loved adventure and offshore fishing. He and his brother spent most of their free time in their boats out in the Gulf. Happy got his name from the fact that he always had a smile or smirk on his face. He was a light-hearted man with few cares and a zest for life. I spent some time with him and his brother out in the Gulf and learned a lot about offshore seamanship and hooking big game fish. I never caught anything larger than thirty pounds but was witness to some pretty sizable monsters coming in over the side.

As I talked to Ray I was feeling the come down effects from my ordeal. I had just spent over six and a half hours in an airplane. The last three and a half were spent anguishing over Rob, his condition, my actions and my decisions. Ray comforted me, but I had witnessed the whole thing and all I could think about was Rob being trapped in that burning airplane.

Physically and emotionally I wasn't in much condition to go on. If Happy was flying the 340 he wouldn't be using The Highway to get Rob anyway. Happy would check through customs in Veracruz and enter the country legally. That would give him access to hospitals or wherever Rob was located.

Since Happy was also a relative newcomer to the business, he wasn't recognizable to the Mexican authorities yet. But, I wasn't so sure of my status. As far as I knew, I could be identified and arrested. Maybe my picture was hanging in some Mexican post office somewhere.

In reality, the police and soldiers cared little about me personally. They could be paid off and would leave us alone unless some *commandante* or political figure needed to make a statement and have one of us stopped. Although ending up in a Mexican prison still loomed over us, the people I feared the most were the renegade authorities looking for a piece of the payoff. Corruption was widespread. The *capitans* of the small regiments wouldn't hesitate to line their own pockets. They would go to great lengths to profit by capturing one of us *banditos*.

Some of the *capitans* were more zealous than others. They would cause us grief even if they'd been paid off. Some were granted unchecked authority to do whatever it took to stop the smuggling. But we were electronics smugglers, not murderers. Our crimes had more of an economic impact and we never really hurt anyone. But *banditos* were *banditos*, and the proud Mexican with a badge had a grudge against us *gringos* thumbing our noses at their bands of soldiers.

As I finished with customs, Happy Boy landed in Brownsville. Ray and I went outside to greet him as he taxied on the customs ramp. He shut down and climbed out of the Cessna 340.

"What's the latest?" Happy said as he hopped down the stairs.

"Supposedly, one of Renaldo's men will be waiting for you in Veracruz," said Ray. "Once you check through customs he will take you to a doctor who will assist you in getting Rob out of there."

"Sounds good," said Happy.

"This is now a medical rescue," Ray continued, "and as I understand it the customs people are willing to cooperate with us."

In addition to his injuries Rob had another problem. He was in Mexico illegally. He had no entry records, and getting on an American airplane bound for the U.S. meant that Happy might have to answer some questions before being allowed to leave. Happy had several thousand U.S. dollars in his pocket to be used for bribes as needed. Everything was supposed to be prearranged, and according to Ray, there should be no problems getting Rob home.

After a brief conversation with Ray and me, Happy left the customs office and got back into the twin-engine Cessna and took off.

It would take Happy a little over two hours to reach Veracruz in the turbocharged twin airplane. We used the 340 mainly for leisure trips in the U.S. It was pressurized and comfortable enough for six people.

Happy was to give Ray a call when he arrived, and call again before he departed with Rob onboard. Ray would have an ambulance standing by in Brownsville to rush Rob to any medical facility he needed.

I called Hal's from a phone in the customs office and requested a fuel truck. Soon the 100 low-lead truck arrived, parked in front of The Spook, and began topping it off. I didn't need to top it off, of course, but since the tanks were dry I wanted to know exactly how much fuel the wings held. Although the book said that the main tanks held seventy-three usable, it wasn't uncommon for that figure to vary by a few gallons from airplane to airplane. The main fuel tanks in these airplanes consisted of rubber bladders, and installation anomalies could alter their capacity slightly.

There are only two opportunities to measure total usable fuel. One is during a maintenance function and the other is when the engine stops from fuel starvation. When the tanks run dry, whatever goes back in is exactly what you've got.

I asked the lineman who was fueling to make sure he filled the tanks all the way.

"Put every drop you can in it," I said.

"We always do for you guys," he answered.

Hal's Flight Line was a good Fixed Base Operator. It was owned by a man that understood what we were doing and knew we needed all the support we could get.

I stood by and watched the meter as the lineman filled each tank. He took care of the mains first, then pulled the hose out to each tip and topped them off. When he finished the left main I looked at the meter and read 37.2—about a half gallon more than it was supposed to take.

The right main came in at 37.5 and together the tips held 28.5 for a total of 103.2 gallons. So The Spook took precisely 2.2 gallons more than the book called for.

Those 2.2 gallons gave me eight more minutes of flying I didn't count on. I'd flown six hours and thirty-seven minutes and burned an average of just over 15.5 gallons per hour.

I also realized that the analog fuel flow meter on the instrument panel was off by about a half gallon per hour, in cruise anyway. That was pretty good for a gauge that was notorious for error.

I thanked the lineman for the gas, signed the ticket and climbed back in the airplane to reposition to Cameron County. The whole day felt surreal and seemed to have occurred days before rather than just hours.

When I landed at Cameron, Wally was waiting for me on the ramp.

"How's Rob?" he asked.

"I don't know," I said. "I don't think it's good, though."

"Shit!" Wally exclaimed as he turned back toward the hangar shop door. "Do you think Rob made it?"

"We'll know soon enough," I said. "I'm going home. Call me if you hear anything."

Once I got home I went inside my apartment, plopped down on my bed and fell asleep. There was much more to do but I was done for now. I dreamed about the mission and woke up several hours later to the telephone ringing. It was Ray and he was irritated. Happy had arrived in Veracruz and discovered that nobody was waiting for him.

"Those sons of bitches don't know where he is!" Ray said. "Renaldo told me they'd moved Rob to a different hospital and that there wasn't anything we could do to get him released. I couldn't even find out what hospital or where it was located. I don't know if they're lying to me or not. I didn't see any reason to keep Happy there all night, so he's on his way home. I'll call you later."

Things were turning ugly. If Rob was still alive he certainly needed intensive medical care, and only a well-equipped hospital would have the facilities to do that. Perhaps they'd taken him to a hospital in another community. But Veracruz was the largest city in the vicinity of the accident.

I had a long night. I didn't do much but sit around and think about Rob. I tried watching TV but couldn't concentrate on anything. At 10:30 Happy Boy called me and said he was back in the states.

"They don't give you any cooperation down there," he said. "I spoke to Ray and he couldn't get any straight answers either. If they get their act together I'll go back down in the morning. Otherwise, it's all a waste of time and right now we don't even know where Rob is."

The next morning Ray called me at seven. The people in Veracruz told him that Rob had died. Rob had been moved from the crash site to a doctor's home, and had died there.

"Have you called Bev?" I said. Bev was Rob's wife.

"No, not yet. I can't seem to get confirmation from anyone. I'll keep you informed."

I called Happy Boy and he said he was planning on going back to get Rob come hell or high water. If they didn't cooperate he was going to knock a few heads.

At about noon I heard from Ray again. This time he was steaming mad.

"Rob is alive and those sons of bitches are holding out on us!" he yelled. "Now they want us to bring more money."

"That's incredible!" I said. "Is Rob still in Veracruz?"

"As far as I know. I sent Happy with ten grand but will wire more if necessary. Those sons of bitches better let him go now!"

Happy flew into Veracruz and checked in through Mexican Customs. We still didn't know exactly where Rob was, but Ray felt that he was finally getting some cooperation and Happy would stay there until he had Rob on board the airplane.

At about eight o'clock that night, Ray called me and said that Happy was on his way back . . . and that he had Rob with him.

"Happy says that Rob is in pretty bad shape, but alive," Ray said. "I've called the hospital in Harlingen and they're going to be waiting at the airport. They may transport Rob directly to San Antonio. There's a burn center there."

I grabbed my car keys and sped to the airport. By the time I got there, Happy had already landed and Rob was in a military medevac transport headed to San Antonio.

"They were playing games with us," Happy said. "I told 'em if they didn't come up with either Rob or his body soon, I was going to kick someone's Mexican ass."

"The important thing now is that Rob is getting good care," I said. "He's on his way to one of the best burn centers in the nation."

Rob's condition was critical. It was still touch-and-go, as his burns were very serious. Things were quiet in the smuggling world and nobody was doing any flying. We were all waiting to hear about Rob.

For the next few days he battled a number of infections. Ray told me that things would be uncertain for weeks to come. Then I got another phone call from Ray. He sounded troubled.

"How's it going?" I said.

"It's bad, Bill."

Ray's voice was so quiet, he was almost whispering.

"Rob's dead," he murmured. "He died about an hour ago."

"I'm sorry, Ray. How are Bev and the kids doing?"

"As well as can be expected."

"I wish there was something more I could have done."

"These things happen," said Ray, "and we go into it knowing that we take chances. Rob understood that. He told me several times how he knew something could happen and didn't ever want me to feel guilty."

I didn't say anything. Ray needed to talk.

"It was his decision," said Ray. "But that doesn't help now. I feel like I failed him in some way. I only wish I could change what happened that morning. I look back and play the whole thing over and over in my head and can't figure it out, Bill. Why did this have to happen to him?"

I hung my head and began to tear up. I couldn't seem to offer any comforting words to Ray. Why had things gone so wrong? Why did I feel so guilty for letting Rob get ahead of me that morning? When things were going well, we all celebrated victory and laughed with one another about how we'd cheated death. But now. . . I took a deep breath and swallowed hard.

"It should have been me," I said.

CHAPTER 11

THE BARNYARD

A COOL MIST SAILED in from the Gulf. Ray strolled into the restaurant looking for Happy and me. He wanted to talk with us on the ramp after we finished our breakfast. It was not an unusual request, as Ray would often meet us on the ramp to discuss particulars about the day's trip.

When Happy and I met Ray on the ramp, he was in his usual matter-of-fact mood. He stood there with his coffee and told us that we'd be flying into The Barnyard today.

The Barnyard? Happy and I looked at each other and then back at Ray. The last time we flew into The Barnyard we nearly wiped out an entire flock of chickens that were feeding on the strip. Ray smiled and assured us he'd spoken to Cruz about that.

"We shouldn't have any more problems with animals there," he said.

The Barnyard was a dirt strip about a thousand feet long, located southwest of Tampico. It was a good *pista* and we considered it to be quite secure. There was a dense area of trees along the entire west side and at the south end, which gave us a good place to unload. We could park two airplanes at a time there, so it was usually a more relaxed atmosphere where we could enjoy some homemade tacos for breakfast. I figured Cruz lived near there, since his wife usually appeared with the tray of tacos.

There was only one serious problem with The Barnyard: the animals. It should have been called the Zoo-On-The-Loose, or even One of These Days, but that was already taken. Almost every landing was a game of dodge-the-goat or pig or cow. The Barnyard, as its name implied, was just that. It felt like landing in a livestock feedlot where the animals roamed free. There was more danger of plowing into a wandering cow than being taken captive by the Mexican police.

It was just three airplanes today. Happy and I were headed for The Barnyard and Buddy was making a run to The Ranch for Raúl. Happy still had to file his flight plan so he told me to go on ahead.

"I'll be about five minutes behind you," he said.

Buddy was about to taxi out. He shouted to me from under his wing: "Hey Bronco, let's do a flight of two!"

"Sure, I'll follow you," I replied, "and you do the talking."

As soon as I was ready, Buddy and I taxied together to customs for our outbound declarations. When we finished I followed him to the end of the runway. The tower cleared us to takeoff as a flight of two. I focused on Buddy's airplane ahead of me and mimicked his every move. We departed Brownsville, and from engine start through takeoff and departure I never said a word as Buddy made all the radio calls.

As soon as we crossed the river, Buddy radioed me and asked where Happy Boy was. I told him that he would be along shortly and I asked him how the weather was at The Ranch.

"It's a little foggy but should burn off by the time I get there," he called back. "You were pretty close this morning. What were you tryin' to do, hitch a ride?"

"I figured you needed a little thrill to wake you up this morning," I said. "And what are you doing looking back? You should be concentrating ahead."

"I don't trust you," he laughed. "You're crazy!"

"That makes two of us," I said.

As Buddy drifted off towards The Ranch, I continued to The Barnyard. I thought about the weather. There was fog spread across the whole region. It was supposed to lift but we never knew for sure when.

I decided that I would stay on course and see how things went. So far the weather was still marginal. Buddy and I had the usual chit-chat as we flew deeper into Mexico. He asked me if I wanted to do some more waterskiing and invited me back out to the *arroyo* (the river) when the weather warmed up a little.

Soon Buddy and I left each other as we headed to our individual *pistas*.

"Be good, Bronco," Buddy told me. "Maybe I'll catch you on the way back."

Soon he was out of sight as he entered some low scattered clouds. He would fly the next twenty minutes down on the deck. We all had our own ways of avoiding detection. Since Guerrero had almost captured me, I spent more time up high and watched my back. Because of the load I couldn't see out most of the airplane and Guerrero would not hesitate to exploit my blind spots if he intercepted me in the air. Occasionally I turned to my left and looked back to make sure I wasn't being followed.

The fog began breaking up, and I could see that Buddy would have no problems getting into his *pista*. We actually liked to have *some* clouds around us because it was harder to be spotted. The authorities were familiar with most of our airplanes and the *pistas* we used. Since The Ranch was not surrounded by trees or mountains, we'd use any camouflage that was available. As I passed directly over The Ranch I caught a glimpse of Buddy coming in from the northeast. I wondered how many airstrips had been used by smugglers and how many were now abandoned.

South of La Pesca the clouds were breaking up just fine. As I approached the lakes to the west of Tampico I started down.

"Hey Happy, you out there?" I called.

"You got him," he replied.

"I'm just about there. The weather looks good."

"Save me a taco!" Happy said.

I picked up the FM and keyed the mic. It was time to contact our receiver.

"Hey, Cruz!" I said.

"It's okay," Cruz squawked back.

We were good to go. I put the FM microphone back in its holder.

I made my usual long and low final just above the trees. As the *pista* came into view I saw a few chickens running around next to the landing strip, and some kind of scurry going on at the turn around point at the far end.

With the throttle closed and the flaps coming up, I pulled back on the yoke, planted it on the end of the runway and began to apply the brakes. I rolled to a stop at the far end and paused before turning around—the unloading crew was frantically chasing a large pig back into the trees.

I spun around and pulled the mixture to stop the engine. I heard my back door being opened and a lot of excited conversation. I stepped out, greeted Cruz, and anxiously anticipated my tacos. Within a few seconds Mrs. Cruz came out from under the trees, carrying a tray. Cruz smiled at me.

"You like a taco, Bronco Billy?"

"*Sí, bueno,*" I replied.

I was about to take my first bite when I heard Cruz's men shouting again. They were running and waving their hands in the air. Cruz threw down his taco and, shouting and cursing, rushed to the other side of the plane.

The pig had returned. It ran wildly in half-circles and threw dirt, pig crap and busted pieces of electronics all over the place, kicking and squealing the whole time.

I quickly moved clear of the activity and so did Cruz.

I swear I saw two or three Mexicans flying through the air that day. Cruz tried to reassure me that all would be well. To me it was business as usual. Just more aggravation and another example of how not to believe everything Cruz said or promised.

It wasn't the goods I was concerned about. Obviously the pig was causing a lot of damage as Cruz's men chased it around. I was worried that the pig might damage my airplane. That swine was trying to take his aggression out on my ride home! If that thing were to come into contact with the aluminum propeller, the paper-thin skin, or any part of the tail, I'd be hitching a ride home with Happy Boy in the back of Peanut Butter. (That's what Wally named our new airplane.)

Eventually Cruz's men got control of things. After clearing away the mess it was time for me to leave. Cruz seemed overly apologetic; in broken English he assured me that there would be no more pig trouble at The Barnyard.

"I take care of *porcina!*" Cruz said. *I take care of that swine.*

As I crawled into the airplane I heard Happy on the FM:

"Hey, Cruz!"

Cruz spoke into his handheld FM transceiver.

"It's okay."

I couldn't bring myself to warn Happy Boy about the pig. I rolled my airplane off the end and headed straight out to the north.

Yeah, right, it's okay, I thought to myself.

In a few minutes my VHF crackled. It was Happy.

"What happened back there?" he asked.

"Did you get to meet the pig?" I said.

"No, but there was busted up packages and pig shit all over the place. Looks like you guys had some fun."

"I didn't even get to finish my taco," I said.

"I think the taco lady split," replied Happy.

An hour and a half later we were back at U.S. Customs in Brownsville, laughing over the whole matter. Ray didn't see the humor in it.

The next morning I flew from Cameron County to Brownsville as I usually did. Ray and Happy were already there. We had no time for breakfast as we had to get a jump on things and possibly make two trips that day.

"I talked to Cruz," said Ray. "He was sorry for the problem yesterday. I told him that we can't use The Barnyard anymore. He said that the rancher has moved all of his animals to another farm and that we won't see anything from here on out."

Happy said something about a commitment he had that afternoon, and Ray asked me if I could take two more trips.

"Sure," I said. "Where are we going today?"

"The Barnyard," Ray said, laughing.

I knew Ray didn't want us going back there but our receivers called the shots as to where the loads got dropped. We tried to convince Cruz that we didn't like The Barnyard and he convinced us that the trouble with livestock was behind us.

The outbound check through customs was routine. Happy was a few minutes behind me again and we exchanged only a few comments over the VHF on the way down. I wasn't looking forward to another morning at The Barnyard.

An hour and a half later I picked up the FM microphone and pressed the transmit button.

"Hey, Cruz."

This time there was no answer. This was not a good sign: our rendezvous times were usually within a minute or two, and we always expected an immediate response if all was well. Again I keyed the mike.

"Hey, Cruz."

Finally the reply came: "It's okay."

I hung up the microphone and wondered if something was amiss. Perhaps he didn't hear me because his volume was turned down. Perhaps he was being held at gunpoint and delayed his response to tip me off. Or maybe he was preoccupied with rounding up a pig!

Whatever the case, I approached the *pista* a little bit higher to get a better look at things before I committed to land. Once a fully loaded 207 is transitioning to idle power at that slow speed and the flaps are retracting, there is no going around. You're committed to land.

Everything looked pretty normal and I saw only a few harmless chickens feeding off to one side. I could clearly make out the truck and spotted one individual resembling Cruz standing off to the side just as expected. For all I could tell, things appeared calm.

I set up to flare, committed to land and kept a close watch. Not only did I need to put an airplane into a short strip but I also had to watch for livestock and gun barrels. Both were able to ruin my day. I touched down and rolled to a stop at the other end of the strip, then spun the airplane around and pulled the mixture. I saw Cruz walking toward me with his usual smile.

"Hey, Bronco Billy!" he said.

"Hey, Cruz, *¿Qué pasa?*" I said.

I told him that Happy Boy would be along soon. I was hungry. I had skipped enchiladas in Brownsville earlier, so I was looking forward to a breakfast of tacos. . . . And there she was, coming out from under the trees, carrying her tray of tacos. She first offered me my portion and then held them out to Cruz. He picked out a couple and told her to make sure I had enough.

"*Sí*, I take care of you, Bronco Billy," he said.

I'd finished my second taco and had started on a third when Cruz looked at me and, still smiling, asked, "You like your tacos, Bronco Billy?"

"*Sí, bueno!*" I replied.

"*Sí, bueno*," Cruz repeated, "and *no more pig*! I take care of him good!"

I laughed as I realized that I was eating a pork taco made from a freshly butchered hog.

"*No more pig!*" we both shouted and laughed.

I headed back to my plane. Happy had just landed. We waved as we passed each other. When I climbed into my cockpit, I stuck another paperclip on the visor.

Those tacos were the best tacos I ever ate.

CHAPTER 12
NO BUBBA, NO!

I T WAS A HOT AND STEAMY South Texas afternoon and I was hanging out at Cameron County enjoying a Budweiser as Wally repaired some engine baffling. Ray drove up with someone in the car with him. I didn't recognize the other guy.

"Bill, I want you to meet someone," said Ray. "This is Bubba, and I want you to get him ready for some flying."

Bubba was in his mid-thirties, a little on the heavy side, and wore a plaid shirt, blue jeans, cowboy boots and a big belt buckle. He had a thick Texas drawl and greeted me with a firm handshake and a smile.

"Glad to meet you," he said.

"Likewise," I replied. "How much time do you have in 207s?"

"Most of my flyin's been in DC-3s and Twin Beeches," he said. "I've got plenty of single Piper time and about two hundred hours in Skyhawks and the like."

"Great, the 207 is just a big Skyhawk," I said. "We'll put some sandbags in one and practice some short field landings. Get in and I'll show you some distance markings on the runway."

As we drove out, Bubba mentioned that Ray had explained the sandbag thing.

"How much did he tell you?" I asked.

"He said you load a plane up with sandbags and see how short you can land," said Bubba.

"Did he tell you how short he wanted?"

"No. Only that we needed to stop as short as possible."

As we reached the end of runway, I said. "Well, here's the deal. You see that blacktop extension of the runway? Well, that is a thousand feet long, and with only twelve hundred pounds of sand you have to be able to stop in about half the blacktop portion."

"You're shittin' me!" said Bubba.

"Did Ray tell you about One of These Days?"

"No, I guess not," said Bubba. "He only mentioned that you guys used a couple of short airstrips and that if I could land short enough in a practice run with sandbags, I would get the job."

"One of These Days is one of our most secure *pistas*," I said. "However, it's a bit tricky. It is eight hundred feet long, dirt and gravel, and has telephone poles along one side and unusable rough ground along the other."

"That seems kind of short," Bubba replied.

"That's not the best part," I said. "You've got to cross a fence and plant it right on the end. Because at the other end there's a gas well a little off to the right side and a three-inch pipe running across the end of the strip. If you don't get stopped in time, KABOOM! It will ruin your whole day. That's why we call it One of These Days. There's zero room for error."

I drove onto the runway and showed Bubba the 500-foot point.

"That's your stop target," I said.

When we got back to the hangar, Wally was already loading sandbags in the back of his truck. Bubba and I pitched in until we had thirty bags. We drove around to Peanut Butter and began loading the bags into the back of the airplane.

"Try not to burn the tires off," said Wally.

I laughed and assured him that it would be a cheap lesson.

"It's not the parts, it's the labor!" he said.

I coached Bubba on some techniques and said that we expected to have hot brakes and burned tires. "You want to brake hard but not skid,"

I said. "If you blow a tire in Mexico you come home on another airplane. And that would be bad."

Bubba climbed in Peanut Butter and began going through the checklist.

"You'd better learn that by heart," I explained, "and be able to do it in about three seconds."

Bubba smiled. "I told you that it'd been awhile since I was in one of these things!" he said.

Wally and I teased Bubba by shouting in our own version of Spanish: *"Hey, Gringo, get out of the aeroplano and put your hands up!"*

Bubba didn't see the humor. As he fired up the Continental, Ray appeared in the side door of the hangar.

"Let's see how he does," I said to Ray.

Ray just stood there chewing on his cigar.

"It wasn't too long ago *you* were doing this," he said.

"I know," I said. "But I think you snuck a few extra sandbags in my tail!"

We watched as Bubba taxied to the end of the runway. After a quick run-up he poured the coals to it, and soon he was lumbering into the air. We had full fuel on Peanut Butter so the weight was pretty close to what we landed at in Mexico. Stopping on a dry, hard surface was a little easier than braking on the different *pistas* in Mexico. But if you could get it down in five hundred feet on hard surface, you should be able to get her stopped at One of These Days. That was the critical one.

Bubba came around and lined up on final. He was making a normal approach, which was way too high for our Mexican *pistas*. Our procedure was to come in at treetop level from five to ten miles out. At One of These Days, you wouldn't actually see the *pista* until you came over a knoll, and—*BAM!*—there it was. Then you would chop the power, get ready to stand on the brakes, and hit the flaps up just a few seconds before your main wheels hit the ground. With the flaps fully retracted you had more weight on the wheels for braking. Leaving the flaps down might result in skidding, and that ate up too much turf. There was a wire fence at the approach end and you had to get as close to it as possible in order to utilize the full length of the strip. Otherwise you

131

would come way too close to the gas well at the far end before coming to a stop.

Bubba came over the threshold at about ten feet of altitude and chopped the power. At the halfway point he was still airborne and I noticed his flaps were still down. This one was a bust. The 500-foot point streaked beneath him and his wheels were still above the concrete.

Bubba didn't try to make a go-around. With seven thousand feet remaining he set the airplane down. We heard the brakes lock up a couple of times before he came to a stop. Then suddenly the engine roared back to life. As Bubba gained speed we noticed that his flaps were still fully extended.

"This ought to be good," chuckled Wally.

"What the hell's he doing?" said Ray.

A fully loaded 207 with the flaps extended will fly, but it was more like a brick than an airplane. It's almost impossible to accelerate and climb.

About the time Bubba got airborne we noticed the flaps begin to retract. As the flaps came up the airplane settled back down and contacted the runway. This would have been the time to chop the power and stop on whatever runway remained.

The engine roared on and Bubba burned up a good three thousand feet getting her back in the air. The weight of the airplane combined with the heat and humidity were working against him.

He finally gained the speed he needed, and this time he climbed to about five hundred feet as he flew the pattern. He was still too high, but it was better than his first attempt.

This time on final Bubba chopped the power a little sooner but still left the flaps down. He hit in the 1000-foot blacktop portion of the runway but skidded the tires excessively and still blew way past the target. He stopped about thirteen hundred feet from the end and seven hundred feet from where he'd hit the runway. I was impressed as this was only his second attempt.

Throttling up again, Bubba began his takeoff roll. He made another a 500-foot pattern and, turning a short final, he chopped the power even sooner and this time slammed the airplane onto the pavement. He still rolled about two hundred feet past the limit. This time he turned around on the runway and taxied back to the ramp where we were waiting.

Bubba was not happy and the main tires had bald spots. The shimmy dampener on the nose gear was coming loose. He rolled to a stop, pulled the mixture and sat in the airplane for a minute staring out the front. As I approached the plane he threw open his door.

"What am I doing wrong?" he shouted.

I rehearsed some of the techniques we used as Wally tightened the shimmy dampener.

Bubba climbed out and we went to the hangar for a soda. I explained the whole timing thing and reminded him about the flaps. Chopping the power earlier was his next biggest mistake and could cost him everything in the jungles of Mexico. There were *pistas* situated in terrain that was unforgiving. If you didn't hit the strip precisely, you'd lose. The best technique was to come in low and slow while carrying more power with the flaps fully extended. You had to drag it in over the trees. That way, when you cut the power, the airplane would naturally drop. Retracting the flaps at the same time helped to plant the bird on the very end of the airstrip. It was all about timing.

Spot landings are a game that most students learn early in their flight training. The instructor runs a chalk line across the runway and you compete with other students. The winner usually gets a new flight computer or plotter or something stupid like that. This was done in light trainers with no load onboard and half fuel. But that is where I learned the technique—not so much the stopping short, but the ability to touch down on a precise spot on a runway.

As Bubba and I sipped on our Pepsis he questioned me extensively about One of These Days. I told him that there was a good chance that his first solo trip would be into an airstrip called The Students rather than One of These Days, and to not get too concerned. On the other hand, One of These Days was a very secure airstrip and Bubba could count on getting in and out of there regularly once he had a couple of trips under his belt.

Wally appeared in the door as Bubba slammed down the last of his soda.

"Ready to go," Wally said.

"Then let's do it," Bubba replied.

133

When Bubba mastered the technique, he would take a ride or two with me into at least one airstrip to witness how things were done. Then, if he still wanted to pursue this type of flying he would take a load himself, with either me or Happy Boy in the other airplane.

Bubba climbed back into Peanut Butter and went right to work. Without delay he taxied to the end of the runway and poured the coals to it as he rounded the turn onto the runway.

"That's more like it," I said to Wally.

Ray headed home, asking me to call him when Bubba got it together.

I had explained to Bubba that he needed to get used to low patterns and approaches. This time he was only about two hundred feet in the air as he rounded the field. His final approach was much lower and flatter too. As he crossed the trees he now seemed to be dragging it in over the last quarter mile to the threshold. Just before crossing the end we heard him cut the power and saw the flaps coming up.

"Now he's gettin' the hang of it," I said to Wally.

This time Bubba stopped only a few feet beyond the 500-foot point. I knew he would have it in the next try or two. Now the only thing Bubba had to learn was to slow the airplane down to just above a stall. So far he'd been a little too fast.

There is a common practice maneuver among pilots called "slow flight." This is where the airplane is slowed down to the point where the stall warning horn begins to sound; and then, with full flaps and landing gear extended, you add just enough power to keep the airplane flying while making shallow turns to the left and right. Turn too steep or pitch up in the slightest and the airplane will stall.

Recovery from stalls can require several hundred feet of altitude as the airplane will naturally nose over and gravity takes over. If you have sufficient altitude, you simply begin flying again as the airplane regains adequate flying speed from the resulting dive. During training, this procedure is always practiced several thousand feet up.

Now what Bubba had to perfect was slow flight just above the trees with no room for recovery. Doing this fully loaded in the hot Mexican countryside can be unnerving. The stall speed of a Cessna 207 with fully extended flaps was about fifty-nine knots. So flying final approach at sixty was perfect. You would actually stall at the point of crossing the end, and touch down just before the airplane pitched over. That was the most desirable way to do it, but it had the least margin for error. To touch down at sixty was acceptable. The airspeed indicator in Peanut Butter had no error either, so Bubba could rely on that for his approaches.

The next pattern Bubba flew actually worried me a bit. We lost sight of him a couple of times. But we heard the roaring engine and saw him as he turned on final. This approach looked more like Mexico than his others.

Crossing the trees, Bubba had it slowed down with a nose-up attitude and lots of power. He cut the throttle at just the right moment and hit the very end of the runway. He came to a grinding halt at precisely the 500-foot point. He'd found his technique! Now, if he could repeat it a couple of times with consistency, I'd be taking a passenger with me tomorrow to show him the ropes.

Bubba made two more successful short landings, then taxied back to the ramp with a smile on his face that we could see from the hangar. He parked the airplane and climbed out.

"I think I got it!" he told us.

"That looked much better, Bubba," I said. "You think you're ready to go south tomorrow?"

"You guys don't mess around," he said, wiping the sweat off his face and neck.

"I'll give you a call after I talk to Ray," I said.

Back in Harlingen I dropped Bubba off at his hotel room and told him I'd talk to Ray.

"Okay, let's make some money!" said Bubba.

After I got home, I called Ray. "I think he's ready," I said. "Wally's putting new tires on Peanut Butter right now."

"Cruz will be at One of These Days tomorrow," said Ray. "You can give Bubba a good taste of the way we do it. I will meet you both at Hal's around 7 a.m. tomorrow."

I got up about five the next morning and drove to Cameron County. Bubba was already waiting for me. I did a quick pre-flight and we both climbed in The Spook and hopped over to Brownsville. We were running about forty-five minutes early so I suggested we have a couple of breakfast enchiladas at the terminal. Bubba eagerly agreed. About the time our order arrived, Ray came in and sat down with us and ordered coffee. He looked at Bubba.

"You ready for this?"

"I sure am," Bubba replied.

"Nobody's making you do anything, you know."

"I think Bronco here will take good care of me," Bubba said.

Ray smiled and looked at me.

"Just so the both of you don't get killed."

After breakfast Bubba and I headed to Hal's to file our DVFR flight plan. I showed Bubba how we filed our Mexican destination as *Piedras Negras*, a legitimate entry point. As far as the Mexican customs knew, we'd be arriving there in about two hours. We never went there, of course, but One of These Days wasn't exactly listed in the Mexican airport directory, and it threw off anyone who might be listening over the phone line or around the corner from the other room.

After checking through U.S. customs Bubba and I climbed in The Spook and called the tower for taxi clearance. At the end of the runway I looked over at Bubba and told him to say goodbye to the good ol' U.S. of A.

"You ready?" I said.

"Ready as ever," he replied.

We took off and were in Mexican airspace about a minute later.

The weather en route was fantastic. It was a beautiful morning—clear and smooth. The next hour and a half was pure pleasure, flying south into central Mexico. There were a lot of landmarks to point out to Bubba and it was easy in such clear conditions.

"You've got to know these landmarks," I said to Bubba.

I pointed out *Las Animal*, *Tiburon Uno*, *Tiburon Dos* and *Las Tigre*. As soon as we passed *Las Tigre* I throttled back and pointed out the general area of One of These Days. We were still about twenty miles from landing but it was time to drop to the deck. As we got closer to the trees I pointed out the landmarks that would aid Bubba in finding the airstrip. There was the barn, the rocky meadow, and finally the knoll that lay just off the end of the strip.

I picked up the microphone of the FM radio and called, "Hey, Cruz."

Immediately the reply came. "It's okay," said Cruz.

As we drew closer I showed Bubba how to stay in the valley below the trees.

"You won't actually see the strip until we're right on top of it," I explained.

I slowed down and set half flaps. As the rocky knoll came up on our left I turned directly for it, lowered the flaps to full and continued to slow down as we flew uphill and over the knoll. As soon as we reached the top, there it was.

One of These Days appeared directly ahead of us, as if out of nowhere, Descending down the back side I cut the power, and just before crossing the barbed wire fence I raised the flap selector to zero. The 207 settled firmly at the end of the airstrip, and I applied as much braking as I could without skidding. As we rolled to the far end I mentioned to Bubba that if he stayed directly in the center he would be fine and not hit the telephone poles on the left. The *pista* itself was only about twenty-five feet wide and there was a good fifteen feet beyond the wingtip to the poles. I also warned him not to drift to the right as the ground got rough and if he went too far he'd lose it for sure.

"Just stay in the middle and you'll be all right," I said.

Bubba didn't say a word but it was obvious that he was a little anxious. He'd been gripping the glare shield since we topped the hill when the *pista* came into view. We rolled out and came to a stop. At the far end I turned right to exit the *pista*, throttled up, spun around to the left and stopped. As soon as I pulled the mixture Bubba exhaled and looked at me with his eyes open wide.

"That don't seem like no eight hundred feet!" he said.

"It's not," I said, "but the book won't let us come in here with less."

The unloaders opened the back doors and greeted Bubba and me with smiles.

"*¿Qué pasa?*, Bronco Billy?"

"*Como estás?*" I said. "How are you?"

"*Ah, muy bien,*" they would reply. *Very well.*

Cruz got out of the truck and walked over to the airplane. I greeted Cruz and introduced him to Bubba.

"*Nuevo piloto, Señor* Bubba," I said. *New pilot.*

"*¿Qué pasa, Bubba?*" Cruz said. "Would you like a *tamale?*"

I told Bubba that this was a tradition with Cruz.

"*Si, muy bien,*" I said. *Yes, very good.*

Cruz smiled. "Bronco Billy knows a little Spanish, eh, Bubba?"

"I know even less," Bubba answered.

"That's okay Bubba. I take good care of you."

The workers finished unloading the plane just as Bubba and I finished our *tamales*.

"Do you think you can handle this *pista?*" I asked.

Bubba took a deep breath and said, "I think y'all are crazy, but I'll do my best."

"You'll be fine," I said. "Just relax, hit the very end and stay in the middle."

When the plane was ready, we said goodbye to Cruz, climbed in, and blasted off. It was an uneventful flight home. We talked about some of the other *pistas* and the quirks and dangers in using them. Bubba wasn't overly excitable, and the prospect of getting popped and sent to a Mexican jail didn't seem to bother him, on the surface anyway.

After an hour and a half we were back in Brownsville and taxiing to customs. I showed Bubba how to check back in. Afterwards we taxied from customs to Hal's for fuel.

Ray was waiting for us. He said that he had another load for Raúl that afternoon if we wanted to take it.

"Sure," I said.

Looking at Bubba, Ray said, "You should go with him."

"I'm in," replied Bubba.

"Where are we going to?" I said.

"The Ranch," Ray replied.

The Ranch was actually on Raúl's property. It was a fun airstrip to fly in and out of. It was in the rolling plains just east of the foothills of the Sierra Madres. It consisted of a portion of a narrow ranch lane that draped over the top of a rolling hill. It had some dips and a slight curve. You could see for miles in all directions; so if anyone was near or approaching, we would all know well in advance.

Our only concern was that Raúl didn't get along with the *federales* and they constantly harassed him. We didn't want to land only to find

Raúl being held at gunpoint by a truck full of soldiers. The Ranch was long enough to take off with a full load, provided a vehicle or piece of equipment hadn't been moved onto the lane behind you after you landed. So I always wanted to be sure the coast was clear before I shut the engine down.

"You should be able to leave by two-thirty," Ray said. "I'll tell Raúl you'll be there at four."

I always liked the days we did multiple trips. It meant more money. On some days I even made three trips into Mexico, usually one for Cruz and two for Raúl. Between Cruz, Raúl and Renaldo, we stayed very busy.

That afternoon, Bubba and I headed south for The Ranch. I showed him some more landmarks along the way and pointed out *Numero Dos*, the *caliza pista*,

We flew in low, following the rolling green meadows, and just as I was able to see the waiting truck its headlights snapped on and off. Bubba and I touched down on the lane. Raúl stepped out of the truck and came over to us. In my broken Spanish I introduced him to Bubba.

In a few short minutes we were unloaded and climbing back aboard to blast off.

"This is just too easy!" Bubba said. "Easy money."

"Yeah, as long as everything goes as planned," I said. "Don't ever forget that the *federales* won't hesitate to pop your airplane full of holes. And if you just happen to get hit by a stray bullet in the meantime, well, that's just tough luck."

I told Bubba about my two experiences with gunfire, leaving out a few details. I didn't want him knowing that he might be riding with someone who was being watched by the authorities.

It was time for Bubba to fly his own airplane. A few days later he and I met at Cameron County. Both The Spook and Peanut Butter were fully loaded and full of fuel. Bubba and I did our preflight inspections and climbed in and headed for Brownsville. When we arrived on Hal's ramp we parked side by side, shut down and got out.

"How'd yours handle, Bubba?" I said.

"Pretty heavy," said Bubba. "A lot heavier than those sandbags."

I pointed at his tires. "You've probably got about fifteen hundred pounds onboard," I said. "Look at your tires. They should be full of air, but they look like they're half flat."

We never bothered to calculate a weight and balance before a mission. We knew the airplanes were overweight and as long as the tail didn't fall to the ramp, the center of gravity was good enough.

After clearing customs Bubba and I taxied to the runway and were on our way. As soon as we left the Brownsville controlled area I tuned in 123.45 on the VHF and called Bubba.

"Welcome to Mehico, Bubba!"

"Glad to be here," he answered.

We passed *Las Animal* and *Tiburon Uno*, flying within a half mile of each other. I called Bubba again.

"Let's start down," I said. "You should try to cross *Tiburon Dos* a couple of minutes behind me. I'll give you a call when I'm over it."

"Got it," Bubba said.

"When you hear me call Cruz on the FM you should be just past *Las Tigre*."

"Got it," Bubba replied. "I'll be right behind you. Save me a *tamale*."

As I passed over the Rocky Meadow I picked up the FM microphone.

"Hey, Cruz."

"It's okay," Cruz replied.

"You get that Bubba?" I said on the VHF.

"I just passed *Las Tigre*," Bubba replied.

"Perfect," I said. "Give us a call on the FM before you land. I'll be waiting for you."

I hopped over the rocky knoll, rolled onto the *pista* and spun around at the end of One of These Days. It was always a rush going in there. I said hello to Cruz and his men started unloading my airplane as we waited for Bubba to arrive.

In a few minutes we heard the sound of an airplane from the northwest. It was Bubba, and he was right on-time. Bubba must have been a little unsure of the location of the *pista* as he was well above the trees. He never did call on the FM. I figured he was nervous and forgot about it. At about the time he should have turned on his final approach, he kept going straight. He flew past the *pista* and disappeared to the southwest.

"Oh, Bubba," Cruz said with a degree of anguish in his voice.

A minute later we heard Bubba again, approaching from the southwest this time. I picked him out and saw that he was headed due north. Again, about the time he should have turned on final approach, he continued past the airstrip.

Suddenly Bubba called us on the FM radio.

"Where is this place?" he said.

Cruz handed me his portable.

"You've passed us twice to our west," I said. "Now it sounds like you're turning around again."

"You're just over the hill, right?" Bubba asked.

"Yeah, look for The Spook and truck to the east of the peak of that hill."

We picked out Peanut Butter again heading in our direction. He was much closer this time—a little too close for comfort. In fact, I wasn't sure he was going to get it turned to final on time.

"We're just off the left of your wingtip," I told him over the radio.

"I got you now," he replied.

Cruz instructed his guys to get ready for the second airplane. Bubba was coming in fast and I saw the flaps drop to full as he turned final. I thought this was another missed approach when I saw him hug the terrain. He wasn't lined up properly; he seemed to be pointed toward me rather than the centerline of the *pista*. Bubba steered left, aligning correctly, and then immediately drifted to his right again.

He was focused on the telephone poles. He'd forgotten the instructions I'd given him and was now lining up with the roughest portion of the *pista*. If he touched down in that area he'd lose it in the ditch and probably damage the airplane.

There was nothing we could do but watch as Bubba crossed the fence, chopped the power and hit the flaps up. He hit the end of the *pista*, realized his mistake, and tried to correct with full left rudder.

It was too late. The soft shoulder gave way and Bubba slid off the edge. He was losing control, and the worst part was that he was headed right toward me!

The right main gear caught a drop-off and spun the plane back straight, but the airplane was now hopelessly bound for the ditch and listing at least twenty degrees. A second later the nose wheel and right main gear failed and ripped away. Bubba came to a rapid and dusty stop about a hundred feet from where I was standing.

"No Bubba, No!" Cruz cried. "No Bubba, No!" He kept repeating as he turned and headed for his truck.

Cruz wasn't sure what to do. I ran toward the downed plane and saw Bubba climbing out. He didn't seem injured and I didn't see any fuel leaking from the aircraft. Dirt and dust floated around everywhere. I got to the plane as Bubba stumbled out from underneath the wing.

"Are you okay?" I said.

"Yeah, I'm fine," Bubba said. "I guess you were right about the rough. Once I hit that ditch back there, it's like there was no way out. I thought I was fine as long as I stayed on the gravel."

Cruz sent his six helpers and the truck to unload the wrecked plane. Once we got it unloaded we needed to move it far enough off the strip for me to take off. Bubba had spun around pointing south, and the tail of the airplane stuck out over the *pista*. The airplane was nose-low in the ditch. The cargo doors toward the tail were too high to reach, so Cruz's men unloaded the airplane through the pilot's door. Once the front half was unloaded the airplane became tail-heavy enough to pull down by hand. Then the crew finished unloading from the back doors.

As soon as the plane was unloaded we tried to pick it up and turn it so that it cleared enough space for me to take off. I showed Cruz's men where to pick up the airplane and what areas they should avoid. Cruz seemed to understand and relayed the directions in Spanish. We struggled to move the crippled airplane but it wouldn't budge.

"You wait here, Bronco Billy," said Cruz. "I get help."

Cruz and a driver climbed in the truck and drove off, leaving Bubba and me and half a dozen Mexicans sitting around looking at each other. The men snickered and mimicked the airplane wallowing through the whole sequence as they twisted and gyrated their bodies. Bubba wasn't amused, but took it all in stride and sat quietly next to the plane. I looked over the damage as I would have to relay the situation to Wally and begin planning the recovery. One of the loaders retrieved the nose gear and we threw it in the back of The Spook. I climbed in the front of the wreck and grabbed the microphones from both the FM and VHF radios.

"Why are you doing that?" Bubba asked.

"Guerrero and some of the *federales* have the same type of radios," I said. "If the wreck is discovered by the wrong people, they might attempt to contact the authorities or guide Guerrero to the site."

Cruz returned in the truck and ten more Mexicans climbed out of the back. We now had plenty of lifting power and were able to raise the airplane and rotate it so that it was clear of the airstrip.

"You can go, Bronco," said Cruz.

I asked Cruz to move the crippled airplane to a level spot after we left.

"*Sí*, I take care of it," he replied. "I call Ray too."

"Okay, we're outta here then," I said. "Hop in, Bubba!"

Bubba and I climbed in The Spook, fired up the engine and headed back to the border. He sat on the floor with his head in his hands. Reality was setting in and Bubba began talking about how upset Ray was going to be.

"The main thing is that you're all right," I said. "These things are expected now and then."

"Oh, Ray's gonna fire me for sure," said Bubba.

I tried to calm his concerns. He knew that cracking up an airplane on his first solo flight wasn't a good start. But on these airstrips it was easy to lose focus. It was an expensive lesson but nobody got hurt and I was sure that Ray would understand. The main thing was to build Bubba's confidence back up. Maybe we could have him fly into The Students next time until he was more comfortable.

I looked back. Bubba lay on the cargo floor with his arm over his face. I thought he was sleeping but suddenly he sat up and looked at me.

"Hey, I didn't get any *tamales*!"

We laughed the rest of the way home. Bubba was going to be fine.

CHAPTER 13

LAWN CHAIR LUNACY

I STILL ONLY HAD my single-engine rating and wasn't legal to fly the twins. I was making good money in my little 207 and there didn't seem to be any reason to go for more. But every time I saw the Aero Commander sitting on the ramp I'd wonder what it would be like to fly it.

Before his death, Rob had made the occasional trip in it. Flying missions in the Commander paid about double what we got for piloting the 207; and based on that, I'm surprised I didn't go after it sooner. Even my old flight instructor Darin showed up periodically to make a run in it. There were only three *pistas* long enough for the Twin Commander: *Pista Negra*, The Students and The Ranch. Darin talked about taking the Commander to Belize a couple of times, and I'd heard of some trips to Guatemala.

On the other hand, we rarely used the Aero Commander because it often suffered mechanical problems.

Wally had been chasing one of those problems for about two weeks. Darin had taken the plane to Brownsville to pick up a load, and on the short flight down the left engine lost fuel pressure and quit running. Fortunately for Darin it quit after he had landed. He said that when he extended the landing gear he noticed the fuel flow was fluctuating, and shortly after touchdown the engine lost power and stopped. The trip was cancelled and Wally came to Brownsville to investigate.

Wally and Darin performed several high-power test runs but were unable to duplicate the problem. They took fuel samples from the wing and engine sumps; the gas was clean. The guys were baffled but assumed there still could be some kind of contamination in the tanks.

Frustrated by the whole event, Wally instructed Darin to take the plane back to Cameron and, on the next mission, sump the tanks before he launched. Wally drove back to Cameron, and Darin flew the Commander there.

When Wally arrived back at Cameron, Darin was waiting for him, and he was madder than hell. The same failure had occurred, except this time it happened on short final.

"It was a good thing that didn't happen on takeoff!" Darin said.

Wally shrugged. "What was I supposed to do, tear the engine apart looking for something that ain't broke?"

The two men had never had any conflict between them in the past, and neither had the type of personality to take things further. They looked at each other and busted up laughing about the whole thing. Darin went home and Wally went back to work.

For the next couple of days Wally looked over the entire fuel system. He didn't find anything obvious but decided to troubleshoot by gradually replacing components one-by-one to see if something was malfunctioning. He looked at the engine-driven fuel pump and figured that it may be wearing out and getting ready to fail. So he replaced that and called Darin for a test flight. Darin circled the field, waiting for signs of another failure. Within ten minutes Wally noticed Darin was making a sharp right turn for the runway.

As Darin rolled out on final, Wally noticed the left engine had stopped rotating. Darin feathered the propeller. He landed without further incident, taxied into the parking area, and shut down on the maintenance ramp. Again, the engine had quit and Wally knew he hadn't found the source of the problem. Darin went home and Wally pulled the airplane back into the hangar for more investigation.

On a hot afternoon Happy and I returned from a second trip across the border, and I was ready to kick back and enjoy a few ice-cold beers with Wally. I noticed he had been test-running the Commander and was taxiing back in. He got out with a smile on his face and said that he had found the problem. Or at least he was pretty certain that he'd found it.

"What was it?" I asked.

"The fuel vent was plugged," Wally said.

"Oh, I guess that'd do it,"

"Yep, and that'd make sense too," Wally said. "It would take about ten minutes to cause a vacuum in the tank and prevent fuel from flowing to the engine."

"But why didn't that show up on the ground tests?" I said.

"I don't know," said Wally. "But funny things like this happen with airplanes. Anyway, it seems to run fine now. I'll give Darin a call."

Wally wasn't a pilot, Happy had gone home and I didn't have any experience in the twin. We decided to practice some hangar flying while we waited for Darin to show up. Wally didn't have any Budweiser on hand so I volunteered to take The Spook and buzz down to the local Maverick Market for a couple of twelve-packs. You never knew how long some of these things were going to take.

There was an old duster strip next to the nearby Maverick Market convenience store. I could land there and taxi off the airstrip and onto the road. Another forty yards and I'd pull the airplane into the parking lot, provided there weren't too many cars or pickup trucks in the way.

The clerk gave me quite the look when I brought my airplane right up the drive and stopped next to the building. There was a guy at the gas pump who was filling his car; he just stood and stared with his mouth hanging open. I guess neither of them had ever seen an airplane at a convenience store before. I loaded a case of Bud in the back of the plane, jumped in and headed back out. I didn't bother using the duster strip for takeoff—I just pointed the Spook down the county road and poured the coals to her.

When I got back to Cameron, Wally called it a day, confident he'd located and fixed the problem. He was beyond ready to let off some steam with a few beers. We sat next to the hangar and, after pounding the first two, systematically polished off one *twelver* and started on the second.

No sooner had we popped the top off the second twelve-pack when Ray's son Dave showed up. He'd had similar ideas and brought his own twelve-pack of Busch. This was quickly turning into a ramp party. About the time we were just getting into the bag and our shouting became more fervent, Darin showed up. He stood there with a big cheesy smile on his face and joined the fun. It was just another typical Friday afternoon.

After he'd finished his second beer, Darin reminded Wally why he'd come out: the Aero Commander sat on the ramp awaiting a test flight.

"She's ready to go," Wally said. "I'd have taken it up myself but I'm too drunk to fly."

"But you're not a pilot!" said Dave.

"Wow, I'm drunker than I thought!" said Wally.

We all busted up laughing as Dave and I picked up our lawn chairs and half a twelve-pack and followed Darin and Wally to the plane. Nobody questioned whether Darin was sober enough to fly. We'd all decided to go for a joyride.

Since there weren't any seats in the back, Dave and I would have to ride in our lawn chairs behind Darin and Wally, who sat in the front two pilot seats. There was no reason to think that anything was wrong with this. Darin and Wally would be strapped in, and Dave and I were just hangin' out in the back.

With the four of us inside, I closed the door and soon we were taxiing to the end of the runway. Darin made a thorough check of the left engine with two or three high-power runs before he made the decision to launch. We lined up with the runway and Darin smoothly advanced both throttles. As we gained speed I noticed that Darin was veering off the centerline to the right. At first I thought he was showing off, and then I wondered if perhaps the beer was kicking in.

As we broke ground I could see that Darin was struggling with the rudder pedals.

"That was a damn impressive takeoff!" Wally said sarcastically. "What were you tryin' to do, fly through the hangar?"

"I can't move the rudder pedals!" Darin shouted.

As we climbed out, Darin banked to the left and flew north, keeping his attention on the stuck rudder.

Then it dawned on both Darin and Wally.

"THE GUST LOCK!" they shouted simultaneously.

Many smaller airplanes come equipped with an external device that's designed to lock the rudder. This prevents damage to the rudder by keeping it from banging around in high winds while the aircraft is parked. The gust locks are wedged between the gap at base of the rudder and the fixed tail surface. These wedges or blocks are normally made of padded aluminum and usually painted red, with long red streamers attached to draw the attention of the pilot on the preflight inspection. The locks are sometimes held in place with straps and must always be removed from the outside prior to entering the airplane. It's normally a part of the preflight walk-around.

Since the Aero Commander has a steerable nose wheel, rudder movement on the ground is not necessary. Many smaller aircraft have rudder-*assisted* steering as the nose wheel is coaxed rather than controlled to the left or right by applying full rudder deflection in the direction you want to turn. But in the Twin Commander you only need to apply pressure at the top of the pedal corresponding to the desired direction of turn. The first few degrees of pedal movement actuates a hydraulic valve that in turn controls the nose wheel. The rudder pedal itself does not move but simply rotates forward until steering is activated. If you keep pushing on the rudder pedal you'll trigger the brakes. The Commander is perfectly capable of being taxied without using its rudder.

Whether it was a simple oversight or the effects of the beer, Darin had failed to do a preflight check, and he'd also failed to do the normal control checks before takeoff. And none of us thought to look the airplane over before getting in.

To further aggravate the situation, the red streamer was missing from the homemade lock device. If the streamer had still been present, Darin could have continued flying and waited for the streamer to flap enough in the airstream to loosen and pull the lock free of the rudder. (This is how many rudder locks are lost and why many Commanders have replacement devices of a wooden, homemade type.)

Unaware that the streamer was missing, Darin flew along, hoping that the lock would become dislodged and fly off the back end of the airplane.

Darin explained to Wally how the streamer would eventually pull the lock out.

"It doesn't have one," Wally said.

Hearing that, Darin quickly banked the airplane and headed back. Wally looked down at the left fuel pressure gage.

"Look! We're losin' the left one!" he said.

This was our "Oh Shit" moment. If an engine fails in a twin-engine airplane that has no rudder control, all onboard are in serious trouble. The rudder is used to compensate for uneven thrust. Without it, the airplane will roll over resulting in a loss of control. The only—and I mean *only*—option was to kill the other engine and land wherever we could. All of us looked around for a suitable landing spot.

Wally explained to Darin that the rudder lock was made of wood and that, with enough rudder pressure, Darin might be able to break it free. Both sides of the cockpit had a set of pedals, so the two men began to apply heavy right rudder...

After a great deal of straining they were unable to free the rudder. Desperate, Darin shouted to try the left, and both men stood on their left pedals, pushing with all their might.

Suddenly the airplane veered sharply to the left as the rudder lock broke free. Darin recovered and we had full control.

Five seconds later, the left engine quit.

CHAPTER 14

IT'S AN AIRPLANE, ISN'T IT?

T HE FOUR OF US realized how close we'd come to turning ourselves into a pile of smoldering ash in the South Texas sand. Darin brought the Twin Commander back to Cameron on one engine.

After we touched down, the tension eased a bit, and Wally looked back at Dave and me.

"I guess that didn't fix it," he said.

Dave chuckled and Darin started cracking jokes as we pulled into the parking space on the ramp.

It took a little more troubleshooting and a lot more Budweiser, but Wally finally discovered a faulty fuel vent that worked correctly while on the ground and only failed when in flight. Simply clearing the obstruction hadn't fixed the problem.

A couple of weeks went by. One afternoon I returned to Cameron from a delivery mission and noticed that the Commander was missing. In its place sat an all-blue Beech Queen Air. Ray had sold the Commander and made a deal on the Beechcraft.

I taxied The Spook to her parking space, climbed out, and walked over to Wally. He was sitting in his lawn chair up against the hangar.

"How's The Spook running?" he said.

"Great," I replied. "Purrs like a kitten. Happy Boy will be along any minute."

I stood there next to Wally, looking at the Queen Air while fiddling with the new rabbit's foot I had in my pocket.

"What do you think of her?" he asked.

"Looks like a B80," I said.

"Yep, I guess Ray made a deal with some guy named Bobby Wilson and it showed up a couple of hours ago."

"We gonna start taking her south?" I said.

"I guess that's the plan," Wally said. "I just need to get a cargo net in her. You ever fly a Queen Air?"

"No. I don't even have my multi-engine rating,"

"Oh well. She needs some work anyway."

I went inside the shop, grabbed a couple of beers and a lawn chair, and sat down next to Wally. I handed him a beer. We watched as Happy touched down and taxied in next to The Spook. He got out and joined us.

"Hi fellas," said Happy, looking at the Beech. "Is that our new bird?"

"That's her," said Wally.

"When will she be ready?"

"Oh, I've got to get a cargo system in her and then there are some issues with the engines."

"Hopefully she's not a piece of junk like the Commander," Happy said.

Flying was pretty steady for the next two weeks, and each time I went through Cameron I asked Wally how things were going with the Queen Air. He'd gotten the engine problems resolved but hadn't installed the cargo net.

I spent several hours staring at the new airplane as it sat on the ramp. It became a real temptation, as I longed for some twin-engine time.

One afternoon I asked Wally if I could borrow the pilot's operating manual for the Beech and look it over. Wally had no problem with that since we weren't expecting to be flying the plane for some time.

The Queen Air was considered a light twin, but a fairly large one. She had a wingspan of just over fifty feet, could carry up to ten passengers plus one pilot, and had a gross takeoff weight of eight thousand, eight hundred pounds. She sat high on her main wheels and had an aft swing-down door with stairs for entry. She was powered by two, Lycoming IGSO-540, 380-horsepower, supercharged engines. The Lycoming was a geared engine, which meant that the propeller shaft turned at a speed slower than the crankshaft.

The Beech was similar to the Aero Commander; that is, she was somewhat of a temperamental beast. Special care had to be taken in engine management in order to avoid damage caused by the gear reduction system. Smooth and slow throttle application was the key to proper power management.

I spent the better part of that night familiarizing myself with the systems on the Beech. The next morning I had a 207 trip to The Barnyard. I took the Queen Air manual with me and thumbed through more of the systems during my trip. When I pulled into Cameron County about noon I'd been through most of the Queen Air systems a couple of times. I had a pretty good idea of the operation of the engines, flaps, landing gear and fuel system.

I approached Wally with the Queen Air manual tucked under my arm.

"You ready to fly that thing?" he said.

"I'd sure like to," I replied.

Back home I'd spent a couple of hours with Darin in a Piper Apache and a Cessna 411. The Apache was a small and simple twin-engine, and the 411 was used for charter flights. While my experience was minimal, I was somewhat familiar with the feel of two fans turning and pulling me through the sky. That was about the extent of my multi-engine time so far. I'd never taken anything out on my own.

"Why don't you take her out for a spin?" Wally said.

"Do you think I can?" I said.

"It's an airplane, isn't it?"

"Do you think I should?"

"Ray's going to need a good pilot soon," said Wally, "and the more time you've got in her, the better. Besides, I'm sure the pay is better."

For me the pay wasn't the biggest temptation. It was the thought of getting twin time and the excitement of flying a bigger airplane. I looked at the Beech for a moment.

"Wally, has she got fuel in her?"

"About half tanks in the mains," he said.

That was it. I'd made up my mind.

I tucked the manual under my arm and walked out to the Beech. I did a quick walk-around and checked the fuel and oil. As I lowered the door I realized that I hadn't read much about the actual flight operations and figured I'd better scan the manual a little more. I ascended the air stair, closed the door behind me, crawled into the cockpit and began to read. I reviewed the before-start and after-start checklists and decided that I'd figure out the actual flying part as I went along. I knew I had a natural ability to fly and was confident that I'd be fine.

Starting her up went smoothly, and once both engines were running I knew that I would have this bird in the air soon. However, I couldn't figure out how to turn the radios on, and for some reason I couldn't find several of the electrical switches I'd read about.

Taxiing was just like the 207—plus, I had the help of differential power from either engine. I had no trouble getting her to the end of the runway. I did a thorough engine run-up and extended and retracted the flaps fully to check that system out. Everything seemed normal.

I looked at the airspeed indicator to get an idea of the aircraft's operating speeds. Airspeed indicators are marked in such a way that a pilot can pinpoint certain critical speeds and get a relatively good idea what speeds to expect. This indicator had two short radial lines—one red, one blue—that were unfamiliar to me. I sat there for a minute, trying to figure them out. The red line was at eight-five knots, and the blue line sat right at about a hundred knots. I figured the red line was the more important one; it probably indicated some kind of stall speed. I had no idea what that blue line was for.

I could have looked it up in the manual, but I was too excited about my first solo flight to take the time. After all, it was just an airplane, and I'd have time later on to learn all those details.

With no radios working I looked around the pattern, carefully pulled onto the runway, and lined up on the center line. I held the brakes and slowly advanced the throttles. The Lycomings came to life smoothly and quite vigorously. I could feel the airframe wanting to go, so at about half-throttle I let go of the brakes. Directional control was a little tricky, but I got the hang of it and was soon accelerating down the runway.

I was so focused on maintaining a straight line that I didn't realize I was getting pretty light on the wheels. The Queen Air was begging me: she wanted to fly.

With a slight release of the forward pressure I was airborne and accelerating quickly. I grabbed the gear handle and raised the landing gear . . . and immediately climbed over the inland bay to the east of the airport.

This airplane was easy to fly and was quite nimble. It had a good, crisp roll and a very stable pitch moment. I turned and headed north. I made a few turns to get a better feel for her, grabbed a fistful of throttles and reduced my manifold pressure. I brought the propellers back to a comfortable level within the green arc on the tachometer. The airspeed settled to about a hundred sixty-five knots and I made a couple of three-hundred-sixty degree turns in both directions. It didn't take long. I felt comfortable in this bird!

I felt I should keep my first flight short, so I headed back to Cameron and eased the throttles back to reduce my speed. The Queen Air had a high landing gear speed limit, and with little deceleration I could throw the gear out and use the additional drag to further slow the airplane without excessive throttle reduction. Soon I was at a speed where I could extend the flaps to set up for landing. Since the fuel tanks were at less than half capacity and I had no cargo, I was pretty light and the airplane performed and handled well. I wondered how she'd do with a full load in her.

To avoid a stall I knew I'd be safe crossing the fence at ninety. There was eight thousand feet of runway in front of me and I didn't feel shy about taking as much as needed. Over the threshold I pulled the power completely out and the airplane floated a good thousand feet before settling onto the concrete. Again, directional control became my priority and I slowed to a quick taxi. I drove the Beech to the far end of the runway.

Wally was still sitting in his lawn chair when I pulled onto the ramp and shut down. I was pretty excited to have completed my maiden voyage with such little effort. The Queen Air was easy to fly and I hoped I'd get the chance someday to take her south.

"What'd you think?" he said.

"Piece o' cake," I replied with a big grin on my face.

"How'd the engines run?"

"They seemed fine. Lots of power."

"Any problems?"

"I couldn't get the radios to work," I said.

Wally smirked at me. "Did you turn on the avionics master switch?"

"Oh crap! I didn't even think of that.

Wally handed me a beer and told me that my flying was done for the day.

A couple of days later I had another 207 trip. When I returned to Cameron I told Wally that I wanted to take the Queen Air out for another spin.

"Sure," he said. "But don't run her dry. I haven't fueled her since last time."

"I'll only be up a few minutes again," I said.

Happy Boy had arrived at Cameron before me and had already gone home, so I was clear to go without anyone knowing about it except Wally, and I knew that he didn't care. I climbed into the Beech and was taxiing to the end of the runway. This time everything was working, including all of the radios. I still didn't know what those red and blue lines were for.

After a short run-up I barreled down the runway and launched upward to do some more maneuvers out over the South Texas brush. My confidence grew by the minute. I made several turns and even a smooth barrel roll.

This thing was just too easy to fly! I decided to go back to the airport and practice some takeoffs and landings. After three touch-and-go's I was able to bring her in low and slow and plant her pretty close to where I was aiming. The same flap retraction procedure I used on my 207 worked on the Beech, and stopping short looked to be almost as easy. However, the Beech was still traveling light, and I knew that the aircraft would react differently with a full load aboard.

After flying for half an hour I checked the fuel gauges and decided it was time to finish up for the day. When I pulled onto the ramp, Wally had Max bring the fuel truck around and park in front of me.

Wally walked over to the Beech and told me he figured I was about dry, so he decided to have her topped off. "I need to check for fuel leaks anyway," he explained. "Besides, you'll probably burn through it in no time."

During the next two weeks I probably went through two full tanks. I flew the Beech almost daily. As far as I knew, no one except for Wally and Max knew about my joyrides. I was careful to wait until Happy Boy left for the day, and I'd always ask whether Ray was expected on the ramp, before I took to the skies.

One day when I taxied in I saw Ray's white Monte Carlo parked at the hangar. My heart stopped. Ray had discovered my secret. I was sure that my career with Ray was over. He'd want to know how I justified taking his airplane out for joyrides. He'd shake his head and tell me that my time was up and that I could pick up my last check in the morning.

I pulled the mixtures and sat there watching as Ray appeared from inside the hangar and walked out to the where I was parked. He looked at the ground the whole way out and seemed to to be chewing angrily on his cigar. I knew I'd have to face him head-on so I got out of the pilot's seat and climbed to the back and lowered the door.

Ray stood at the bottom, scratching his ear and looking over the plane as if he expected to find some damage.

"How's it running?" he said.

"F-fine," I said. "She runs good."

"You got any problems with her?"

"No. It's an easy airplane to fly."

He nodded. "You wanna take some trips in her?"

That threw me off. Did he really just ask me if I wanted to fly deliveries in the Beech?

"I don't have my multi rating yet," I stammered.

"Aw, those are just details. I've got some work coming up with her soon, and you can take the trips if you're up to it. By the way, how much time you got in her?"

"Oh, just an hour or two," I said.

"Yeah, right," he said, looking at me in disbelief.

I couldn't believe my ears. I'd just switched from figuring out how to pack my furniture to landing this airplane on a Mexican *pista*.

"We'll probably just be taking her in and out of *Pista Negra* and The Students for now," Ray said.

"What about One of These Days?" I said eagerly.

Ray's cigar drooped in his mouth.

"You *are* crazy!" he said. "I'll see you later."

That was the start of my twin-engine flying. Although I didn't possess the training, knowledge or license, I handled the Queen Air with ease. It wasn't long before I was taking her south and pulling in the extra money that went along with it. It was addictive.

I was also taking a new direction in my career. Making money was now my greatest aspiration. I was still addicted to the adrenaline of flying dangerous missions across the border, but the additional pay gave me an entirely different kind of high.

Because the airplane could carry heavier loads, I found that my new skills were in higher demand too. Soon I was receiving phone calls from operators I barely knew. The fact that I didn't have my multi-engine license was just an inconvenient technicality. I didn't need it.

I'd upgraded my *bandito* status. I was skilled, I was in demand . . . and I was becoming very rich.

One late morning as I pulled the Queen Air onto the ramp after taking a load south, Ray met me at the entry door. I could tell something was bothering him.

"Here, dammit!" he said. He thrust a fistful of money at me. "Take this and go get your multi-engine rating."

Ray's conscience was beginning to bother him. Or maybe he knew that it was only a matter of time before the FAA caught me during a customs inspection. Whatever the case, Ray was right. I took the money and arranged for lessons and a check ride in San Marcos. I got it done, and I returned to Ray as a legitimate twin-engine pilot.

I was now a legal pilot, doing illegal things, but I was raking in the cash. Life was good.

Or was it?

CHAPTER 15

THERE HAD TO BE MORE

I LEARNED EARLY IN LIFE that without strong convictions, a man can get himself into dangerous situations. Many of us go through periods in our lives when we cast caution to the wind. We feel immortal. In the foolishness of our youth we somehow manage to escape the wages of our sin. Some of us do, anyway.

At the tender age of twenty I had an exciting life built on lies and deception. My criminal activity was limited to a country for which I had little respect. I viewed Mexico as a kind of third-world territory, bumbling in its attempts to thwart our clandestine enterprises. I had conquered Mexico and defeated the forces trying to stop me. I now had a name and an infamous reputation of which I was unashamedly proud.

I can't tell you why I did what I did, nor can I attribute my behavior to a lack of discipline in my upbringing. I had a normal childhood, and my parents taught me sound values and morals. I saw good examples that I could emulate. Why I strayed, I may never know.

Yet there was something in me that was lacking, a hole in my moral tapestry. I would learn many years later that it wasn't so much a deficiency in my character as a sinful nature that I kept feeding. I was a mirror image of the man I should have been. I was identical in form yet the exact opposite in many character traits.

I didn't understand temptation or its true cost. I was clueless about the power sin had over me, and I returned to it time after time to feed it. I made regular flights into a foreign country, broke their laws and evaded their pursuits. With each flight I fed the demon inside me. He spoke lies; he distorted truth and bent reality. He controlled my thoughts and reinforced my pride and tickled my ego. Each paperclip on my visor represented a medal earned through my unscrupulous livelihood.

I was losing a battle over my heart and soul. It would take something much more powerful than man's law to force me back into the real world.

Deep down, I always knew that a powerful God had spared me from being shot, captured or killed. But on the surface I denied Him. I listened to the demons that whispered in my ear. I thought the odds were always in my favor.

I managed my life as if I was playing a slot machine. Each mission was a pull on the lever. I figured that when I ran out of quarters, I'd stop.

But I was already on my third bag of quarters.

I remembered setting goals and limits for this job. I told myself that I would stop at just twenty flights, pocket my winnings, and move on. I could leave the smuggling business, debt free with enough to find legitimate employment while living comfortably.

I remembered when I reached twenty paperclips on the visor of my airplane. Out of twenty trips I'd had only a few tense moments. So I went for more. I crossed more hurdles and escaped more potential disasters. I became callous and numb to my situation. Capture? Jail? Beatings? Death? They were just words.

The paperclips gradually overtook the visor. Trip number 100 had come and gone long ago. I was flying constantly, not only for Ray but a couple other operators as well. In a little over two years I'd forgotten about my original goals. I'd become dependent on my little Mexican connection. I'd developed an insatiable appetite for perilous adventure and money.

One day Ray brought me my paperwork and I didn't even notice that there was no paperclip. It didn't matter; I'd fallen out of the paperclip habit anyway. The visor was no longer an accurate account of my missions.

I was more interested in my money and how it was accumulating. Funny thing, though: it *wasn't* accumulating. My lifestyle had become expensive and extravagant. Between the drugs, the parties, and airplane joyrides (for which I would buy my own fuel), I had very little cash set aside for my future. I assumed the money would continue to roll in.

There is a universal truth about sin: "It will always take you farther than you wanted to go, keep you longer than you wanted to stay, and cost you more than you wanted to pay."

One morning I awoke to someone banging frantically on my apartment door. I got up and threw on a robe. When I looked through the peephole I saw a young lady whom I'd gotten acquainted with quite some time ago. She looked very distraught outside in the early morning sunlight. I wondered if she'd been in some kind of accident. I quickly opened the door. Her look of anguish changed to one of relief; she embraced me and began to cry.

"I thought you were dead, I thought you were dead!" she sobbed.

"What are you talking about?" I said.

"A friend of mine told me, she said. "He works for the border patrol and heard that Bronco Billy had been killed on the *Yucatán*. I thought it was you! Oh my God! It was horrible."

After she calmed down she told me that her friend got his information from an illegal alien who'd been arrested in Brownsville for possession of narcotics. As he gave his statement he casually mentioned the name Bronco Billy.

Evidently, Bronco Billy, or whoever he was, had been running dope out of Belize when an engine caught fire and his airplane exploded and crashed. The sensational story had major political value and made many Latin American news releases.

As far as Guerrero, the Mexican army and police were concerned, Bronco Billy was dead.

I was free.

No one was hunting me now. I could fly my missions without having to look over my shoulder. Now I could fly more, deliver more cargo, make even more money.

With a razor blade clinched between my fingers I bent over the kitchen table. I put my face to the mirror, and with a deep breath I snorted another dose of confidence.

PART II

The Jamaica Chronicles

CHAPTER 16

PEDRO'S POINT

THE LETTER MY FATHER had sent was encouraging. *We'd love to see you, and we are all hoping you make it home for Thanksgiving,* it said. I hadn't made any plans for the holidays, and as usual I'd left my schedule open for last-minute changes. I read the letter several times, hearing my father's voice in my head, telling me how much he loved me. He knew I was flying cargo into Mexico. What he didn't know was that every time I got behind the controls of an airplane I was dodging local authorities and breaking Mexican laws.

After arriving in Texas, I quickly found myself in the pilot's seat of a Cessna 207 flying boom boxes and tape recorders deep into the lush tropical landscape east of the Sierra Madres. The landing strips were short and barely suitable for an oxcart let alone an airplane, and I was playing an ongoing game of cat-and-mouse with the Mexican army and a few bounty hunters.

We—my fellow pilots and I—were in it for the money, and we gorged ourselves on the frequent shots of adrenaline that came normally with such a dangerous job. Our appetite for adventure could not be satisfied and we constantly craved more. We took greater and greater risks . . . and, in doing so, we became increasingly foolish.

But even in such a high-risk environment, the daily exposure to danger numbed our senses and we became callous to the possible consequences. Having an adversary became the attraction rather than the deterrent. Yet those who pursued us were corrupt and could be bought with bribery. But no matter how much payola we shelled out, we were always in danger of being double-crossed.

We were always taking chances. If it wasn't the Mexican authorities or the horrible landing strips, it was the weather. We'd fly blind in the clouds and descend with nothing to guide us except our compass and hope to break into the clear before hitting a mountain. There were ways of improving the odds but there were always those times that we'd have to push it just a little further.

I'd already survived several life-threatening events. I'd escaped gunfire from soldiers and from a bounty hunter who'd become familiar with my movements. I witnessed mishaps that resulted in destroyed airplanes and loss of life. Through all of this I learned how to survive and whom I could trust.

Along the way I'd been given a new name. As "Bronco Billy" I was counted with those flying cargo planes on missions centered on self-indulgence.

I was hanging out in my apartment one afternoon with Kara when my phone rang. When I answered it I didn't recognize the voice on the other end.

"My name is Francisco," he said. "I'm a friend of Darin's. I heard you were a good stick. Can you do some part-time work for me?"

I told him that I'd probably not be available but was interested to hear more. He told me that he didn't have all the details but would like to meet and talk about it.

"When?" I said.

"Right now," he said. "You pick the place."

I put my hand over the phone and looked at Kara.

"This guy wants to meet with me right now about some part-time flying job," I said.

She raised her eyebrows. "You'd better make it a public place," she said.

I had a pretty good idea what he wanted me to do. I could have told him "no thanks" and hung up the phone. But I also knew that this gig could reenergize me while making a nice contribution to my strongbox.

"Can you call me back in fifteen minutes?" I asked.

Francisco wasn't happy. "You've got to be kidding me," he said.

"You mentioned that you were a friend of Darin's," I said. "I think it's only reasonable that I check that out."

"Okay, I suppose you're right," he said. "I'll call you back in half an hour."

I hung up and immediately called Darin. He told me that Francisco was an old acquaintance and a straight shooter.

I'd had regular contact with Darin during my time in Texas. We confided in one another about whom we were working for and what we were hauling. The skills I possessed opened up many opportunities, and I was picking up odd jobs flying for other operators. I was carrying a wider variety of cargo into more remote locations and I even brought a few suspicious packages back to the U.S., neatly stowed in the nose baggage. I was so comfortable with U.S. Customs that I rarely worried about passing through, and I never questioned my employers about what I was bringing in. On one assignment I received a very nice cash bonus shortly after bringing back what I was told was a bag of sugar.

That's how I liked it: the less I knew the better. Trouble was I could still go to jail. In a court of law my ignorance of the true identity of the cargo would be irrelevant.

Any time Darin and I talked about an operator over the phone—whether we were working for that operator or not—we were very careful about what we said. We never talked about flying or a particular airplane. We never uttered incriminating words or statements because we knew that law enforcement agencies regularly tapped phones in our area. To protect ourselves, Darin and I used a system of code words so we could get the information across without giving away anything to whoever might be listening in. So when Darin mentioned that Francisco was "a straight shooter" I knew right away that Francisco was looking for a pilot to carry a load of guns.

When Francisco called back exactly thirty minutes later I told him to meet me at the swimming pool of an apartment complex across town from where I lived. I figured the pool area wouldn't be busy at that time of day, and it was surrounded by apartments that were just beyond earshot. The tenants would be able to see us but not hear our conversation.

I turned to Kara. "Would you mind waiting for me while I take care of this?" I said.

"No problem," she said. "The less I know the better. I'll just go home. Call me when you get back, okay?"

An hour later I was sitting in a chaise lounge next to the swimming pool. I wore a bathing suit and tee shirt—just another guy relaxing on a sunny day. When Francisco arrived, we took one look at each other and laughed. He'd dressed in a similar outfit to mine. I immediately got a sense that he and I would get along just fine. After some small talk we got down to business.

"You ever fly a Beech 18?" he asked.

"Yeah," I said, "but not for some time."

What I really meant was that I'd only flown that type of aircraft twice and that I didn't have much time in it. But I'd learned that if you wanted a job in this business you had to be creative with your résumé.

I had some experience with the model 18, also known as a Twin Beech. I'd flown with Darin into *Pista Negra* a couple of times several weeks before. Darin gave me the controls and let me fly the trips while he watched closely from the right seat. It reminded me of my blood hauling days. The controls took a little getting used to, but I caught on quickly and Darin had great fun watching me fumble around. He showed me all the systems and controls. I felt like I was back in the Midwest, getting some twin-engine time with my old flight instructor.

Francisco told me that Darin had flown for him many times and had recommended me for the job. We chatted for a while, mostly not about aviation, and got comfortable with each other. Then came the pitch. Francisco lowered his voice.

"How would you like to make five thousand dollars for a single trip?" he said under his breath.

I already knew what he was talking about but I had questions that needed to be answered.

"Where am I going, and how do I get paid?" I asked.

"We've got a *pista* in Mexico that is on the Guatemalan border," said Francisco. "There will be one man who speaks English and he will have your money in U.S. currency. You will leave from McAllen Airport at 3:00 a.m. sharp."

"How will I find the *pista*?"

"You will not be going alone. You will have a passenger to make sure the offloading goes smoothly. He can guide you to the *pista*." Francisco shrugged his shoulders. "All you have to do is fly."

"Why isn't Darin taking this trip?" I asked.

"He is also going, but in another airplane. He will be taking a DC-3 to the same place."

It was all starting to make sense. Whoever was funding this trip needed two airplanes for the haul, and I was the lucky one to be invited along. The trips I'd flown with Darin just a few weeks ago had been training flights: Darin was checking me out in the Twin Beech. No wonder he put me in the left seat from the start! He wanted to see how quickly I learned to handle the more complex airplane. Apparently I'd passed the test.

"Why didn't Darin come to me about this flight?" I asked.

"He could have," Francisco answered, "but I wanted to meet you before we took the trip. I own the merchandise and I like to know who is handling it."

That sounded good to me. The boss needed to take a look at his new employee.

"When do we leave?" I said.

"Tomorrow."

"Wow!" I said. "That soon?"

Francisco nodded. "Your airplane will be loaded and fueled and sitting on the Customs ramp at McAllen. That is when you will meet Pedro. He's the guy going with you. Darin will meet you there too and will have instructions for you then."

"I have to call Ray and tell him that I won't be available tomorrow," I said.

"Ray already knows that you are taking this trip for me," Francisco said. "I called him right after I called you."

I felt somewhat ignorant. There was a lot going on that involved me, and I had no idea about any of it. Now the plan was in motion and all I needed to do was show up at McAllen Airport the next morning, and fly to Guatemala and back.

Francisco reached into his pocket, pulled out an envelope, and handed it to me.

"This is a deposit for your services," he said.

As soon as Francisco and I parted company I immediately headed to Darin's house. I had a lot of questions. On the way over I opened the envelope and counted ten hundred-dollar bills. That would keep my interest up until tomorrow, anyway.

I knocked on Darin's door and his wife Kathy greeted me and ushered me inside. I sat with Darin in his living room, but we talked only sporadically about our next mission. He wanted to keep Kathy out of it as much as possible, so he and I mainly just talked about flying. He said that he'd see me in the morning and to go home and try to get some sleep.

When I returned to my apartment, getting sleep was the last thing I was able to do. I was charged with the excitement of this new mission. I thought about the extra five grand I was going to make and I was pumped to get the chance to fly the Twin Beech. I decided not to call Kara. It could wait until I got back. I finally nodded off around 11 p.m. only to be awakened an hour and a half later by my alarm clock. I scurried to get ready and drove through the dark Texas night to the McAllen Airport.

As I parked my car I could see both the DC-3 and the Twin Beech parked near Customs on the unlit part of the ramp. I walked out onto the asphalt and saw three men standing by the tail of the Douglas. It was Darin, his copilot, and Pedro. Darin waved as I approached the group.

"Good morning, Bronco Billy!" he said.

It was the first time he'd called me by that name. He introduced me to Pedro and the copilot the same way. Then he took me by the shoulder and we walked to an empty part of the ramp.

"These trips," he told me, "will be much less frequent than your normal electronics loads. Francisco has a limited supply of merchandise." Darin grinned. "Every now and then you might get a phone call about some part-time work like this."

I nodded. "Sounds good to me."

Darin gestured at the Twin Beech. "You're all set," he said. "You've got full fuel and about three thousand pounds in the back. That's about what we had going into *Pista Negra*, so you'll do fine. I'll take off first in the Doug and you follow right behind me. I'll leave my lights on until you can tuck in close and match my speed."

I looked at my airplane, sitting patiently in the darkness.

"Adjust your power to keep up and let me know when you're locked on to me. Then I'll shut off my lights and you'll need to keep me close and in your sights until the sky starts to get light," Darin said.

"How about radio communication?" I said.

"We can talk on the FM. If we get separated Pedro knows where the *pista* is. Just hold a heading from the McAllen one-fifty radial and if the weather is good you'll see the lights of Coatzacoalcos just before dawn. Just aim for that. Any other questions?"

I shook my head.

"Good," said Darin. "We should be airborne in about twenty minutes."

It would take me that long to reacquaint myself with the Twin Beech. I felt wide awake and alert as the adrenaline was back in flow. Pedro and I crawled into the airplane, scrambled over the wooden crates in the cargo bay, and buckled ourselves into the two front seats. I laughed at the thought of even using seatbelts as there would be no chance of surviving a crash landing or ditching the aircraft.

We were ready to go. The outbound customs declaration said nothing about our true cargo and everything had been arranged the day before. Darin and I got both engines running on our aircraft and taxied together to the end of the southeast runway. The Twin Beech was a little tricky to taxi, and visibility from the cockpit wasn't that great. Pedro just sat quietly, not saying a word.

Darin and I paused at the end of the runway for a couple of minutes, waiting for the engine temps to reach normal. Then we did our run-up checks at the same time. Everything looked good and I taxied onto the runway, lined up behind the DC-3, opened the oil shutters and locked the tailwheel. I was still a little unfamiliar with how the Beech would perform so I gave Darin a little distance before I throttled up and released the brakes. We rolled down the runway, picking up speed, and lifted off. The takeoff was smooth and the tail actually came up sooner than I'd expected with the heavy load in the back. I had a good visual on the Doug as we climbed to five thousand feet.

The moonlight illuminated the silhouette of the larger plane in front of me. I called Darin on the FM and told him that I had a good bead on him and that he could shut off his lights.

"I hope you're the only one that's got a bead on me," he replied, laughing.

We headed out across the Mexican night, crossed the beach of Laguna Madre and headed out over open water. The winds were light and I didn't need to make any course corrections. For the first hour I kept the Mexican shoreline to my right and the DC-3 in my windshield. Pedro had fallen asleep soon after takeoff so there wasn't much conversation going on in the cockpit.

As the night sky slowly yielded to the brightening eastern horizon I put a little more distance between Darin and me. Pedro came to and seemed disoriented for a few minutes. It was then I learned that he didn't speak English.

The Twin Beech was running smoothly and I spent the time managing the fuel and reviewing the flight manual as Pedro dipped in and out of consciousness. I too was beginning to feel the heaviness of sleep as my adrenaline was being replaced by my lack of rest.

Once when Pedro came to I made a gesture with my hands, simulating a steering wheel, and asked, "You fly?"

"*Sí*," he replied, and immediately took the controls.

I soon realized that Pedro was familiar with the Beech and that although he wasn't a pilot, he probably had more stick time in it than I did. I took advantage of the situation to get some shut-eye. In a few minutes I was slouched down and comfortably dozing in my seat.

"Bronco! Bronco!"

I realized that Pedro was calling for me. I shook off the grogginess and looked at my watch. I'd been asleep for an hour. Pedro had steered us just east of the city of Coatzacoalcos. We were right on course. I felt refreshed from my nap and got excited as we approached the Mexican shoreline. We would be landing in about an hour.

Pedro unfastened his seatbelt, went to the back, and returned holding what looked like an M16 semiautomatic rifle that he'd pulled from one of the gun crates. He had a big grin on his face. It made me a little nervous.

Pedro propped the rifle against the forward bulkhead and returned to his seat. I figured that he'd pilfered a rifle for himself. He just sat there and smiled.

We roared over the coastline and headed into Mexico. Darin's DC-3 was about two miles ahead of me. After twenty minutes over land, Darin made a shallow turn to the west and we followed. Pedro sat up in his seat and pointed at a small mountain range ahead. Before long we were maneuvering around brown and green peaks that seemed to come right up to join us. I peered into the distance and saw several mountains that were well above our altitude.

The radio squawked. It was Darin.

"Where are you, Bronco?"

"A few miles behind you," I answered.

"Pedro knows the way from here and will keep you pointed in the right direction. Drop back a few more miles and give us a chance to get turned around at the far end of the *pista*. It's not much different than what you're used to."

I slowed the Beech down, dropping farther back from the DC-3. Pedro started to point rapidly, straight ahead of us.

"*Pista, pista, pista,*" he said.

I looked ahead and saw a long narrow road that Darin was headed for.

"I see it!" I said.

Pedro heard me but kept right on pointing at the landing zone. I didn't see anything else that looked suitable to land on.

Darin came up on the FM again:

"All clear, Bronco." he said.

"*Sí,* I'll be right there," I said.

I throttled back and began to slow down. Suddenly I realized I had no idea how long this *pista* was. I only assumed that it was at least as long as *Pista Negra*. I didn't have much experience in the Twin Beech. I had a high-risk load in the back, and I was lacking sleep. I began to question my abilities. I could screw this up real bad.

I thought about calling Darin on the FM but he was already on the ground and probably wouldn't answer anyway. From my vantage point the runway looked to be at least three thousand feet in length. I threw the gear and flaps out and slowed the airplane for landing. I reached down, checked the tail wheel lock, and aimed for the road.

At about a mile into my final approach I could tell that the *pista* was plenty long. I let out a long breath and relaxed as I pushed the mains onto the dirt and rolled the aircraft down the smooth-dusty *pista.*

Four and a half hours after leaving McAllen, Texas, I was on the ground and taxiing to the northern border of Guatemala. At its southern end the road dipped sharply. Darin rolled his plane to that point and spun around, using an open field that spread across the road. There were no areas suitable to park off the road, so Darin and I turned our airplanes around and pointed back to the north, ready to depart once we were unloaded.

Two small box trucks were waiting next to the road. Darin had already popped open the cargo door on the Doug and a group of men were unloading crates.

Pedro got out of his seat, grabbed his M16 and climbed in the back. I glanced back and saw him remove an ammo magazine from an opened crate and I heard him put a round in the chamber. I turned around and looked out the windshield. Several of the workers on the ground wore similar rifles over their shoulders. It seemed like everyone was armed but me. I began to get nervous. Then I saw Darin through a back window behind my wing. He appeared to be unarmed, which made me feel a little better.

No sooner did I shut down that a pickup truck with a fuel tank and oil drum in the back pulled in front of the Twin Beech. A couple of little natives jumped out of the truck, grabbed some hoses, and started to put fuel in my wings and oil in my engines. The guys were quick and efficient. It was almost like being back at Hal's.

Pedro bailed out the back and stood in front of the door opening, bearing his rifle. I crawled over the crates, got out of the Beech, and took a piss behind the tail. Darin walked toward us. Close behind him was a short tubby guy who looked like a Latino version of Ray. He was holding two manila envelopes, one large and one small. When he and Darin reached the back of my airplane the short little guy introduced himself:

"I'm Juan," he said. "I need to please inspect your load."

Pedro, who had been guarding the door, moved aside as Juan climbed aboard. He selected two crates from different locations in the back of the plane. As soon as he opened the first one I looked inside. I didn't see any rifles. We were actually carrying ammunition—three thousand pounds of ammunition! My blood suddenly ran cold. I looked at Darin with my mouth hanging open and couldn't think of anything to say. Darin just stood there with a big grin on his face.

Juan reappeared from the airplane. He handed me the small envelope and Darin the larger one. A truck pulled alongside the Beech, and several natives scurried to offload the crates. Darin and I sat nearby and chatted about the haul. Pedro never left his post and continued to guard as the men emptied the airplane.

About then a small native man appeared. He was holding two grocery sacks.

"Time for breakfast!" Darin said.

We thanked our host. Inside the sacks were some very special breakfast *tamales* from a local Guatemalan home. They were fantastic.

The natives finished loading both trucks. They jumped in, cranked up the engines, and drove south across the Guatemalan border, which was just a hundred feet from where we were parked. In that remote location borders had little meaning to the locals.

Juan returned to his white Chevy pickup, which he'd parked behind the DC-3. He drove around to Darin and me behind the Twin Beech.

"Thank you," said Juan. "I hope to see you again soon!"

With that, Pedro strolled around the tail of the Beech, threw his weapon in Juan's truck and climbed into the passenger seat.

I looked at Darin. "Isn't Pedro going back with me?" I said.

Darin shook his head. "He's a Guatemalan and only comes to the States to escort the cargo. He usually rides in the jump seat of the Doug with me on the way down."

At that point nothing surprised me. With all the people and weapons around, I felt secure on the ground but was beginning to get anxious to head back to Texas. Darin finished his *tamales* while I inspected the fuel and oil caps on the Twin Beech. It would be a long ride home but I had an envelope full of cash for my efforts.

I waved the envelope around and thanked Darin for all the fun.

"You know your way home, right?" he said.

It wasn't the first time he'd asked me that question. It took me back to the not too distant past when my flight instructor entrusted me to sharpen my skills of piloting airplanes.

"I think I can make it," I replied. I climbed into the Beech and closed the door.

CHAPTER 17

ISLAND HOPPING

I WAS FLYING A Twin Bonanza that Bobby had loaned us, headed for the tropical island of Jamaica, but I was shivering. The aircraft was running well, but I couldn't get any heat in the cockpit.

I'd flown south along the Mexican coast for an hour, then turned to the southeast and headed across the Gulf. In a couple of hours I'd look for the *Yucatán* Peninsula. It was still dark to the east. I figured I'd see the lights of Mérida (the capitol city of *Yucatán*) and later the island of Cozumel by dawn.

The Twin Bonanza, or "T-Bone" as they are commonly called, was cruising at about fifteen thousand feet and the night sky outside was near freezing. I tried to keep warm by covering myself with a blanket of navigation charts, but it didn't seem to help much. At that altitude the engines burned less fuel. Even with the auxiliary tank we added to the plane, I needed to conserve all I could in order to make the trip back. I'd be taking on fuel in Jamaica, but only a limited amount.

All things considered, though, it was a beautiful night for flying and once I left the eastern shores of Mexico there were five hundred miles of open water until I came ashore somewhere between the cities of

Campeche and Mérida. I navigated off the Tampico VOR until its signal faded and disappeared. Then it was dead reckoning until I picked up Merida's beacon. Ideally I'd come ashore and fly just south of Merida, fly for an hour over land, and cross open water again for another six hundred miles.

My only checkpoint before reaching Jamaica was Grand Cayman Island, which should be just off my left wing. If I passed north of Grand Cayman I would likely enter Cuban airspace. If I passed too far to the south, I would miss Jamaica altogether and run out of fuel over the eastern Caribbean Sea.

I adjusted my course slightly, calculated wind and drift, and crossed over the northern shores of the state of Campeche. I headed across the *Yucatán* and began to pick out its eastern shore at about dawn. Now my objective was to cross the southern tip of Cozumel Island before heading out over the Caribbean. Once I was east of Cozumel and beyond radio navigation range I would have to dead-reckon for an hour until I began receiving the radio beacon from Grand Cayman. From there I should be able to locate the island of Jamaica.

The Twin Bonanza was pushing against a light headwind of about ten knots out of the east-southeast. A high-pressure system dominated the entire region, meaning the weather was predicted to be clear and the winds light. There were no systems expected from the western Atlantic for several days.

I could now see features on the ground over the eastern *Yucatán* and could pick out Cozumel Island up ahead. I headed right for it.

With the sun coming up in my windscreen I passed over Cozumel Island at its southernmost tip and adjusted my course for Jamaica. I wanted to track slightly southeast until I picked up Grand Cayman, and pass to the south of that island.

With nothing left to do and some time to kill, I dug into my duffle bag and pulled out a couple of candy bars. I unlatched my seatbelt and crawled over the fuel tank to the back of the plane, where I grabbed the box that held the life raft and emergency flares. Ray had thought it would be a good idea to carry this stuff, but it took up so much room that I wasn't sure where to stow it on the return trip. The raft was a small two-man model that Ray had picked up at a local sporting goods store in Brownsville. I wanted to check out the inflation device so I reached in the box and pulled out a rubber hose attached to a small volume bellows. It was a foot pump!

Oh great! I thought. *If I happen to ditch in three feet of water I can just stand there and inflate the raft by hand.*

I disconnected the hose and tried pumping the bellows. That's when I discovered that the check valve had been installed backwards. The pump was sucking air instead of blowing it out.

Fantastic! Now I'm going to drown for sure.

I tried to remove the check valve but had no luck. It was glued into the hose and permanently attached to the pump body. I'm sure the manufacturer did that for liability reasons. They didn't want anyone tampering with the device and die because of it. *Brilliant!*

Things were running smoothly and I figured I'd make it to Jamaica just fine. On the return trip I'd have a ton of pot stuffed in the plane. If for some reason I had to ditch in the ocean, it was highly unlikely that I'd survive anyway.

As I said, I was flying a Beechcraft Model G50 Twin Bonanza. This one had long-range fuel in the wings and a 210-gallon aluminum tank placed behind the cockpit. The extra fuel tank inside the cabin was illegal as hell, but what did we care? We got the idea from companies that exported airplanes overseas. They installed similar tanks to give their airplanes enough range to cross the vast bodies of water between stops around the world. After I landed in Jamaica there would be two drums of aviation fuel waiting to be dumped into the wings. That would give me enough fuel to get back to Mexico, plus about forty-five minutes of reserve. If everything went as planned I might even have enough to reach the States from there.

I'd be landing in Jamaica all alone, but on the return trip I'd have a female passenger. Ray had arranged for her to come to the U.S. and work for him as a housekeeper.

Things would be quite cozy for the seven-hour trip back to Mexico. The front seats in the T-Bone were actually a small bench pilot seat, and a narrow single right passenger seat that had been removed. The passenger and I would have to squeeze onto that small bench seat for the entire ride back. The airplane was also equipped with a "swing over" control column, a signature piece of equipment in early model Beechcrafts. A single control post extended from the lower center of the instrument panel, angled to the left or right, with a control yoke or wheel attached to the end for the pilot to steer with. This device had a locking mechanism that could be released either on the ground or in flight, allowing the entire control column to swing over top center and lock in the opposite side position. By moving the control column, a pilot could fly the airplane from either the left or right seat.

Since crossing Cozumel Island I'd taken a final course check before tracking off Merida over open water. The next leg was a six-hundred-mile poke. There was a lot to think about for the next three and a half hours. I wondered if I'd see any ships crossing beneath me and if anyone in them would spot me passing overhead. I thought about the raft a lot and how long the airplane would stay afloat if I had to ditch. With the wing tanks about half full and two hundred gallons of fuel in the cabin the aircraft would probably stay afloat for several minutes before disappearing beneath the waves. I was wearing a "Mae West" style life preserver, strapped to my waist. If I ended up in the drink, the raft and my Mae West were the only things that could keep me from drowning. Hopefully I could ditch close to a passing vessel and get picked up soon afterward.

I was reminded of an incident that happened to a friend a couple of months earlier. He and a companion were touring southern Mexico and the *Yucatán* in his single engine Mooney when he decided to take a shortcut across the southern end of the Bay of Campeche. About an hour and a half out of Campeche they experienced a rough running engine so they immediately headed south for land. Soon the engine quit and they were forced to ditch. Fortunately, below them were calm seas and a small fishing vessel. He made a perfect emergency ditching and the airplane remained intact and came to rest only about a thousand yards from the small ship. The fishing crew had spotted the small plane prior to impact and was already making preparations for a rescue.

Thinking that the airplane was about to head straight to the bottom, the passenger panicked, threw open the door and bailed out. With the airplane still afloat the pilot stepped out on the wing and threw a life preserver to his companion. The pilot then proceeded to assist his friend in climbing back onto the wing of the small plane. They both waited only a few minutes while the fishing boat came alongside and launched a dingy. They pulled up close to the Mooney and both my friend and his companion stepped off of the airplane wing and into the dingy and were taken back to the boat safe and sound. My friend told me that the only time he got wet was while helping his buddy back up onto the wing of the airplane to wait for their rescue. He said that the Mooney stayed afloat for nearly thirty minutes before filling with water and sinking.

Over open water and an hour past Cozumel I tuned in the Grand Cayman VOR and waited for the nav to lock on. Thirty minutes went by. No signal. I was about two hundred fifty miles from Cozumel Island. Where was Grand Cayman's VOR? I tuned in a different radio beacon and finally got a bearing of 250 degrees off Grand Cayman. That was good news. I should see Grand Cayman Island very soon. A few minutes later I looked out and saw an island about thirty miles northeast of me. It was Grand Cayman. I adjusted my course and tracked outbound on the Grand Cayman non-directional beacon until that signal faded. I was then close enough to Jamaica to pick up the Kingston VOR. I was right on course.

My plan was to descend to the surface of the water and fly low for the last hour of my trip. I headed for the deck. When I hit two thousand feet of altitude I could see Jamaica ahead in the distance. I'd found it! It was no miracle with modern navigational aids. But crossing the Gulf of Mexico and most of the Caribbean non-stop, alone in a small plane, under radio silence, can wreak havoc with your head.

Now I needed to stay off the south coast of Jamaica until I passed the western tip of the island. At about midpoint I looked for a peninsula—the southernmost point in Jamaica. I needed to cross close by that peninsula and head into the bay. I had a handheld FM transceiver and I picked it up and made a call to someone on the ground.

"Everything okay?" I asked.

"Good to come, okay to land," came the reply.

I hit the coast, flew west of a small hill, and spotted the landing strip dead ahead. After seven hours and forty-five minutes of flying I was rolling out on a dirt airstrip west of Kingston, Jamaica. There were eight people waiting for me. After I spun the airplane around and shut down, one of them stepped up onto the wing and looked into the cockpit.

"Welcome to Jamaica, mon. I hope you are Bronco Billy?"

"That's me!" I said. I pulled myself out of the cockpit and headed for the trees to take a leak.

"We've got some fuel for you," he said. "You relax and we take care of every-ting."

There was a box truck parked off the turnaround with two thousand pounds of marijuana in the back. A pickup truck pulled around the front of my airplane. I saw two drums of fuel in the pickup, ready to be pumped into the wings.

They backed the box truck up to the plane and began to pack in the forty-pound bales of pot. Meanwhile, two guys frantically began hand pumping fuel into the left main and auxiliary tanks. One guy stroked the pump while the other held the hose in the filler port. After they finished with the left side they traded positions and repeated the process on the right.

Shortly after I'd arrived, a white man came up to me and introduced himself as Mike.

"I believe you have som'ting for me, mon," he said.

I crawled back into the airplane and grabbed a brown paper bundle from the cockpit. Inside the bundle was a wad of cash: money for the ganja. I handed it to the man.

"T'anks mon," he said. "I'll count it now if you don't mind."

He opened the bundle, placed the money on the wingtip of the plane, and counted out forty thousand dollars in U.S. currency. The cargo being loaded into the plane had a street value of over $1.5 million. That was one hell of a markup.

Ganja cultivation and trade was illegal in Jamaica, although at that time possession of the substance was considered a gray area. The authorities were aware of the economic boost that the pot-growing industry brought to the country and often looked in the other direction. Rather than arresting and prosecuting the growers, Jamaican authorities often took payoffs and kickbacks instead. Ganja was everywhere and it seemed as though everyone was partaking in the lucrative cash crop—at least in the circle of people I was involved with.

After Mike finished counting the money he gestured to someone in a small shed at the end of the strip. A small woman emerged from the hut and walked toward us.

"Dis is Marta," he said. "She is going home wit' you, mon."

Marta carried a little duffel bag over her shoulder. She was a small woman, probably in her mid-fifties, and wore a modest flowered dress and no jewelry.

"Good morning sir," she said to me with a smile. "Where would you like me to sit?"

"Right next to me in the cockpit," I answered.

"Okay den. I be waiting, sir."

With that she sat down underneath the wing and waited quietly while the others finished packing the bales and pouring the fuel.

I looked at Marta. She didn't seem like much of a talker, and I wondered how much conversation we'd be able to generate on the trip back. I was in this for forty grand, and Ray had promised to throw in a little something extra for the passenger. It sounded fair to me.

While the work continued I added a couple quarts of oil to each engine. I needed to keep the airplane running smoothly for the next six hours.

The loading crew moved away from the plane as I did a quick walk-around, checking the back door and the fuel caps. I had just enough time to eat a sandwich I had brought and stuff some trinkets they had given me into the small space underneath my seat. I checked the back of the plane; every nook and cranny was filled with ganja. The guys had done a bang-up job of stuffing all fifty bales into the airplane, with a couple stuffed near the doorway across from the pilot's seat.

It was time to go. I shook hands with Mike.

"We see you again Bronco," he said. "Say hello to Ray for me."

I crawled into the cockpit and helped Marta get in the seat next to me. She looked nervous.

"You ever fly before?" I said.

"No, sir."

"No worries," I said. "I'll teach you."

"No t'ank you sir," she replied. She didn't seem to be kidding.

I shoved the mixtures forward and cranked up each engine. Once they were running smoothly I simply pointed the airplane back down the strip and advanced the go sticks to full power. The T-Bone accelerated slowly as we rumbled across the ground. With her heavy load the plane sluggishly lifted off and began to climb in the hot and steamy Jamaican morning. I reduced power to avoid overheating and we settled into a gentle climb of a few hundred feet per minute. The slower climb meant I'd burn more fuel getting to altitude.

We had a long climb ahead of us and I noticed the engines were already getting hot.

Marta was very uncomfortable flying. I wondered how she was going to make it all the way home.

"Don't worry, Marta," I said. "Everything is going to be all right."

She didn't say anything, just clutched the seat and stared straight ahead.

As soon as we cleared the coast I leveled out slightly trying to let the added airspeed cool the cylinders.

Suddenly the left engine sputtered. At first it was a single blip and then it surged violently and the airplane yawed to the left. The engine was failing!

Not only were we yawing and rolling to the left but the nose was beginning to pitch up. I looked out the left side for evidence of oil or fire. I couldn't see anything unusual, but I was obviously losing power.

As the motor continued to sputter, catch again, sputter again, and catch again, I forced the controls forward in an attempt to regain some lost airspeed. It didn't seem to be working as we continued to pitch up. Our airspeed was getting critically low. Why wasn't I able to correct anything?

I looked at Marta and realized why. In her panic she had grabbed the horizontal section of the control column and was pulling on it with all her might. She had no idea that she was placing us in grave danger. If the airplane had slowed much more it would have stalled and rolled over on its back, sending us downward. We were only a few hundred feet off the water and would not have had time to recover from the loss of control. If I didn't take immediate action, we were going to flip inverted, plunge into the water and die. I pushed hard on the controls.

"Marta, *stop*!" I yelled.

She didn't respond. She was frozen in place, her hands wrapped around the control column, hanging on for dear life. No matter how hard I pushed at the controls to counter what she was doing, nothing had any affect.

"Don't pull, Marta!" I shouted as I tried to pull her off the controls. "Stop it!"

I couldn't free her grip. She glared straight out the front window with a look of terror on her face. It was time to take action.

I aimed my right elbow at her and popped her square in the face. The sharp blow stunned her and she released the controls and collapsed to her right against a bale of ganja.

Suddenly the airplane lunged downward toward the water and I was barely able to recover. When we pitched over with the nose down, the windmilling engine caught briefly and surged again. I finally figured out the problem: fuel contamination. There must have been a good dose of water mixed in with the gas. I hadn't drained the sumps before we left. I was in a hurry and assumed the fuel to be pure. Big mistake. With the good engine at full throttle and the other surging violently I forced the airplane around and headed back to the airstrip in Jamaica.

Normally I'd have feathered the propeller of the bad engine. This causes the propeller blades to twist at the hub, align themselves with the slipstream, and stop turning. A windmilling propeller creates a lot of unwanted drag. With a feathered prop it's easier to maintain enough airspeed to avoid loss of control and become instantly inverted.

My left engine was still giving me short bursts of desperately needed power. The overloaded airplane would not fly on one engine and was barely flying now. The best I could do was nurse the aircraft back to the airstrip and land it in one piece.

We were a hundred feet off the water when I regained control and headed back to land. Now my objective was to climb and clear the hills that lay between us and the airstrip. They poked up about three hundred feet above the surrounding flatlands. We were headed back and I struggled to coax the old girl into giving me just a couple of hundred feet.

In less than a minute I'd encounter the rising terrain. The hills to the right were too high but to the left there was a break and a small valley. I began a very shallow turn to the left and barely made the valley with only a few feet between us and the hill under our right wing. Just squeaking through I headed directly for the airstrip. It was only a few miles inland and we were coming in at a sharp angle and were not lined up to land. I carefully maneuvered around until we were headed right for the end. The airplane yawed with every surge from the left engine. We were coming in fast and I'd have to throttle back before landing or I could lose control and roll up into a ball of fire on the airstrip.

At the last second I extended the flaps, lowered the landing gear and yanked both throttles back to idle and killed the left engine. We hit the end of the strip hard and fast and I pushed on the brakes as hard as I could. We skidded and swerved in the dirt and gravel and slid to a stop at the very end.

Marta sat up, bleeding from her nose. She didn't say a word but pulled a handkerchief from her bag and began cleaning up her face.

Outside there was nobody around. Everyone had left. In the silent calm with the dust settling around us I looked at Marta and smiled at her with a sigh of relief.

"We had an engine failure," I said.

"Okay," was all she said.

I reached under the seat, grabbed the FM radio, and tried to raise someone on the other end. But there was nothing. They had their money and had no reason to stick around after seeing us fly off and disappear over the hills.

I reached across Marta and opened the door for her.

"Let's get out and I'll see what I can do," I said.

She sat there, still holding her handkerchief to her nose. Still dazed she hesitated to get out. I looked at her nose.

"Sorry 'bout that. I had to fly."

"Okay," she replied.

We climbed out of the airplane and Marta headed right for the shed next to a sugar cane field. I took a look at the aircraft. The right engine had been running at full power for several minutes and was still smoking and crackling from the heat.

I crawled under the wings and began to sump the tanks. The heavier water will settle to the bottom, where it can be drained from low points under each wing. I went to the left side and pushed the sump open. At first all I got were a few drops. I closed the sump and opened it two or three more times and got nothing but a few drops of water and what looked like rust sediment. I kept working the sump until a steady stream began to flow. The first gallon was all water mixed with flakes of rust.

It was that combination that was causing the problem. I was getting a plugged line from the sediment; then, with the water and fuel sloshing around, the line would become open as the engine died. The pickup tube would sometimes take up fuel and sometimes water, and then plug up again from the sloshing sediment. It was a vicious cycle. The right wing only had about a cup of water and no sediment.

I sat on the ground and looked at Marta in her little shed. She was just sitting there, looking somber. She knew we had failed. I wondered what she thought of the whole episode but then I realized she was unconscious for the most exciting part. I smiled at her but she ignored me and went back to attending to her sore nose. I felt terrible. I sat there for a few minutes thinking about what to do. Our choices were limited, but maybe with Marta's help we could find someone to help us out.

CHAPTER 18

THE ESCAPE

CRAWLED OUT FROM underneath the wing and stood in the sunshine for a minute, wondering how much fuel I had burned and whether I had enough to reach Mexico on a second attempt. I looked at my watch and decided I'd burned off about thirty minutes of fuel. But taking off and climbing out again would probably burn up my reserve and we would land in Mexico on fumes. If we came up short the choices were either to plow into a dense area of trees or ditch in the Gulf. Neither option was appealing. I grabbed the FM and made another couple of attempts to raise someone, without success.

Marta was still sitting in the shed, cleaning her bloodstained blouse.

"Hey, Marta!" I said. "We need to contact someone for some more fuel."

She thought for a moment and said, "I have a brother in Spanish Town."

"Is that near here?"

"No sir, it a ways."

I wasn't sure what to do. I still needed to drain more fuel from the left wing to be sure the tank was clear. I had given away all the big cash and didn't have anything substantial to barter with except for a couple hundred dollars and my Buck knife. Fortunately the predominant language in Jamaica was English. Even then I sometimes struggled to understand the local dialect and slang.

"Someone be coming soon, sir," Marta said.

I nodded. "I just hope they're on our side."

At the far end of the airstrip a figure appeared. Someone was walking our way.

"Look, Marta," I said. "Do you think they're friendly?"

"I t'ink so sir," she replied.

The figure got clearer as it approached. It was a tall man and he was carrying a machete. I began to get nervous. I didn't realize that the machete was a common tool used in the country and many of the men who worked in the fields used them for cutting cane, coconuts and bananas. To me the machete was a weapon, and I was defenseless.

Marta came out from the shed and we both stood there waiting.

"Dat mon a farmhand," Marta said. "He good mon, sir."

I recognized him. He was one of the men who had loaded the airplane earlier. I felt a rush of relief. Maybe he'd help us.

I was supposed to meet Ray and the receiving team in Mexico at 6 p.m. The flight back would take well over six hours, and if everything went smoothly we could make it just in time. However, the left fuel system could still be contaminated, resulting in more engine problems. We had a good stretch of water to cross and I needed mechanical perfection to ensure the protection of life and property. A forced landing in the ocean would be a death sentence and the odds were beginning to stack up against us.

I also realized I hadn't brought a life preserver for my passenger. In fact, Ray never mentioned that I should carry a personal floatation device. That was an idea I'd gotten from speaking to a helicopter pilot who regularly flew out to offshore oil platforms. The raft was useless and I would have had to resort to the buddy system should Marta and I find ourselves afloat in the middle of the Caribbean. It wasn't a comforting thought.

The man walking toward us raised his machete in greeting.

"I'm Reggie," he said. "Why you come back?"

"Where can we get some more fuel?" I asked.

"Ders no gas, mon," he replied.

"Is there any way we can get some?" I said.

"No mon, we haffi find de pig."

I had a hard time understanding what he was saying, but I did grasp that getting aviation fuel was going to be a bit of a challenge. The "pig" was the truck that had carried the two drums of fuel that caused all of my problems.

"All I need is about twenty gallons," I said.

"No mon, we haffi find de pig," Reggie repeated. "I take you to get some."

For the first time since I'd launched out of Cameron County earlier that day, I was a little scared. As I stood there trying to figure out how to gather this ball of twine that was unraveling on me we heard the sound of an airplane coming in our direction. Reggie looked up and motioned for us to get under the wing and out of sight. He and I crouched under the wing but Marta headed back for the shed and waited there. Soon a single engine Cessna arrived overhead and began circling the area.

"It's a spotter plane," Reggie said.

The spotter plane made a tight pattern and was setting up to land.

"You must hide now!" Reggie said.

The Cessna made its turn onto final approach to land. Marta was already making for the sugar cane field that lay just behind the shed. Reggie motioned for me to follow her.

"I watch what they do," he said. "You go hide!" He got up and ran for the trees next to the cane field.

I shot out from under the wing and sprinted for the cane field, right behind Marta. As I hit the edge of the field the spotter plane was just touching down. I struggled in the dense sugar cane and pushed as deep into the field as possible. The sugar cane was dense and the ground was covered with two inches of standing water. It was a muddy, mucky mess, and I could barely move through it.

When I got as far as I could, I dropped to my knees and lay down to hide. We heard the Cessna roll to a stop several hundred feet from the fully loaded T-Bone. The Cessna sat there idling for a minute, then taxied back and took off directly over our heads. After the airplane passed I heard a noise a few feet from where I was lying.

"Marta, is that you?" I asked.

"I'm over here sir," she called from a different direction.

191

I didn't know what the sound was but I didn't stick around long enough to find out. I struggled to my feet and pushed my way back through the path I'd made coming into the cane. Marta wasn't far behind me. Muddy and wet, we emerged from the cane field. Reggie was walking towards us from the woods. We met near the shed.

"Dey is comin' soon," Reggie said. "De babylon be here soon."

"Where can we go?" I asked.

"I take you to a house. You will wait der and I get help for you."

The spotter plane headed off towards Kingston and soon we could no longer hear it. No doubt they'd radioed in our position and requested a ground team. We needed to get out of there before they arrived, or we might not live long.

Reggie instructed me to get anything out of the plane I wanted and to follow him. I grabbed my and Marta's bags. I didn't want to leave the airplane there, and I asked Reggie how long he thought we'd have to be away. He didn't know and seemed to be more concerned with leaving the airstrip.

With Reggie leading the way we walked down a narrow lane to the north. Marta brought up the rear and started to sing in a quiet voice. She had a big smile on her face. I had my doubts as to whether she would have gotten back in the airplane with me after the ordeal I'd just put her through.

The airstrip was located in the middle of a large agricultural area to the west of Kingston. We walked a half mile around the cane field, and then headed through a grove of grapefruit trees. The grove opened into a pasture where we followed a barbed wire fence line that bordered a dense area of trees on the east. We were halfway to the opposite end of the field when Reggie suddenly turned toward us.

"Get down!" he hissed.

All three of us scrambled over the fence and rushed into the woods. We crouched behind some trees. Reggie lay flat on the ground with his head buried in the base of a tree. Marta crouched down; facing the tree she was behind. I lay with my back against a tree, attempting to make myself as small as possible.

"What is it?" I whispered.

"Soldiers!" said Reggie.

"Do you think they saw us?"

192

"Can't tell. I don't t'ink so."

We heard them getting closer. They were coming along the fence in our direction.

Reggie and Marta were natives to the area, so I wondered why they too were hiding. Couldn't they just pop up and introduce themselves to the soldiers, then leave? I learned later that Reggie was a known drug trafficker and Marta was wanted for robbery in Kingston and Spanish Town. That explained Marta's willingness to leave Jamaica on an airplane full of ganja. There were more legitimate ways of getting out of the country, but when you're on the lam your choices are limited.

My hopes of leaving that day were fading fast as I heard the soldiers getting closer. My heart was pounding. I thought it might give us away. I was certain one of them would see us.

We remained motionless while twenty Jamaican army troops marched by, only a few feet away. They were heading toward the airstrip and my only hope of getting out of there. Foolishly I thought that maybe they would find that we had left and turn to pursue us and leave the airplane alone.

The troops were now well past us. We scrambled to the other end of the field, away from the soldiers and the airstrip. After walking for another thirty minutes we came upon a clearing. An old abandoned building sat on the opposite side. We ran across the clearing and into the building. It was a single-level structure, about sixty feet square, with one large room and several smaller ones. The few windows were all busted out and in the large room there was a huge pile of broken glass that covered the entire floor and was piled up against one of the walls. We were holed up in an old soft drink bottling factory.

"Wait here," Reggie said. "I'll get help and I will probably be awhile. Don't be goin' anywhere."

With that he left Marta and I alone.

Kingston is the capitol city of Jamaica and a unique, crowded metropolis. We were outside of the suburbs. Beyond the citrus groves and cane fields around us were densely populated villages and small cities.

Inside the former bottling plant there was no place to sit except on broken glass or on the floor in one of the interior rooms. Marta and I used our bags as makeshift seat cushions and sat quietly. We talked softly and learned a little about each other. Two hours passed.

Marta told me that she had made up her mind about flying.

"You didn't like it?" I said.

She shook her head. "I am stayin' put, sir."

I couldn't blame her. I felt terrible about knocking her senseless and apologized to her more than once. I think she understood the reason I did it. Every time I mentioned it to her she said the same thing:

"Dat awight, sir. We still bredrin."

We talked some more about the United States and her attempt to leave Jamaica and her family behind. I was slowly learning about the country I was now stranded in. I asked her about the sugar cane field and the noise I heard while hiding there.

"Could that have been a snake?" I asked.

"Maybe sir. Maybe alligator," she replied.

I didn't know whether she was kidding, but I decided to stay out of sugar cane fields from then on.

It had been almost three hours since Reggie left. We hadn't heard or seen any commotion in the area, and the traffic on the nearby street seemed to be getting congested. Then we heard a vehicle pull up outside. We ducked down out of sight. A voice called to us.

"Marta?"

Marta sat up and looked out the front window of the building.

"Here!" she said.

It was Marta's brother.

"You must come with me," he said.

We grabbed our bags and got in the car.

"What's your name?" I asked.

"Just call me Jancro," he said. "Reggie said they are looking for you."

"Did he tell you why?" I asked.

"I know why," he said. "I was there helping earlier today."

I felt a little embarrassed at not recognizing him, but things were moving pretty fast. Jancro said he would drop off Marta at a house up ahead and try to get me out of the area.

We drove about a mile. Jancro pulled the car over and Marta got out.

"I see you again, sir," she said to me.

She turned and walked to the side door of an old stucco house. Jancro turned the car around and drove back in the direction of the bottling plant.

"We cannot go that way," he said, pointing behind us. "There is a town with many policemen."

Just before reaching the bottling plant, Jancro turned up a narrow lane and pulled into the driveway of a small tin-roof shack. Inside the shack was a rickety wooden bar. In front of it, two old men sat at a table playing dominos. Jancro greeted them and asked to use their phone. They pointed to the phone on a table behind the bar and Jancro made a couple of telephone calls. He had his back turned to me so I didn't pick up any of the conversations he was having. When he was done he hung up and turned toward me.

"We'll stay here awhile," he said. "You want a Red Stripe?"

"I need to use the phone," I said.

"You cannot call outside Jamaica on this phone," he said. "I will see that you have a phone soon."

We waited in the makeshift bar watching the game of dominos and drinking warm Red Stripe beer. It tasted really good but I was getting hungry. Jancro must have picked up on that fact and offered me some salt pork. I said yes. Jancro left for a minute and came back with a brown paper bag full of salty dried pork pieces. They were very tender and tasted great with the Red Stripe beer.

We finished our salt pork and another Red Stripe and Jancro said it was time to leave. We got in his car and he explained to me how he was going to take me to meet someone who would move me to a safer place. We drove down the road and suddenly Jancro turned left onto a narrow lane.

"There is a roadblock up ahead," he explained.

We drove up the lane and up a steep incline. The car was beginning to struggle. Before we got to the top Jancro turned right and drove through a farm lane next to a cornfield. We followed that field for about a quarter mile, turned right again and headed back down the hill. We came out on the main road, bypassing the roadblock by no more than a hundred feet, and we both laughed aloud.

"I showed them!" said Jancro.

I didn't quite understand why I was being cared for so much but I wasn't going to question the efforts of those who were protecting me. So far everyone I'd come in contact with was friendly and helpful.

Jancro continued down the main road for another mile, then pulled off and headed down another narrow lane. Two blocks later he stopped the car.

"This is as far as I can take you," he said.

I looked around and didn't see anyone else.

"Now what am I supposed to do?" I said.

"I'll wait here with you until your ride shows up," he said.

Five minutes later a red van came up the lane behind us. I felt nervous again. The van blocked our exit. Two men stepped out and strolled toward the car. Jancro greeted them. They seemed friendly enough and laughed a lot about the whole situation. One of them thrust his hand toward me. I shook it.

"You must be Bronco Billy."

"That's right," I said. "How do I get out of here?"

"You'll be spendin' the night in Jamaica," he said. "You'll like it. My name is Thomas, and"—he jerked his head toward his partner—"this is Bob."

Thomas explained that as a white man, I'd have some trouble hiding in Jamaica, since the police were looking for me. I agreed. Thomas told Jancro that he was taking me to his house. I thanked Jancro and reached into my pocket and pulled out my Buck knife. I handed it to Jancro and told him it was a token of my appreciation. He smiled and thanked me and said that he'd see me again.

"Follow me," Thomas said, leading me to the back of the van. He opened the doors. The back row of seats had been removed.

"The police are looking for you," he explained. "They know you are a white man from the U.S. They've captured your airplane and have set up roadblocks to catch you." He pointed inside the back of the van and continued: "We can get you through the roadblocks and take you to a safe place where they will not find you. Are you ready, Bronco Billy?"

Bob jumped into the van and lifted a floor panel, exposing a hole in the floor. Underneath was a small hiding place, barely big enough for a man to fit in.

At first I was a little hesitant. I questioned whether I would even fit in the space and asked Thomas how long I would have to remain under the floor panel.

"Only until we pass the roadblock," he said. "If you don't hide they will find you. Then we will all go to jail."

The alternative wasn't acceptable so reluctantly I crawled into the back of the van and, lying on my side, curled up and crammed myself into the hold. Bob smiled and replaced the false floor panel and a rubber mat on top of me. Inside the compartment it was hot, smelly and loud. I was right next to the muffler.

The truck started up, turned around and headed back down the lane. For me it was a rough ride but Thomas and Bob had quite a good time. I smelled the familiar fragrance of ganja mixing with the exhaust gases. When we got to the main road I began to shake. It was a combination of fear and being crammed into the small space.

As we pulled up to the checkpoint I thought I would be discovered because I was shaking so much. I tried to calm myself down. The police opened the back of the van and questioned Thomas about his whereabouts, destination and intentions. Thomas answered calmly. The conversation seemed to take forever. I could hear other vehicles pulling up behind us and both cars and trucks passing us in the opposite direction. I thought at any moment the floorboards would fly open and I'd be greeted by a welcoming party holding machine guns pointed at my face.

Suddenly it got quiet. The van doors slammed shut and Thomas hopped back in the driver's seat. We slowly pulled away from the checkpoint.

I couldn't take it any longer. I pushed up on the floor panel just enough to take in some fresh air.

"Hey Bronco," said Bob, "we made it. It's all good now, mon."

I kicked the floor panels open and ejected myself out of the cubbyhole.

"That was awful," I said.

I was sweating profusely and breathing heavily. I felt lightheaded from the exhaust fumes.

"Now where are we going?" I asked.

"You relax now, mon," Thomas said. "We need to go for a good drive."

We started up a winding road into the mountains. I crawled into one of the middle seats and took in the many sights Jamaica had to offer. Turn after turn we continued farther into the hills. I saw several settlements, mostly tin-roof shacks and small groups of women carrying a variety of goods on their backs and on their heads. Sometimes we had to slow for a banana cart or a few wild goats roaming along the road. About thirty minutes later we came to a town.

"This is Linstead," said Bob. "You want a Red Stripe?"

My tongue was sticking to the roof of my mouth and my throat felt dusty.

"Yeah, I could sure use a drink," I replied.

We pulled over onto a widened shoulder, got out of the van and walked toward a small wooden building. It had a rusty tin roof, was weathered, unpainted and only had openings for its windows and single door. We stepped inside, onto a dirt floor. Nearby was a small wooden bar and a couple of countrymen sitting and staring at me. Thomas ordered up three Red Stripes and the man behind the bar pulled them out from underneath. The beer was as warm as the tropical afternoon but tasted very good. I was thankful for anything wet at this point.

I stood there drinking my beer as Thomas and Bob conversed with the locals. I couldn't understand everything they were saying. To follow the quick banter of the local dialect, heavily mixed with slang, took all of my attention.

After finishing our Red Stripes we got back in the van and continued into the hills. We passed several small settlements and changed roads a couple of times. We tracked along a hillside lined with banana trees. I could see out over the Jamaican landscape: a beautiful, lush, green paradise. We pulled onto a single-lane road and slowly maneuvered along for ten minutes. I soon realized why we were going so slow: there were several severe washouts in the road and to misjudge any of them would send us tumbling down the hillside. Fortunately there was no other traffic on this section of road.

"Here we are, Bronco," Thomas said as he lit up another ganja stick.

We pulled into a driveway to a modest stucco home with a tile roof and a couple of barns in the back. There were chickens and goats running around freely, plus the usual dogs and cats that one would expect on a farm. I saw a half dozen kids playing volleyball with their feet and a couple of older men sitting on the porch playing dominos.

A woman appeared in the doorway of the house, wiping her hands in her apron.

"That is Sarah, my wife," Thomas said as we came to a stop.

"Who's with you?" said Sarah.

"We've got the pilot."

"Oh God, what happened?"

Thomas told her the story. When he was done, she looked at me.

"You stay with us awhile, okay?" she said. "What's your name?"

"They call me Bronco Billy," I answered.

"I like the Billy," she said. "I'll stick with that."

Sarah was a typical Jamaican woman, totally dedicated to her family, the mother of five—three playing volleyball and a couple of younger ones still in the house. She was a sweethearted yet strong woman who definitely dictated matters around her home.

Thomas led me into the house, offered me a soda, and introduced me to his family. They were very close to one another and all lived in the two houses side by side. In addition to Sarah I met the children, mother, father, grandparents, brothers, aunts and uncles, and a couple of cousins, who were all sharing together on this small banana plantation. The women were busy cooking and grating coconut, the men were playing dominos; the children were all playing volleyball or some version of hacky sack. One uncle was out back sitting outside a shed. In front of him was an iron pot on a propane burner. He had a couple of crates of bottles and a grocery sack sitting next to him.

"What's he making?" I asked.

"Hash," answered Thomas.

"What do you mean?"

"You know, hashish," Thomas said, "from the Sinsemilla."

To them this was as common as an outdoor barbecue, as if the uncle was boiling corn or cooking up a batch of ribs. I stood and watched as he mixed the concoction of marijuana with rum in the simmering pot. Everyone except for the children and a couple of the older women smoked ganja. They all preferred sinsemilla; it was the unpollinated female marijuana plant. Sinsemilla was potent and readily available to all Jamaicans. It was the Marlboro of Jamaica.

Thomas led me back in the house and talked with Sarah and his mother for a few minutes. They were cooking up yams and ackee fruit. Ackee is an indigenous tree in the tropics. The seeds have a covering that is edible and delicious when ripe. When they are not ripe they are poisonous. When cooked, ackee resembles scrambled eggs. The yams were white and looked like a larger version of our common potato. They were mildly sweet, fibrous and delicious.

I felt welcome in their home; everyone was kind and well mannered. The older men played dominos almost nonstop. It was obviously the most popular game among the older adult men in Jamaica at that time.

Thomas showed me to a small bedroom and said I could bed down there for the night. It was late afternoon and I was beginning to feel a little worn out from the day's excitement. All I could think about was contacting Ray back in Mexico but I had no idea how he could be reached. And so far, except for the one in the bar earlier, I hadn't seen a single telephone. I asked Thomas if he had a phone and he said he did but that I couldn't use it to call the U.S. "All calls going outside Jamaica are traced," he explained. "We use a phone in Linstead for all business calls outside the country."

As I sat watching the women cook, Thomas tried to call Mike but didn't get an answer. He told me that Mike lived on the other side of the island and probably hadn't spoken to anyone since he left us on the airstrip that morning. I asked Thomas when he thought I could get to that phone in Linstead and he told me that he would take me there later that night. I figured that I'd call Ray's home and tell whoever answered that I was all right but stranded. I ate some yams and ackee with homemade bread, asked Thomas to let me know when it was time to go, and decided to take a nap.

Sometime later, Thomas entered my room.

"Hey Bronco, let's go make the call," he said as he shook me.

I was in a deep sleep and came to a little confused, but quickly I was back in Jamaica and the reality of my predicament was back as well. I got up and followed Thomas to his van. We drove back down the hill, turned onto the main road, and soon we were back in Linstead.

"I'll take you to a phone you can use," Thomas said. "It can't be traced."

We pulled into a small driveway in front of a tall privacy fence painted all black with a walk-through gate. Thomas walked along the fence, onto a concrete porch, and up to the door of a large stucco building. He knocked on the door. An oriental man appeared, chatted briefly with Thomas, then retreated back inside the building and closed the door behind him. Soon the small gate in front of the van opened slightly. I could see the Chinaman's face as he stuck his hand through the gate opening and motioned for me to follow him.

"He will take you to a phone," Thomas said.

I got out of the van and followed the man through the gate and into a large open court. He led me onto a concrete loading dock under an overhang. Fastened to the wall was a wooden box with a hinged lid. He lifted the lid, revealing a telephone.

"You use this," he said. "Dial zero-one first."

He disappeared through a dark doorway. I picked up the phone and dialed zero-one, then got a dial tone. I called Ray's home number. After several clicks and a few rings, Sandy, Ray's wife, answered.

"Hello Sandy? This is Bill."

"Oh my God! Are you all right?" Sandy cried. "Ray's been calling. He's worried sick about you."

"I'm okay," I replied. "We had some trouble with the airplane. When is Ray coming home?"

"He was going to wait in Mexico all night for you. We didn't know what happened and when Ray called Mike in Jamaica he said that he didn't know where you were but that he'd seen you take off."

"I don't think Mike knows yet," I said. "Tell Ray I'm all right but we had to turn back because of engine trouble."

"Okay. How can Ray get ahold of you?"

"I don't know yet," I answered, "Tell Ray I will call again when I get the chance."

"Be careful," Sandy said, and with that she hung up.

I stepped off of the loading dock, walked back across the courtyard, exited through the wooden gate and got back in the van with Thomas. We backed out of the driveway and headed for his home.

CHAPTER 19

THE COCKPIT COUNTRY

W HEN WE GOT BACK to Thomas' house late that night, a
few of his friends were waiting for him. Bob was still
there and Jancro had shown up with a new friend named
Patrick. We all sat on the porch and smoked sinsemilla for hours and
talked about airplanes and Jamaican culture. I was stoned out of my
gourd but my new friends seemed to be perfectly normal. They laughed
at me and joked about my sensitivity to ganja. I'd smoked a lot of pot
before and even had some of this potent stuff come my way. But it
seemed that this stuff had a little extra kick to it.

Jancro was the heaviest toker and insisted I try to keep up with him.
They thought it was great sport watching me as I zoned in and out over
and over again. There was nothing I could do but kick back and ride this
one out. Marijuana had an atypical effect on me. Instead of the normal
mellow relaxation that most people experienced, I became hyperactive,
shaky and nervous. I would often engage in physical activity while my
friends lay around and wondered what was up with me.

Hours later I could see the morning light in the east. My new friends
were either asleep in their chairs on the porch or had gone to bed. I sat

and watched the sky brighten, and just before sunrise I was finally able to go to sleep.

At ten o'clock Thomas' mother came into my room and asked me if I'd like some breakfast.

"That would be awesome!" I said.

"You were up late," she said. "I tried not to wake you too soon."

My throat was raw from the night before. Some eggs and cool juice was just what I was craving. Thomas' mother served eggs with salt pork and a fried version of the yams from the night before. The orange juice was fresh squeezed and it all tasted wonderful. My cohorts were already up and milling about the yard. I stepped outside to a rash of jesting and name-calling. They all laughed and greeted me. They didn't have many opportunities to smoke with such an amateur. Funny thing was, I didn't think of myself as an amateur. It was incredible, their resistance to the effects of the weed.

Thomas walked up to me and said that he was going into town that afternoon. "You can ride along and use the phone at the Chinaman's place," he said.

After lunch, Bob and Patrick left but Jancro stayed. He and Thomas and I jumped in the van and drove to Linstead. When we arrived, I got on the telephone again and dialed Ray's home number. This time Ray answered. Needless to say, he was glad to hear my voice.

"We didn't know what happened to you," he said. "I called Mike last night after I'd talked to Sandy and told him that you'd turned around. He was as surprised as I was. Where are you staying?"

"With one of Mike's friends," I answered. "The police are looking for me and we had fun dodging them. I'm hoping to get some fresh fuel and get out of here soon."

"Yeah, but that might be a problem. Mike told me that the airstrip owners probably know about your return and might have the plane guarded."

"The army is all over it, that part I know," I said. "Can we pay 'em to look the other way for a while?"

"I'll do what I can," said Ray. "Communication is horrible to say the least."

"Okay. In the meantime, they're taking pretty good care of me," I said.

"What happened?"

"I think I got some bad fuel."

"They told me there wouldn't be any water," said Ray.

"I'm not sure if it was the water or the rust," I said. "Either way, I wasn't about to venture off across the Caribbean with an engine spitting and sputtering."

"Call me if you get any news. Is there anything else you need?"

"No I'm fine. I'll talk to you later," I said, and with that we hung up.

Thomas and Jancro joined me in the courtyard and said they needed to use the phone themselves. They were going to call Mike. He had direct communication with the owners of the airstrip. I walked across the courtyard and leaned against an oak barrel and waited. Thomas called Mike and they spoke for a few minutes. After Thomas hung up he looked at me.

"Mike says that the owners of the airstrip are giving us three days to get the airplane off."

"That's great," I said. "Let's go back and you can take me to the plane."

Thomas shook his head. "It's not that simple, Bronco. You have a plane full of ganja sitting abandoned in the middle of a field we don't own, and armed guards waiting for you to come back. The property owners want us to pay off the soldiers."

We were using a makeshift airstrip that was owned by other dope smugglers. Whenever they wanted they could pay off the authorities and do their business without any interference. It seemed that Mike hadn't paid them for use of their airstrip yet, and when they'd heard that I was parked on their property they weren't willing to pay off the guards on our behalf. The fact that there was a ton of dope on the plane made matters worse. Whoever showed up would be immediately arrested no matter who they were. So the strip owners just sat back and waited to see what we were willing to do to recover the airplane and its cargo.

"Mike will talk to Ray about bribing the guards," said Thomas. "Mike says that is risky because the guards cannot be trusted and the police chief wants to make a name for himself by capturing an American ganja smuggler. You are a prize pig to him, Bronco Billy."

"So what are we going to do?" I asked.

"We are going to go home and wait a couple of days. Maybe the airstrip owners will make a deal with the police since they're anxious to use their own airstrip."

There was nothing more I could do. I was helpless. The whole matter was in the hands of the authorities and some smuggler kingpins. It was a bad combination and I didn't like it one bit. We headed back up to Thomas' house and arrived in time to drink some Red Stripe and sample some of Uncle's latest batch of hash. It did the trick, all right. I was up most of the night.

The next two days I hung around the homestead playing volleyball, hacky sack and learning to play dominos. My hosts were entertaining and they wanted to show me all of their tricks.

One day I walked out back and saw Thomas' grandfather sitting with a small board on his lap and a small pile of brown leaves at his side.

"What are you doing?" I asked.

"I make a cigar," he said. He held up a few of the leaves.

"That sounds interesting. May I watch?"

"Sure, Bronco. I'll teach you how."

I pulled up a stool beside him and watched as he stripped several leaves of their stems and bunched them together. He then formed the cigar into a tube using another leaf. As the leaves became bound by the outer leaf he rolled the bundle on the board on his lap using his hands and a broad blade knife. Then he took another clear leaf and wrapped the whole tube in it and twisted one end and cut the other end square. Again he rolled it with the knife and made it into a perfectly symmetrical cigar. I thought the process was complete, but he reached underneath his seat and pulled out two halves of a wooden block. It was a mold with ten cutouts shaped like cigars. The mold was half full of completed cigars. The grandfather explained to me that the sticks needed to rest in the mold for a while.

"How long?" I asked.

"Depends."

"On what?"

"Depends on how badly you want a smoke," he laughed.

He reached into his pocket, pulled out a freshly rolled cigar, and handed it to me.

"You can smoke this one for yourself," he said.

I thanked him and bit off the twisted end as he handed me some matches.

The cigar was wonderful. I'd smoked some cigars before but none seemed to have this much flavor. It was spicy and aromatic and blew a smooth heavy cloud. It burned a little strangely but I enjoyed it all the same.

I sat there smoking my cigar and watched the grandfather finish filling the mold. About then Thomas came around back.

"Grandpa has you smoking cigars now?" he laughed.

"These are great!" I said, adding half-jokingly, "and he's going to teach me how to roll them."

Grandpa nodded. "I show you how, Bronco."

With a great deal of patience he helped me fumble through the process and I came up with a loosely packed, cone-shaped contraption that didn't resemble a cigar in the least. Grandpa smiled and pointed at it.

"Let's see you smoke that," he said.

Thomas walked away laughing as I made a feeble attempt at smoking my creation. It wasn't as easy as Grandpa made it look.

Soon Thomas appeared on the back porch. He was smoking a joint.

"Grandpa used to work as roller in the Royal Jamaican cigar factory," he told me. "He could roll a cigar a minute."

I was now in my fourth day of being a fugitive. Thomas pulled his van into the driveway and told me that I needed to go to Linstead with him and call Ray. I jumped in the van and as we headed down the valley Thomas explained that Mike had tried to bargain with the owners of the airstrip but the whole thing fell apart. If we didn't have the plane off by tomorrow they would push it to the side and burn it.

"You need to call home," said Thomas, "and have some money wired into a Jamaican bank account."

"How much do they want?" I asked.

"Forty thousand dollars in U.S. currency."

When we arrived in Linstead I dialed Ray's home number but didn't get an answer. I tried a second time with the same result. Thomas and I decided to hang out in Linstead for a while and try the phone call later.

Linstead was an interesting town. Thomas drove me from one end to the other. I saw one- and two-room buildings painted in pastel colors of yellow, green or pink. All had tin roofs and many stood with their front doors wide open or missing altogether. There were people everywhere. The town was a combination of relaxed village life and busy metropolis. We visited a street vendor for some jerk chicken and Red Stripe. We stood on the side of the street eating and drinking. Afterward Thomas went to the van and pulled out a sinsemilla stick and lit up. I didn't partake in it as I wanted to have a clear head when I spoke with Ray later on. We drove to a roadside shack where Thomas talked with a couple of men as I stood nearby and downed a couple more Red Stripes. I was growing fond of the warm Jamaican beer and they went down easily.

After two hours we tried to call Ray again. The Chinaman's place was actually a restaurant and although I never entered the dining area I did enjoy some of the cuisine as I was treated to a couple of appetizers while spending time there.

This time when I called, Ray answered right away.

"We need to come up with forty thousand dollars by tomorrow or the airstrip owners will burn the airplane," I told him.

"I can't get an account number from these guys," Ray replied. "I got in touch with the guy who is supposed to be the owner. He originally thought that we were acting on our own and was under the impression that you had the money on you. When I explained to him that you'd used the money to purchase the cargo, he didn't listen and insisted you were holding on to it."

"That's crazy!" I said. "Didn't Mike tell them that he had the original forty grand?"

"I don't know," Ray said. "But there is the issue of the cargo. Evidently this guy paid off the guards to get it off the plane and wants to be reimbursed to let us have the T-Bone back. He said that he doesn't know who Mike is and wants to meet with you for an exchange of the cash."

"I don't have it," I said. "Mike took it and counted it out right in front of me."

"There's no way they will let you leave without paying for it. I think we got caught up in a feud between Mike and the airstrip owner."

"What are we going to do?"

Suddenly the line went dead. There was nothing, not even a dial tone. I went back to the van and told Thomas what had happened.

"That Chinaman, he did it," Thomas said. "We got to go."

Was there someone listening to my calls? I felt caught up in something much more complicated than I'd originally thought. I knew the Jamaican drug trade was a dirty business, but the drug trade is a dirty business no matter where you are. The airstrip we used was rented or borrowed from another operator, and that was a recipe for corruption. The agreements that took place between the two parties were underhanded. And to interfere with someone's plans to make some serious cash on his own airstrip had to cause a great deal of hostility.

Thomas and I sat in the van for a few minutes discussing our options. He was becoming agitated over the whole scenario and warned me that I might not have an airplane by this time tomorrow.

"These men are no good," he said. "I wish Mike had never dealt with them."

"What can I do about it now?" I asked.

"Nothing right now Bronco," he said, "we have to talk to Mike and find out what we can do."

We headed back into the hills. Thomas and I explored all the possible events that could have happened. We didn't fully know the relationship between Mike and the landowner or what, if anything had been agreed upon. Thomas assured me that Mike wasn't the type to try to cheat anyone out of their fair share. Whatever the case, we had a problem and I was at the sticky end. I hoped that money wasn't the issue with Ray or Mike. I hoped they had enough compassion for my well being to make every effort to resolve the situation.

I was feeling very alone and the sudden cutoff of the phone call with Ray didn't help matters. I began to mistrust people—people who so far had taken pretty good care of me, people who had gone out of their way to see that I was protected from the authorities who were now hunting for me. I began to feel homesick and wished I'd stuck with my nice little Mexican radio-hauling gig. I remembered something a friend had told me,"Try to avoid the temptations and promise of high returns and the thrills of high risk," she said. Maybe she was right.

We pulled into Thomas' driveway. Jancro came up to us.

"Mike called," he said. "He wants me to go to the strip tomorrow and talk to the owners."

"I'll go with you," I said.

"You can't go, Bronco," said Thomas. "You would mean a nice reward to them."

My fate was in the hands of some dope smugglers I'd never met. I walked with Thomas and Jancro to the house, kicking and cursing the whole way. It was getting late in the day and Sarah had made some fish with vegetables. We ate and spent the rest of the evening playing volleyball and listening to Bob Marley tapes. Bob Marley was like a national hero to these people. They spoke of him with admiration, respect and even reverence. To them he was a symbol of a free spirit and righteousness. They were eager to tell me about him and what he meant to each of them personally.

I began to imagine a lengthy stay in Jamaica. The potential course of events lay precariously at my immediate future. If things didn't go right I could lose my only ticket home. *I could become a permanent fugitive in this country*, I thought. Somehow, something had to happen in my favor. I kept going over it all in my mind, but I knew that the whole matter was completely out of my hands. If things didn't improve soon I thought about forming a plan of my own.

The next morning Patrick and Jancro drove to the low country. Neither Thomas nor I knew how long they would be. It was to be a day of waiting and wondering. I wanted to call Ray but figured it'd be a waste of time until I had some news.

Shortly after lunch, Thomas' phone rang. It was Jancro. I couldn't make out all of what was said but I didn't like the tone at all. Thomas cursed and shouted and slammed the phone down on the hook.

"They burned the plane," he told me. "Jancro said that there were no guards anywhere and they burned the plane. It was completely destroyed. He is on his way back."

"I've got to call Ray," I said.

We arrived at the Chinaman's place and I dialed Ray's home. The first thing I said when he answered was, "They burned the plane."

Ray was shocked. "Those sons of bitches are liars!" he said. "They told me they wouldn't. I can't believe it. Why would they destroy a perfectly good airplane?"

"I guess they're some pretty underhanded people," I replied.

"I think our problem was much bigger than we thought," Ray said. "I'm not sure how I'm going to do it, but I'll make some kind of arrangement to get you home."

"Okay," I said. "When should I call you next?"

"Can you give me a couple of days?" Ray asked.

"Sure, I think I'll be all right."

"Don't worry, Bill. I'll get you home." He hung up.

Back at Thomas' house I spent the next two days being just another member of a Jamaican family. Part of me was in denial: I couldn't believe they actually burned the airplane. Jancro told me he'd seen the charred remains of what was once a fine piece of Beechcraft machinery. I wondered how much fuel the airstrip owners had stolen before setting the aircraft ablaze.

My life and well-being were now totally dependent on a man fourteen hundred miles away and a group of people I barely knew. There was nothing more we could do but laugh it off and enjoy one another and have fun with our cultural differences. My friends enjoyed teaching me all I needed to know about being a Jamaican.

Mike had called Thomas several times in the past couple of days. On the last occasion he told Thomas about a plan to get me out of Jamaica. He said that the airstrip owners were going to load a DC-3 bound for Florida in two days. For forty thousand dollars I could hitch a ride back with them. They were probably landing somewhere near the Everglades, and I had to let Mike know by tonight if I wanted to go.

The possibility of hitching a ride home was tempting. But hitching a ride on a plane full of marijuana caused me concern. As I said before, drug trafficking is a dirty business. People are engaged in it for one reason and one reason only: money. They are willing to take huge risks for equally huge returns. Sometimes they do it out of desperation. They may be on the verge of financial ruin and trying to settle overwhelming debt. They may be indebted to thugs. Or they may just be taking a shortcut where the ends justify the means. That's what I was doing. I didn't get into this to hurt anyone, and I didn't concern myself with the damage and suffering I would be indirectly inflicting on people as a result of my actions. I was into it for the fast buck. At twenty-one years of age I wasn't looking at retirement but wanted all the worldly possessions easily within my reach. It was greed, nothing less. Self-gratification was my highest priority.

But now I was scared. I didn't know these dope smugglers. I didn't know any of the people I'd be dealing with. I knew Ray pretty well and had grown to trust him for my safety. He'd always treated me right and paid me very handsomely for the risks I took. But this was a different situation. I was not able to depend on Ray, and the challenges of communication didn't make matters any better. I hadn't spoken with him for a couple of days and thought it might be a good time to go visit the Chinaman.

We arrived in Linstead shortly after dark and once again the Chinaman was courteous and obliging. When Ray answered his phone I asked him if there were any new developments.

"They want you to catch a ride back to Florida in a couple of days," he said.

"Yeah, I heard. What do you think of that?"

"I don't know, Bill. These are the same guys that burned our plane."

"Yeah, makes me nervous," I replied. "I don't think I like it."

"Don't do it then. I've got another plan. Give me two more days and I'll have all the details worked out."

"Okay. Just get me out of here."

"I'll do my best, Billy,"

And with that we hung up.

Back at the van, I told Thomas to let Mike know that I wouldn't be going on the upcoming flight.

"I think that's a wise move, Bronco," Thomas replied.

Two days passed. I was now well into my second week of waiting around. I was sitting on the front porch with Thomas when Jancro arrived.

"We've got to take Bronco to Mike's," he said. "The police are in Linstead. They're asking around for anyone who has seen an unfamiliar white man. They were at the Chinaman's place when I came up here."

I ran inside Thomas' house, grabbed my bag and stuffed in the extra shirt and shorts that Thomas had given me. Thomas, Jancro and I jumped in the van and were on our way.

"Where does Mike live?" I asked as we pulled out of the driveway.

"The Cockpit Country," Jancro said. "It's up the road some. On the way to Montego Bay."

The Cockpit Country. I liked the sound of it. I had visions of the wreckage of countless flights scattered among the Jamaican jungles. I found out later that it had more to do with the geological characteristics of the hills in the area. The "cockpits" were cave-like formations set in the sides of the steeply rising terrain. Oh well, it was a nice fantasy anyway.

It was getting late in the afternoon when we reached the road to Linstead and turned north. We went up and down through winding roads for about an hour, and then stopped in Browns Town to grab some food. After our quick bite we continued on. The roads became narrower and soon we went up a steep hill, through a dense wooded area, and emerged in a clearing. We'd reached our destination.

Mike's home was located on a two-hundred-acre plot of jungle and was perched on the side of one of a thousand hills overlooking a small mountain ridge. I saw a large white ranch home with a wraparound porch and a couple of outbuildings. It was a beautiful, lush setting, fitting for the head of a ganja business.

Mike met us on his front porch.

"Hello, Bronco," he said to me with a smile. "How was your stay with Thomas?"

"I was treated very well," I replied.

Meeting up with Mike again made me feel better. I knew I was in the hands of someone who had power and might be able to help me. Mike offered us iced tea and snacks and we all gathered on the porch. Mike's wife Kim soon appeared with beverages and a tray of brownies.

Mike and Kim had no children. They lived easy peaceful lives with a bird and three dogs in a three-bedroom house. They seldom entertained any guests.

We sat on the porch drinking our tea and eating the brownies. It wasn't long before I realized that the brownies had been baked with a very special ingredient.

"We have special Jamaican brownies for you, Bronco," said Jancro. He laughed at me.

It was all so casual. Ganja was their way of life. It was even a staple in their diet. I wasn't accustomed to the frequent intake of THC, so I usually abstained from partaking. Not wanting to offend Mike or Kim I finished my brownie and sat there getting stoned while Mike, Thomas and Jancro laughed and talked for what seemed like hours. Once again, I was up fidgeting most of the night.

In the morning I met everyone in the kitchen for breakfast. Kim had prepared Eggs Benedict. I looked at Mike.

"Are you sure I can handle the Hollandaise sauce?" I laughed.

As we ate, Mike explained what was going on.

"Bronco, the airstrip owners were not happy with us," he said. "Your coming back was not part of the plan."

Mike was to pay the airstrip owners for a one-time use of the landing area. When they saw an airplane full of ganja parked on their property they thought it was another operator and not Mike. They paid off the police to allow them to take the ganja off of the plane. The police argued that the airplane belonged to the airstrip owners. And they insisted the owners pay more ransom to have the airplane recovered.

When the airstrip owners refused, the police threatened to secure the airstrip indefinitely. The airstrip owners had bargained for a load of ganja at a discount and no longer cared about the airplane. That's when the deal was made to burn the plane.

"At first they gave us three days but then the police insisted that the plane be burned immediately," Mike continued. "After they burned the plane, the police agreed to return them landing rights only after they gave up some information on your whereabouts. That's when they told the police you were staying with me in Linstead. Linstead is where the airstrip owners think I live. We knew that keeping you near there was becoming risky and I decided to bring you to my house, so here you are."

Now I understood why we'd failed in our attempts to bribe the guards. Bribery and payoffs were normal for our business, but there was another factor involved: the local police chief was looking for political gain. The airstrip owners had enough clout to avoid interference from authorities, but a wildcat smuggler like me would make for some spectacular headlines: AMERICAN CAUGHT IN JAMAICA. It was just another battle in the war on ganja.

"Soon after they burned the plane," said Mike, "they called me and said that they would be loading a DC-3 bound for Florida in two days and for forty thousand dollars you could ride it home."

"Kind of steep, wasn't it?" I asked.

"Bronco," Mike said, "that money was to bribe the pilots for your passage. You would have been able to identify them."

After breakfast Thomas and Jancro left to run some errands. Mike showed me around his property. His home was large by Jamaican standards, but for a ganja kingpin he lived a modest lifestyle. He had a detached single-car garage that housed a four-door Toyota and a moderately-sized outbuilding where he kept an American-built Jeep. Kim cared for several beautiful flower gardens. There was tropical greenery everywhere. They enjoyed their peaceful private refuge and needed little else. Mike spoke very little about his business, preferring to focus on matters directly affecting my situation. I had seen some of his farming and processing on my scouting trips to Jamaica with Ray a few months before, so I had a fairly good idea of the size of Mike's operation.

As we rounded out the tour I began to feel a little light-headed. At first it was barely noticeable but within an hour I told Mike and Kim that I wasn't feeling well and wished to lie down.

I awoke a few hours later with a full-blown attack of the flu. I was barely able to move. My entire body ached and my stomach felt as though it had been ripped open. I felt as if I'd been poisoned but was too helpless to do anything about it. I was a prisoner in my room and only on occasion did Kim appear to tend to any personal needs I had. I wasn't eating and tried drinking water but couldn't keep a drop down. In my delirium I totally lost track of time. I had an extremely high fever and became weaker every day. It was one of the worst bouts of flu I have ever experienced.

When I finally awoke, Kim was standing in the doorway to my room. She smiled and asked me how I was feeling. Although I was still quite weak, I felt remarkably better.

"Is there something I can get for you?" she asked.

My mouth was bone dry and my bed was soaking wet from the fever. I asked if she had any juice.

"Sure," she said. "I'll be right back."

It was late afternoon when I was strong enough to get around. After downing what must have been a gallon of orange juice I put on a robe and found my way to the living room. Mike and Kim were watching television and greeted me as I appeared in the door.

"What day is it?" I said.

"It's Thursday," said Mike.

I'd arrived at Mike's on a Friday and had lain down before noon on Saturday. I'd been out for about five days.

"We didn't know if you were going to make it," said Mike. "Kim called the doctor and we were just about to go get him."

Kim fixed me a bowl of fruit and toast with jam. It was the first solid food I'd eaten in nearly a week.

Another day passed before I was feeling any strength. Mostly I sat on the porch with Mike and Kim. Thomas and Jancro had gone back home to check on things. Evidently the police had looked all over Linstead for me. They questioned several people who told them about seeing an unfamiliar young white man around the neighborhood. I worried that Thomas and his family would be identified as having helped me.

"Don't you worry, Bronco," Mike said. "Thomas is very well liked in Linstead. Besides, anyone who says they saw you doesn't know Thomas. Those who do will say nothing."

"I hope you're right," I said.

Mike had spoken to Ray while I was ill. Ray told him that the window of opportunity had closed. He had a friend that was a captain on a cargo ship docked in Montego Bay. The ship was to stop in the Dominican Republic and Puerto Rico before heading for Miami. He was willing to smuggle me out, but the ship had left port on Monday.

Ray was looking into other options. Maybe I could ride home on an airplane or a boat. As good as that sounded, there were problems with both possibilities. I had no entry documents, which would raise a red flag when I went through customs. Attempting to board a vessel bound for the U.S. without the proper paperwork usually resulted in an arrest. Getting that paperwork in Jamaica was practically impossible. Then there was the problem of clearing U.S. Customs in Miami or wherever I tried to enter the United States. Mike assured me that Ray would be calling soon with a good plan and I would be home before I knew it.

The next day Mike showed me around the area. He pulled his Jeep out of the shed and we headed down his road. He took me to several beautiful tropical settings. Even on this small island the hills seemed endless. We drove through dark, covered jungle and emerged on a bridge overlooking a deep valley. All around us were flora of deep greens with sprinkles of brilliant red and yellow. It was a beautiful and peaceful place. We stood on that bridge, gazing across the vista, as Mike pointed across the valley to the area where he was born.

"How did you get into the ganja trade?" I asked.

"My father was a white man from the Dominican Republic. He married a Jamaican woman he'd met there," Mike said. "They settled in the village across that valley. He was a tailor and made women's clothing for many years. After I grew up I moved to Falmouth where I worked in a vegetable warehouse for two years.

"One day a man approached me and asked me if I'd like to help him unload a truck. That evening he took me to a farm near here and I helped him load two hundred kilos of ganja into a small plane bound for Florida. He paid me the same amount of money that it took me a month to earn at the warehouse. I was hooked."

Mike quit his job at the warehouse to work for his new friend. Soon he was able to purchase the ganja farm and the airstrip. It was a cash deal, and from what I understood there were few records of real estate transactions.

A while later I was looking at a calendar in Kim's kitchen and realized I had been stranded in Jamaica for nearly a month.

My God! I thought, *I wonder if anyone in my family is looking for me.*

When I first moved away from home I would call my parents about once a week. After about a year the phone calls became less frequent. My father would write me on occasion with little notes of encouragement. I was a long way from home and appreciated my parents' concern for my well-being. It wasn't until much later that I told my father some of the details about my line of work—but only enough so that he knew I was gainfully employed. I could tell that he suspected I was involved in something less than respectable.

Our Mexican operations were all legitimate from a U.S. point of view, and I justified my actions that way. But getting stuck in Jamaica? I never thought I'd get into this kind of a mess. I considered myself lucky though. I'd heard stories of other people getting mixed up in dope smuggling and ending up dead. Lies and betrayal in this business were as common as corn in Indiana. But Indiana was a long way from Jamaica.

It was time for me to make a phone call. I asked Mike if I could make a call to the U.S. and he told me that he only called outside Jamaica at certain times. He knew people in the telephone business and they warned him of any law enforcement wiretaps. They gave him specific time frames where interference was least likely. Most of the time the phone was disconnected. Mike was very careful and knew that the telephone service in Jamaica was a potential trace to his whereabouts and activities. He would connect his phone for short periods of time in the afternoons as that was the prearranged time for calls to be made and received.

"Be listening, Bronco," Mike said. "If it suddenly gets hard to hear the other person, hang up right away."

Later that evening I called home. When my mother answered, I braced my emotions. I had to remain strong and assure my parents that things were just fine and normal for me.

"We haven't heard from you in awhile," said Mom. "You must be busy doing a lot of flying."

"Yeah, it's been busy all right," I answered. "How are things at home?"

"We're just fine. Your dad will be disappointed he didn't get to talk to you. He's out at the country club tonight. Its men's night. Do you know when you're coming home yet?"

It was as though she knew where I was and that coming home was my biggest problem. I tried to hold back any emotion in my voice and continued to speak as though nothing was amiss.

"No, not yet," I said.

"We're having everyone here for Thanksgiving. Are you still certain that you won't be able to make it?"

Fortunately, I'd already warned my folks that I'd probably miss Thanksgiving that year. I told them that I would be flying during the holiday and wouldn't have time to get back. The real reason was that I wanted to be on my own and had been invited to share the holiday with Kara and her family.

"I'm pretty sure I'm not going to make it, Mom," I said. "I'm doing fine and will let you know when I can get home. Tell Dad I'll call again as soon as I can."

"Okay Bill," she replied. "Have a good night and we will talk to you soon. We love you."

"I love you too," I said, and with that I hung up.

Now I had to call Kara and let her know that I wouldn't be making Thanksgiving with her either. I asked Mike if I could make another phone call and he said that it would be fine. I called Kara's home and her mother answered. She asked where I was and said that they'd been trying to call me for weeks.

"We thought maybe you went back home and never said goodbye," she said.

"No, I've just been real busy," I replied. "Is Kara there?"

"No, she's at Jennifer's, and I don't believe you've been that busy."

Kara's mom Jo Anne was an intelligent woman. She taught college-level subjects at a private school. I had interesting conversations with her and enjoyed her intellect and humor. The fact that I was dating her daughter always seemed to steer the conversations towards that relationship and away from more intellectual matters. She asked me one time what my I.Q. was and I jokingly told her that it was over 200. She never took me seriously after that and referred to me as her "pseudo-intellectual." In our more heady conversations I was sometimes challenged to keep up with her but fumbled along as best I could. She would get frustrated and return to her gin and tonics.

"I won't be able to make Thanksgiving," I told her.

"We were fairly certain you wouldn't," she said.

"Tell Kara I'll be out of town for a while and that I will call her when I get back."

A pause. "Where are you, Bill?"

"I'm traveling on a freight run," I said.

"I don't believe you," she replied. "Be careful and call when you get back."

Jo Anne knew about my work and was one of the people who warned me about getting mixed up in drug trafficking. She only trusted a few individuals. For some reason I was one of them. I never wanted to do anything to break that trust.

Thanksgiving came and went and nothing was out of the ordinary for us in Jamaica. The weather was incredible. It rained at night but the days were mostly sunny and warm. Kim bought me a good supply of clothing. The jeans and shirt I'd worn the day I arrived were clean and neatly folded and tucked into a drawer in my room. There was very little for me to do around the house. Kim spent most of her days working in her flower gardens, and a hired gardener took care of the grounds. Nothing needed repair or painting or anything. Mike made an occasional trip to the nearby town for groceries and sometimes returned with news about what was happening around the island.

My ill-fated flight out was the last of the season; there would be no more until after the first of the year. The busy time came twice a year. Otherwise it was a time of rest and relaxation and a time to enjoy some of the fruits of their labor. I too enjoyed my time, but I learned to pace myself.

One evening Kim came in the house. She was crying. One of the dogs was dead in the front yard. Mike and I went outside and found the dog stretched on its side with its head lying in a pool of vomit. Mike called for the other two dogs. There was no response. We walked around the back of the garage and found another dog . . . dead and lying in a similar manner.

We continued to call for the third dog but didn't hear or see anything in response. Kim came outside and joined in the search.

"What do you think happened?" I asked.

"They've poisoned my dogs," Mike replied.

"Who?"

"The locals," he said. "They think I am here illegally and that I stole the land. They want to drive me off."

We continued to look all around the property for the third dog but never found any trace of him.

"That dog wanders off," Mike said. "Maybe he avoided the poison."

We never found any evidence of poisoning except for undigested meat in the dead dogs' vomit. I asked Mike how long this harassment had been going on and he told me that it was the first time they went this far. He said that usually they would park down the lane in the cover of the trees, sneak up to the house and throw bags of goat manure, then run back to the trees.

"I never know when they are going to come," said Mike, "but if I ever catch them I will shoot them on sight."

That night Mike, the gardener and I wrapped the dead dogs in burlap, threw them in the back of the Jeep and headed off into the jungle. On the way down a winding road the gardener began to sing a chorus of "Shall We Gather at The River." We stopped on a bridge over a deep valley that had a small river running far below us. Mike and the gardener heaved the burlap bags over the side rail. Mike looked at me.

"Maybe you want to jump too Bronco?"

Suddenly I began to get nervous.

I looked at him and the gardener standing there in the headlights on the bridge. They were both grinning.

"I'm afraid of heights," I said.

They both broke out laughing. Mike put his hand on my shoulder.

"Let's go home," he said.

It was the only time I felt frightened around Mike. He seemed to be a good man and hadn't done anything to break my trust to this point. He always carried a sidearm in a holster whenever he ventured off his property, and this night was no exception. What really made me nervous was that he'd placed his hand on the weapon when he asked me if I'd like to jump. It was dark and we were on a remote back road deep in the hill country. It was a long drop to the streambed below, and it was unlikely that anyone would ever find my decomposed body.

From then on I was a little more cautious when dealing with people I didn't know well. That night three men got back in the Jeep with two still laughing and one twitching nervously. We drove back to Mike's house and sat on the porch and talked about dogs the rest of the night.

One afternoon I noticed Mike wiring up his telephone. He set the phone on the table and walked away.

"Are you expecting a call?" I asked.

"Maybe Ray will call today," he said.

Within an hour Mike's phone did ring. It was Ray. Mike spoke briefly, then offered me the receiver.

"Ray needs to speak to you."

I took the phone from Mike and put it to my ear.

"Bill, I've got some good news," Ray said on the other end. "I will be sending a couple of guys down there soon to take you back to Florida. I want you to meet them in Kingston in a few days. I don't know the exact date yet but I need you to be ready to go."

Ray explained the details until it was clear to me how this thing was going to be executed. He said that I was to tell no one else of the details and be ready to go with a twenty-four-hour notice.

My conversation with Ray was encouraging. It sounded like a good plan but it was risky. And once again I would be placing all my trust and well being in the hands of people I didn't know.

I hung up the phone and told Mike that it looked like I was getting out of Jamaica. Mike called Thomas to give him the news. Thomas said he hadn't seen the police in Linstead for a couple of weeks and everything seemed to be back to normal.

I was to stay with Thomas until I got the final word from Ray. It had been just over five weeks since I'd landed in Jamaica. I envisioned myself at home in Texas, seeing my friends and getting back to my normal routine. Even though I was excited about the news, the thought of leaving the solitude and safety of my Jamaican refuge caused me a bit of anxiety. I was about to be placed into another high-risk situation. I would be going back into the region where, just a few weeks before, I was a wanted man.

Kim called from the kitchen for us to come to dinner. We knew that my stay was coming to a close, so the three of us had a relaxing dinner, enjoyed each other's company, and prepared for my departure the next morning.

CHAPTER 20

COMING DOWN

T HE NEXT MORNING Mike, Kim and I were all up early. I stuffed my clothes into a larger duffle bag that Kim had bought me in town. We sat on the front porch and enjoyed our morning coffee and a cinnamon roll. Afterward Mike said that he'd like to get started so I thanked Kim for her generous hospitality. She embraced me affectionately and wished me well.

I threw my bag into Mike's Toyota Camry and we headed for Linstead. It was the end of week six of my residence in Jamaica; I'd been holed up with Mike and Kim for a little over a month. I thought about my family back home and my friends back in Texas and wondered if I should make some calls to see if anyone had reported me as missing. Mike said that I could call from Linstead after we arrived there.

It was a beautiful morning, not unlike many mornings I'd seen in Jamaica. The skies were clear and the dew was all around in the cool and still morning air. I'd thought about living there permanently, but thoughts of home kept creeping back into my mind. If I didn't leave eventually I would have to break the news to my parents. I didn't want to think about their reaction. I'm sure my father would have gone to great lengths to have me rescued, legal and diplomatic, negotiating with the government for my release. It was highly unlikely he'd have succeeded without my serving a jail term while the whole matter was sorted out. And once I was incarcerated, there was no telling how long I would be waiting. It could easily be weeks, months or perhaps even years before the Jamaican courts would cooperate. And the financial costs would certainly be staggering. It was best that I trusted Ray . . . for now at least.

We arrived in Linstead before lunch and drove over to the Chinaman's. I pulled the receiver out of the wooden box and dialed home. Mom answered.

"Where are you, Bill?"

"I'm okay," I replied. "What's going on there?"

"We've been trying to call you for days. Don't you ever answer your phone?"

"I'm sorry Mom. I've been really busy."

Mom had every right to be irritated. It'd been weeks since I called home and Thanksgiving had come and gone without so much as a hello. She insisted that I explain my lack of communication to her. She called my dad to the phone.

"Hi Dad, how are you?" I asked.

"We're all fine here," he replied. "We've not heard from you for a while. Is everything all right?"

"Yeah, things are just fine here."

"We missed you on Thanksgiving. We had Grandma and Grandpa out for dinner."

My Mom picked up another extension. "Why didn't you call?" she asked.

"Well, it's good to hear from you now, Bill," said Dad. "Are you at home?"

"No, I'm over at a friend's house right now," I replied. "I was just feeling a little homesick and realized I hadn't called you guys in awhile. I miss you."

"We miss you too. When do you think you'll be able to get home?"

"I'm not sure Dad. I might fly home for Christmas."

"I think you should. I'll pick you up at the airport."

"I'll work on that, Dad."

We said our goodbyes. After I hung up I called Kara and told her that I'd been out of town for a while and that I wasn't sure when I would be home. She was a little more understanding than my parents regarding my lack of communication.

"I don't know what you're up to," she said, "but I guess you know what you're doing."

"I'm just visiting some friends," I said. "I'll tell you more about it when I get back. Oh, would you mind stopping by the apartment and checking up on things?"

"I already did that," she said. "I've been picking up your mail three times a week too."

"Thanks. I knew I could count on you."

Kara knew I was an independent sort and never really questioned my whereabouts or activities. We were good friends but hadn't known each other long enough to share all the details of our lives. Since she was privy to my day job she knew about its inherent dangers. I didn't expect her to help me out like she did, but I was very grateful. I often wondered if it was her mother who instructed her to take care of my personal matters. It seemed that everyone back home was concerned but not alarmed at my extended absence. For now it appeared that my secret was safe.

I finished my calls, and Mike and I headed for Thomas' house. When we pulled into the driveway Thomas came out.

"I think you'll be going home soon," said Thomas. "I can feel it."

We went inside and sat in the living room and talked about how the plan would be carried out. Mike said that the two individuals would likely have all the required papers that indicated I was in the country legitimately. They would have airline tickets showing I'd arrived sometime in the recent past. He assured me that these documents would pass inspection by any Jamaican customs agent. He himself had traveled to the U.S. once using forged papers. It didn't sound that difficult, but I still knew that I was putting it all on the line and that it was in the hands of strangers. I wasn't sure why Ray was sending two people to rescue me. That only seemed to complicate the situation.

Sarah came out of the kitchen with a tray of cooked pork, fruit and vegetables and we had lunch. Afterward Mike got up and said he was going to return home. I thanked him for all his help and friendship and told him what a good caretaker he was.

"Maybe when you come back to Jamaica I will see you again," he said.

"I hope it's under better circumstances," I replied.

Thomas and I watched Mike drive away. Then Thomas turned to me and said:

"Would you like to go into Linstead and hang out with Bob and me?"

"Sure, that sounds fine with me," I replied.

"You can roam freely now. No one is looking for you."

"Are you sure?"

"No problem, mon!"

Thomas and I got into a small four door sedan that he owned and drove into Linstead and stopped at a tin shed were Bob came out and jumped in the back seat. We toured Linstead then meandered along a scenic road through more of Jamaica's picturesque surroundings. In the middle of all of this beauty I couldn't help but wonder about the local economy. The unemployment rate was staggeringly high but in general the people seemed content in this paradise.

We drove down the road along the Rio Cobre River. After a few miles we pulled the car to the side of the road and Thomas pointed directly above us to a single rock that protruded horizontally from the hillside. Bob was trying his best to keep from busting up but like most Jamaicans he displayed his laughter freely.

"Do you see that rock up there, Bronco?" asked Thomas. "That's a very special rock in Jamaica. What does it look like to you?"

I stared at the rock for a minute. Judging by Bob's continued snickering I knew that the answer was something phallic.

"It looks like part of the male anatomy," I said.

"That's right, Bronco," Thomas said. "But that's not all. That rock is pointed at something even more special to a Jamaican."

Thomas directed my attention to another rock formation across the river.

"What does that rock look like, Bronco?" he asked.

I was beginning to understand where this was going. With both hands Bob was slapping his thighs and bouncing up and down so hard that I thought he was going to bust.

"Well, I'm not sure, but it kind of looks like a cave," I answered.

On the opposite river bank was a formation affectionately known as the Pum Pum Rock.

"And that one sort of resembles a part of the female anatomy," I said.

Bob burst out, "Ha ha, I think you can figure it out now Bronco!"

"It's like a national landmark," Thomas said. "The two rocks go together and it's in all the brochures."

Well, I doubted I'd see it in that context in any brochure, but it was obviously an infamous set of landmarks that all the locals got a huge chuckle out of.

After that we decided that it was time to kick back with a couple of Red Stripes and hang out at their favorite watering hole. We had a fun afternoon and I will always remember their friendship.

That night we hung out at the house and played dominos and hacky sack, smoked up a storm, and sang Bob Marley tunes. I can't speak for all Jamaicans, but during the parties I'd experienced with Thomas, his family and friends, the people were never loud, boisterous or out of control. It was more of a peaceful get-together in which to enjoy one another's company. They loved life and loved each other very much.

Nobody really ever went home from these gatherings. Everyone simply found a place on the porch or in the house where they could quietly nod off. I found my way back to the room I'd used before and lay there drifting while listening to Reggae music and the soft stillness of the Jamaican night.

The next morning I awoke to a commotion out on the porch. Thomas' father had brought home a Christmas tree. I got dressed and went out front to find him fumbling with a small evergreen. He was looking for just the right place in a corner on the porch.

"Ah, good morning, Bronco," he said with a big smile.

He found a spot that seemed suitable and stepped back to take a look.

"What do you think?" he asked.

"Looks fine," I said.

The familiar sights and sounds of the holiday were comforting. But I felt an empty feeling in the pit of my stomach. I was coming down off of my six-week high. Reality was beginning to take hold. A symbol of hope was there in front of me in a simple wooden stand, and yet I felt hopeless. I wished that I'd never been tempted by the money and adventure of this whole thing.

As I stood there on the porch, staring at the evergreen, I thought about my childhood and the many happy Christmases I'd celebrated with my family.

Thomas appeared in the doorway. He saw the look on my face.

"Hey Bronco, you okay?"

"Yeah, I'm just suddenly a little homesick," I replied.

"Would you like to help decorate the tree?" he asked.

I was honored to be included in their celebration of Christmas. And when Thomas' father brought in a small box of decorations he began to sing carols as he pulled brightly colored balls out one by one. That empty feeling was soon replaced by the joy that was surrounding me. I was glad to be part of this family tradition and even though I was far from home, the love found at home was all around me.

Sarah brought in a tray of refreshments and the four of us sat on the porch admiring the tree and recalling Christmas memories. It was curious how many things we had in common though our cultures differed so greatly.

Thomas went inside to take a phone call. When he returned he said that I needed to make a call to Ray. He said that I could use his phone and helped me dial to gain access to a secure line. Within a minute I was talking to Ray.

"I want you to get a room at the Pegasus Hotel in Kingston," Ray said. "At noon tomorrow two guys will call you with instructions."

"Who are these guys?" I asked.

"They are two guys who are able to get you out. They've done this kind of thing before. One of them is named Kenny and the other they call Buckets."

"Is it safe?"

"I've never met them but a good friend of mine in Miami knows both of 'em," Ray replied. "They come highly recommended."

"Do I use my real name when checking in to the hotel?"

"No. You will check in under the name Bill Barber," Ray answered. "But all of the customs documents will be in your real name. These two guys will have all the details for you tomorrow. Don't worry, I want you home too. I feel responsible for this whole mess."

I hung up the phone and told Thomas that I needed to go to Kingston. I felt excited but very nervous at the same time. We finished breakfast and I grabbed what few clothes I had and I graciously thanked Sarah for all her hospitality.

"You be good now, Billy," she said. "I hope I get to see you again."

Soon we were on our way to Kingston. I was now Bill Barber, tourist. And tour I did as we took in the sights on the road to Jamaica's capitol city. Things didn't look much different until we arrived in downtown Kingston at the Pegasus Hotel. Instead of shantytowns lining the roads, I was now in a city of steel, glass and concrete. Thomas pulled his car up to the curb of the hotel and I stepped out. The sidewalks lined paved roads next to high-rise buildings. I could still see the poverty around us but I was definitely transitioning to an urban culture and leaving the simple Jamaican life behind.

Thomas stood on the driver's side of his car, staring up at the tall hotel.

"You'll be okay from here, Bronco Billy."

I reached across the top of his car and shook his hand.

"You've been a good friend," I said. "I hope to see you again."

With a hearty laugh Thomas got back in his car and drove off. I watched him speed down the hill back into the world to which he was accustomed. I turned and gazed through the glass doors of the hotel. Soon I would be home.

CHAPTER 21

OUT OF JAMAICA

I WALKED INTO THE LOBBY of the hotel, approached the front desk and checked in. Everything was arranged; I even had a reservation. Bill Barber was to stay for five nights. To me it seemed a little odd that I'd be there that long but I didn't ask any questions and scribbled a signature on the room card. The room had two double beds. I threw my duffle bag on one and plopped down on the other and drifted off to sleep lying there thinking about the events that would unfold in the coming days.

A loud bang jolted me awake. I got up and looked out my window. Twelve floors down, a delivery truck had backed into the garbage dumpster across the street. It was getting dark and the sights and sounds of a bustling city were all around me. It didn't take long for me to get used to the environment. I hadn't been away from modern civilization for that long. I ordered room service and watched Jamaican television late into the night.

The next morning I awoke, ordered breakfast in, and spent several hours staring out the window. In the distance I could make out the international airport. I watched DC-9s, 737s and commuter planes arrive and depart. I was too nervous to venture outside the hotel, but I did make my way to the observation deck on the top floor. It was a bright clear morning and the visibility was unlimited. To the north I had a spectacular view of the lush Blue Mountains, and to the south was the beautiful blue Caribbean. I looked to the west in the direction of the landing strip and imagined that I could actually see it. It was probably twenty miles from where I was standing. I spent a couple hours on the observation deck, drinking strong black coffee and gazing across the island. Then I returned to my room to await the phone call from my rescuers.

Noon came and went without a call. I began to get nervous. Maybe they missed their flight or perhaps they were detained by Jamaican Customs. It was about 1 p.m. when my phone finally rang.

"Is this Bill Barber?" said a husky voice on the other end.

"Yes," I answered.

"My name is Kenny. We are in the lobby and would like to come up and meet with you."

At that moment I was terrified. I knew that I'd been a liability to my employer. And now that I knew what he was capable of doing, I began to wonder if conspiracy to murder wasn't beyond his conscience. I was young and gullible, but not so naïve to allow this. It would have been a quick job of entering my room, putting a bullet in my head, and then leaving with no one ever seeing us together. Suddenly the reason for my false name also began to make sense. It would have given my assassins more opportunity to escape. I'd had a good six weeks to contemplate my situation, and being eliminated from the picture was certainly an option to my co-conspirators. I paused for a moment.

"I'll come down and meet you," I said.

"Okay, we'll be in the lobby," Kenny answered.

When I got to the lobby I saw two men sitting together. They were both dressed in polyester slacks and button-down shirts. One of them stood up and extended his hand.

"You must be Bill," he said.

"I am."

"I'm Kenny and this is Buckets."

Buckets stood up and shook my hand. "I know it's unusual but the name was given to me when I was in the navy," he said.

These guys looked like a couple of hit men, all right. Kenny was in his mid-fifties, about six-foot-two and must have weighed about two hundred thirty pounds. Buckets was a bit more formidable. He too was in his mid-fifties, but he stood about six-foot-five and had to be pushing three hundred pounds. Buckets had huge hands; his sleeves rolled up on thick forearms. On his right arm was a tattoo of an anvil with a lightning bolt running through it. He had wavy blonde hair that swept across his forehead.

Both men looked like they'd lived hard lives, and I had no idea what either of them intended to do with me.

"Can we go somewhere and talk?" Kenny asked.

"Sure, how about the pool?" I answered.

We walked through the lobby and found a patio near the pool, where we sat in the afternoon sun. Kenny didn't ask me any questions but reached into his back pocket and pulled out an envelope with several documents in it.

"These are your papers that we will use to get you out of here," he said. "I've got all the stuff you'll need, including airline tickets that show you came down here with us about a week ago."

Then Kenny handed me the forged papers one by one.

"Here is a copy of the customs paper you filled out when you arrived. It has your real name on it and all you'll have to do is sign this and we'll be all set to leave. Do you have identification with you?"

"Yeah, I've got my driver's license and pilot's license right here," I said.

"We don't want them to know you are a pilot," said Kenny. "I'll take that and keep it in a safe place until we are through security on our way out. Do you have a passport?"

"No," I said.

"I didn't think so. What would you need that for anyway?" he laughed.

I handed Kenny my pilot's license and medical certificate, and folded the fake airline ticket stub and customs declaration and put them in my pocket.

"Take care of those, Bill. We can't get another set for some time if you lose them."

Buckets just sat there smiling as Kenny explained the plan for getting me out.

"Here's how we're going to do this," said Kenny. "I am your father, Buckets is your uncle, and in about a week you are going to get married. Your uncle and I decided to throw you a bachelor party and bring you to Jamaica for one last hurrah before you take the plunge. Your uncle is one heavy drinker. He's loud and boisterous and doesn't take crap from anyone. You, being young and inexperienced, are ready to go home and recover from your own drinking binge. I too have been in the sauce since we arrived and I am in no mood or condition to carry on a conversation with anyone. All I want to do is get you home where you can begin a life of marital bliss with your new bride. Our flight leaves tomorrow morning and we are going to get you through security without them even questioning us."

It all sounded crazy to me but something about the way Kenny was explaining it made me feel confident that it would work. Buckets kept nodding his head as if he knew he was going to enjoy this. These guys may have been mafia but for now they were my ticket home. They weren't hired to kill me but to smuggle me through Jamaican security and onto a plane bound for Miami. The documents all looked legit even though there were some hand scribbles that were illegible. I figured that was all part of the ruse.

"Do you have any clothes that are more of a tourist type?" asked Kenny. "We need you to look as much like a tourist as possible."

"I've pretty much got what I'm wearing, and some plain colored tee shirts," I said. I hadn't gone shopping and the only clothes Kim picked out for me were plain and simple.

Kenny nodded. "I want you to go down the street to some of the tourist shops and pick out a new tee shirt. Make it look like you're a tourist. Make it loud and have lots of print on it." He paused. "Have you got any money?"

"A little," I answered, "but only American."

"That's great. Try using that first. Here's some Jamaican money if you need it." He pushed some local currency into my palm. "Oh, and get yourself a hat."

"Where are you guys staying?" I asked.

"We're staying with you," Kenny said. "You've got a double room, haven't you?" "Okay, but where am *I* going to sleep?"

Buckets piped up for the first time. "Don't worry, we'll get along just fine," he said.

I thought it was strange how they knew I had two beds in my room, but then I remembered I had a reservation that I hadn't actually made. Maybe that's why I was told to use a last name different from my own. Maybe they couldn't remember my real name.

"Buckets and I will be in the lounge the rest of the afternoon," Kenny said. "You can join us if you like. We'll probably get something to eat about eight o'clock."

"I think I'll just hang out here at the pool," I said.

The two men got up and walked with me through the lobby. They hit the lounge and I headed out the front door to find a souvenir shop. I wasn't too particular and picked up a couple of new shirts and a hat as instructed. I headed back to the hotel and sat in my room for several hours alone watching television. Soon I was fast asleep.

It was dark when I heard a knock. Groggy and disoriented, I rushed to the door.

"Who is it?" I mumbled.

"Bill, let us in," came a voice from the hall.

I snapped to and without hesitation opened the door and the two men walked in. Kenny and Buckets each chose a bed. Meanwhile I found some extra blankets and a pillow in the closet and stood there looking at the two men who were now comfortably lounging around.

"Where am I supposed to sleep?" I asked.

Kenny gestured at the floor between the two beds. "I want you to make yourself a bed right here between Buckets and me."

I did as I was told. Soon the two men were fast asleep as I lay there thinking about the day ahead. I was nervous and had trouble falling asleep with two strangers on either side of me. I imagined that this could be their opportunity to take me out. I lay there for hours waiting for one of them to awake and make his move. They never did, and I nodded off just before dawn.

It wasn't long before Buckets was awake and getting himself ready in the bathroom. Kenny followed. I gathered my things together and put on my new shirt. Our flight home was scheduled to leave at eight o'clock and we would be right-on-time.

We checked out of the hotel and hailed a cab. On the way to the airport Kenny rehearsed the plan with Buckets and me.

"Now remember," he said, "this is how it's going to go down. You are my son and you are sick and hung over and you just want to go home. I don't want you to say a word except to briefly answer any questions that the security or customs officers ask. Buckets and I will do everything we can to distract them and keep them from scrutinizing you or your paperwork. Once we are on the plane you are on your own. Buckets and I have separate seats and we won't speak to you again. Got it?"

"Got it," I replied as the cab pulled up to the curb in front of the airport terminal.

"Do you have any questions about clearing customs in Miami?" Kenny asked.

"No, I'm pretty familiar with that part," I said.

As Kenny paid the fare Buckets went into his act and literally fell out of the cab and into the street laughing. Several pedestrians came to his aid. As soon as they approached him Buckets would shout that he was all right and, blurting out expletives, he successfully discouraged anyone from getting too close.

While Buckets was pretending to stumble around in the street, Kenny and I got out the other side of the cab and walked past the distracted security guard. Once we were inside the terminal we paused and waited for Buckets to catch up. When he came through the door Kenny shouted at him and we staggered down the concourse to the security checkpoint. I shuffled along with my head down, saying nothing and looking at no one.

The plan was working: everyone's attention was on the two men who weaved and argued as they pulled me toward the gate. Buckets began to sing as he took the lead and approached a security guard, who was obviously not looking forward to dealing with us. When he arrived at the podium Buckets stumbled again and fell. Kenny pushed me to the side and chastised Buckets for his behavior. As the two men argued the security guard looked at me and held out his hand for my ticket and paperwork. He glanced at the documentation and handed it back to me.

Another security officer patted down my duffle bag and pointed me toward the gate. As security dealt with the two men I walked away, thinking the strategy had worked and I was on my way home.

Suddenly a voice shouted, "Sir, wait." My heart froze.

I turned to see one of the security guards motioning for me to return. I thought something had gone wrong. When I got back to the podium the security guard jerked his head at Kenny and Buckets, who were still making a ruckus.

"Sir, we need your assistance to help control your relatives."

Buckets had dropped his paperwork on the floor, and Kenny was helping him pick up the scattered documents. I bent down and helped. Kenny and I each took one of Buckets' arms and escorted him toward the gate.

Our flight was already boarding. The three of us staggered past the boarding agent, onto the ramp, and up the air stairs of the Air Florida 737. Kenny's and Buckets' seats were several rows behind me. As he passed by, Kenny reached into his pocket, pulled out my pilot's license and medical certificate, and handed them to me.

I felt . . . a sense of freedom. I was pretty certain there'd be no more foul-ups. I'll never forget the secure feeling I got as the flight attendant closed and locked the cabin door. Soon the aircraft engines spooled to life and the Boeing pulled away from the gate. My senses were all firing at the same time.

As we rolled off the runway and into the air I peered out the window, searching frantically for the airstrip I'd arrived at several weeks before. I spotted it but didn't see any signs of the burned-out Twin Bonanza. I sat back in my seat as we climbed out to the north. The entire incident was coming to a close, and soon I'd be back on American soil.

CHAPTER 22
WELCOME HOME

W HEN THE AIRPLANE touched down in Miami I knew that everything was finally behind me. I awoke from the nightmare. I felt a rush of anxiety as we taxied to the terminal. I didn't glance back at Kenny and Buckets; I figured they wouldn't need to speak to me again. We walked off the plane and up the jetway into the terminal and toward U.S. Customs.

I chuckled as I fought my nervousness, remembering how familiar I was with our Customs' system and procedures. There were three lines and since I had no checked baggage I was able to get right in. I felt a hand on my shoulder and turned to see Buckets standing behind me. He seemed less threatening now, standing there with a huge smile on his face.

"Thanks," I said.

I really meant it. Here was this man who barely said a word, and when called on he stepped up and provided cover and distraction by being loud and boisterous. But now he was back to being the quiet type.

"Welcome home," he said. "And Merry Christmas."

Soon the customs agents waved me through. I was a legitimate U.S. citizen again. I wanted to run around the terminal and shout how happy I was.

I looked around for Kenny and Buckets. I couldn't figure out where they could have gone, but I saw no signs of the two men anywhere in the crowd. It was a little eerie. I walked up the concourse and through the terminal to my connecting flight. My next stop was in Houston. From there I'd take a Texas International DC-9 to Brownsville.

I stopped at a pay phone to call Ray.

"Glad to have you back," he said when he answered.

"I'm glad to be back," I replied.

"Call me before you get on the plane to Brownsville and I'll meet you at the airport and give you a ride to Cameron County to get your car."

We didn't say much more. Soon I found myself in Houston thumbing through my tickets and boarding passes. I boarded the Texas International flight for Brownsville. It was a short flight and we landed in south Texas at about 10 p.m.

Ray was waiting in the terminal. He extended his hand and welcomed me home. He didn't press with too many questions but asked how I fared while stranded in Jamaica; he wanted to know if I was comfortable and well cared for. I explained the whole thing to him and told him that I was treated well. We talked briefly about the Twin Bonanza. Ray seemed to be less concerned about the airplane. I was relieved to find out he hadn't placed any of the blame on me.

It was a thirty-minute drive to Cameron. On the way Ray filled me in on some of the events that'd been happening in the area.

"There was another murder," he said. "Another cop."

A few weeks before I had left, a Texas highway patrolman had been brutally shot and left to die on the side of a road in south Texas. No car had been identified and a major investigation was underway. The senseless crime made local law enforcement pretty jumpy. At one point it seemed as if everyone was a suspect. The news media was all over it. As expected they picked up on the story and sensationalized the whole event.

The story was still hot when another killing occurred. That homicide was similar: a sheriff's deputy was killed on a county road not far from the town of San Benito, near Harlingen. The authorities believed the two murders were committed by the same assailant.

Ray pulled into Cameron County and I grabbed my bag and thanked him for the ride.

"Be careful, Bill," he said. "Again, I'm really glad you're home. I'll call you in a couple of days." He pulled away and disappeared into the night.

I found the spare key to my 280Z where I'd hid it under the rear bumper and got in. It felt good to be back in my little "Z" car. I turned the key. As the straight six sprang to life all of the familiar sounds and smells were once again part of my routine. I headed for home.

It was a comfortable South Texas night, so I rolled down the window and basked in the cool fresh air. The fragrance of the camellias and citrus was thick and smelled wonderful. I popped in a cassette tape, a little driving music for the final leg of my journey. I'd be at my door in half an hour—less if I opened the throttle and let my "Z" car do her thing.

A short distance from Cameron County was a small village called Bayview. The road made a couple of quick sharp turns as you passed through, and I couldn't resist. I dropped down a gear and punched my way through.

On the other side I let her go a little and found a nice comfortable speed of about seventy-five on the narrow two-lane county road. Since it was late at night, there was no traffic and I figured that I could make some good time getting home.

Not far out of Bayview I noticed a car pull onto the county road and head in my direction. I thought nothing of it, as any patrolman would have waited for me to pass before he popped me going by. I eased up a little and could see that the approaching car was slowing down. I tried to see if it was a patrol car but I couldn't tell in the darkness. I looked in the rearview mirror and shuddered as I saw the car pull off the road and turn around to follow me.

I braked and got under the speed limit. If a police car was behind me, I didn't want to add charges to the speeding ticket I might be about to receive.

The car came up close behind me and followed close for about two miles. I wondered why a policeman would follow so close. I was obviously speeding just a mile or two back. Maybe it wasn't a cop. I began to wonder just who it was that might be lurking behind me. Then I thought about the killer Ray was talking about. I unconsciously pushed down on the accelerator pedal.

Soon we were both back up to about seventy miles per hour. There were still no flashing lights to indicate I was in any sort of trouble for breaking the speed limit. It was obvious this pursuer either wanted to harass me or pull over for some unknown reason. Again I thought about the cop killer, and in my nervousness I made the decision to just let her fly.

The 280Z had a 2.8-liter, fuel-injected, six-cylinder engine with a five-speed manual transmission. I'd added high performance injectors and induction mods to further boost the horsepower. I'd never taken her to the top end, but did have her at a hundred and twenty a couple of times. I figured I'd run her up and see if my pursuer had similar gumption.

As we passed a hundred and ten miles per hour my pursuer started to drop back. Since there'd been no lights or sirens I was certain I wasn't being followed by law enforcement . . . so off I went to run away from the chaser. I took her up to one twenty and sat there, as the other guy had dropped out of the race. I figured I'd get a good distance ahead of him and then drop back to see if he was still intent on following me.

I slowed down to about eighty and could barely see him in the distance. I figured he was probably some local wanting to run up against a "Z" car with his American-made vehicle. My Datsun was sporty gray with rally wheels, sport mirrors and a racing strip down the hood. She looked fast and occasionally invited challenges.

I continued on for a few minutes, leaving my pursuer in the distance. He'd given up and dropped back.

As I neared the turn to San Benito I approached a set of curves. About a mile ahead I saw flashing lights. My first reaction was that there'd been an accident. I slowed to about sixty. I saw at least three emergency vehicles but I couldn't make out much else. As I hugged my way through the first turn I saw what was ahead. It was some sort of roadblock. I didn't know who it was for, but I had a sinking feeling that I might have something to do with it. As I pulled off to the side I looked again in my mirror and saw a patrol car with lights flashing, coming toward me at full speed.

I put the car in park, set the brake and waited. The roadblock was set up just outside of San Benito, about a quarter mile from where I was sitting.

My pursuer slowed as he came up behind me. The cars ahead of me started to move my way. I was quickly surrounded by police cars and excited police officers running toward me with their weapons drawn. Two of them stopped directly in front of me.

"Get out of the car and lie face down on the ground!" one of them yelled.

I exited the car and put my hands in the air. I could hear several officers shouting, "We got him! We got him!"

As I lay on the ground the officer who'd been chasing me came up and jammed his foot between my shoulders just below my neck. I could tell that the arresting party was about to begin—these guys were pumped. I heard several of their comments and realized these guys thought I was the cop killer! Evidently the cops received a tip that the murderer had been seen along this stretch of road. I was about to become suspect number one. More police vehicles arrived and more officers with guns drawn ran in my direction.

I felt a sharp pain in my side as someone's boot found a soft spot in my ribcage. This was followed by several more kicks. I heard many comments identifying me as "the one" and how I was resisting arrest. I didn't say a word. I couldn't. The wind had been knocked out of me.

The officers handcuffed me. I lay on my face on the asphalt, my hands bound tightly behind my back. Someone lifted me by my wrists and threw me face-first on the hood of a patrol car. He grabbed my hair, and as he pulled my head back against my shoulders he attempted to kick my feet apart to spread my legs. My left knee gave way and I fell on the ground in front of the vehicle. With the help of a second officer I was again lifted by my wrists and thrown onto the hood.

Sometimes we say the wrong thing at the wrong time.

"It's no wonder someone's shooting you guys," I said through the pain.

Oops. Bad move.

The officer who'd chased me from Bayview grabbed my hair, pulled my head from off the hood, and slapped me square in the face. Then he dropped my head back onto the hood.

"Shut up, killer!" he said. "We oughta take it out on you right now!"

My face stung. I kept my mouth shut and barely noticed the cold steel barrel jammed in the back of my skull.

Of course the cops soon learned that this was a case of mistaken identity. I overheard some disagreement among the officers. They were arguing about the address on my driver's license. They also noticed that I was a pilot. They seemed a little confused.

I was loaded into a squad car. We passed through Bayview and entered the small coastal town of Port Isabelle. At the station house two officers pulled me from the car, escorted me inside, and showed me the door to a small single jail cell. I sat on the bench, still handcuffed and bleeding from my nose and busted lip. I overheard more arguing in the front office. There was some sharp disagreement as to how I was arrested.

Soon a sergeant I hadn't seen before came into my cell and took the handcuffs off me. He closed the cell door and said he'd be right back. He returned to the front office and continued the shouting match with one of the arresting officers. Before long the sergeant returned, opened the cell door, and motioned for me to follow him.

He offered me some water. I gladly accepted. He handed me a towel to clean the blood from my face and showed me into his office in the back. I sat in a chair next to his desk. He sat down and began to fill out some paperwork.

"I don't know what happened out there," he said, "but I'm going to find out."

"I was just going home," I said.

"Did anyone read you your rights?"

"Yeah, on the ride here."

"Look," he said, "just tell me what happened and why you are here."

I explained everything that had happened after I got in my car at Cameron. I told the sergeant how I thought I was being chased by the cop killer. He nodded.

"Did you know you were speeding?"

"Yeah, I was doing about seventy when he turned around," I said. "But he didn't turn on his lights so I didn't think it was the police."

"Tell me that again," he said.

"I told you he followed me for a few miles with no lights. I would have pulled over right away if he had turned them on. I was worried about my own personal safety so I decided to try outrunning him."

"Did you know he clocked you at a hundred and ten?" he asked.

"That's when he started to back off," I answered.

"No, he followed you at a hundred and ten _before_ you started pulling away. He wasn't sure how fast your car was, so he dropped back and got on the radio."

"I don't know how fast I was going," I said.

"I'm glad he backed off when he did, but basically you outran him," said the sergeant. "And I don't blame you. This officer has done this before. That's how I know you're telling me the truth."

The sergeant shook his head and continued filling out the paperwork. Just then the arresting officer appeared at the door and stood there, looking at the sergeant and me. The sergeant looked up and noticed him watching us.

"He outran you, buddy," said the sergeant.

"You gonna call the judge?" asked the officer.

"Yeah, but that's not your job. I've got your report and all the facts."

The officer turned and left. The sergeant leaned back in his chair and smiled at me. He asked me why I was out on that road that time of the night. I told him I'd been out of the country for a while and had just returned.

"This is some homecoming, huh?" he asked.

"Yeah, I never expected to get thrown in jail my first night back," I said.

"I've got two choices," he said. "I could keep you for the night and your fine would be set in the morning, or I could call the magistrate and have him set your fine right now. What would you like me to do?"

Spending my first night back home in a cold, damp jail cell wasn't my idea of freedom, so I elected to have the magistrate decide my punishment. It was 12:30 a.m. when the sergeant made the call. He explained the highpoints of my incident and arrest. I overheard the judge yelling at the sergeant over the phone.

Things calmed down. The sergeant hung up the phone and shook his head.

"After hearing him yell, I expected worse," he said. "Your fine is two-fifty. Have you got that?"

"No, but I can get it," I said.

"Okay then, you can make a call."

With that the sergeant pointed to the phone on his desk. I picked up the phone and called Ray. After I explained the situation to him he agreed to come bail me out.

Ray showed up an hour later and paid my fine. He agreed to drive me home so we got in his car and started out for Harlingen. On the way I explained the whole incident to him. All he could do was shake his head and laugh.

"Welcome to the good ol' U.S. of A," he said.

He dropped me off at my apartment and I retrieved my spare key from its hiding place under the carport. When I opened the door I saw a note from Kara lying on the coffee table. The note explained that although she didn't know where I was, she suspected that if I were in jail somewhere, I'd be out sooner or later and to let her know what the score was. Kara had paid my bills and collected my mail while I was gone. I was extremely grateful and couldn't wait to let her know that I'd returned.

Everything else in the apartment seemed normal. Other than some moldy cheese, Kara had taken care of the perishables in my refrigerator. I was now feeling weary from the long day and it was getting past 3 a.m. In the cupboard I found a jar of pickles and a bottle of Scotch. I poured myself a neat three-finger of single malt and tilted the glass to my lips. I was finally home.

CHAPTER 23

TANKS FOR THE LIFT

R AY CALLED AND ASKED if I'd like to come over for dinner. He wanted to talk about my time in Jamaica. He assured me that all was well and that there were no consequences from the loss of the airplane or the load.

Before dinner we sat in his living room and talked about making another trip. James, the owner of our Cessna 340, supplied the money and wanted us to configure the Queen Air for a long over-water haul. We'd learned from our mistakes and decided to make the trip without the refueling in Jamaica. For the Queen Air, this meant installing a 210-gallon aluminum tank and adding a 250-gallon bladder on the cargo floor behind the aluminum tank. The plan was to burn off the wing tanks enough to transfer from the aluminum tank. Then we'd systematically pump the bladder into the aluminum tank before reaching Jamaica. The cargo could then be loaded on top of the empty bladder that was lying fully collapsed on the floor.

But there was one problem: we didn't have a practical way to transfer fuel automatically from the bladder to the aluminum tank, and burning directly from the bladder was impossible because of vent issues. The fuel would have to be pumped manually from the bladder to the aluminum tank. I told Ray that I could set the autopilot and crawl to the back to do the transferring. Ray thought about it for a minute.

"No," he said, "I want you to stay at the controls. Our only option is to have Bubba in on this and have him crawl to the back and operate the manual pump."

At first I didn't agree but Ray assured me that it wouldn't affect my share of the money. After some more discussion I agreed to let Bubba in on our little enterprise.

While Ray and I made plans, Sandy finished setting the table and she called us into the dining room.

"What are we having?" I asked.

"T-bones," Sandy replied.

I looked at Ray and couldn't keep from laughing as he struggled to convince me that there was no correlation. Nevertheless it was a funny coincidence.

A few days later I went to Cameron County to see how the tank mods were coming along. Wally had installed the 210-gallon aluminum tank and the 250-gallon bladder as planned. He had about 50 gallons of fuel in each and had installed an electric boost pump from a DC-3 as a transfer pump. He'd placed the boost pump on the floor between the two pilot's seats, with all the hoses and wiring lying loosely about. The bladder tank had a manual bung-style hand pump attached to it for transferring fuel to the aluminum tank.

"James will be here later tonight and wants you to take him to Wichita Falls," Wally said. "That'd be a good test flight. You should be able to round-trip it without taking on fuel."

Wally was right. With the wing tanks full and a hundred gallons in the cabin tanks I'd be able to make it with plenty of reserve. We could fly for an hour and a half and then have over an hour to transfer fuel into the wings. I figured we could empty the aluminum tank and test the manual pump before getting to Wichita Falls.

James wasn't a pilot, and in his mid-sixties was too old to be crawling across fuel tanks to pump fuel. He didn't seem to mind my suggestion that I set the autopilot and leave him alone in the cockpit while I shimmied back to stroke the pump handle. I only needed to be back there long enough to test the system.

James showed up shortly after sundown. As darkness set in we took off for Wichita Falls. The smell of aviation fuel was a little strong inside the airplane and we were both concerned. Since the airplane interior was unpressurized, I pulled the vent window open to evacuate some of the fumes. It helped for a while.

After an hour of flying through the dark Texas night I thought I'd give the transfer pump a try. I grabbed a handful of loose wires and located the makeshift bundle that held the toggle switch. I adjusted the position of the pump to be sure that none of the hoses were kinked, and with one simple flip of a switch, the pump whirred to life. Things seemed to be working well.

James and I sat for a minute, anticipating a successful transfer . . . when suddenly a loud *pop* and flash of light filled the dark cockpit. At first I was stunned but knew right away what had happened. I looked down at the pump lying between us and saw that the wiring was smoldering.

I grabbed the switch and cut the power. Wally had direct-wired the old boost pump without the use of a *Cannon* type connector. He'd soldered the wires directly inside the housing and then filled the cavity with silicone. Evidently the hardened silicone had caused a short.

I looked over at James. He was clinging to the glare shield in front of us and was staring out the front window. He'd undergone heart surgery several months before, and I worried that this sudden jolt of adrenaline might have caused a blip in the ol' ticker.

"James, are you okay?" I asked. "James?"

At first he didn't respond. Then, still clutching the glare shield, he turned his head and looked at me.

"Are we still alive?" he said.

"I think so."

"I didn't sign up for this," he said.

I reached down and grabbed the pump. It was still very hot. I turned on the cockpit floodlight and raised the pump into view. All of the silicone had been blown out of the plug and the wires were badly burnt. James stared at it.

"You're not going to turn that thing back on, are you?"

"No," I said. "Do you think I'm crazy?"

"I think I'm crazy for coming along," he replied.

I set the pump down and checked my wing tank gauges. All was well; I'd just have to take on fuel in Wichita Falls for the return trip. That meant I'd need to allow a lineman near the airplane. Thankfully, it was dark so there was little chance he'd notice anything unusual about our little Queen Air.

James and I were soon laughing about the whole incident. The situation had been completely out of our control. The problem was born back at Cameron County and consummated the moment I hit the switch. Evacuating the fumes just before turning the pump on was just a coincidental act. But it may have made the difference between our landing safely in northern Texas and plummeting to Earth in a burning airplane. With a hundred gallons of highly flammable aviation fuel sloshing around in a makeshift system, we were very lucky indeed.

I dropped James off in Wichita Falls and arrived at Cameron County at 1:30 in the morning. The next day Wally discovered the burnt pump and fuel still in the tanks. He could see what had happened and imagined the whole scene pretty accurately. By the end of that day we had a brand new pump installed, with a proper connector and wiring harness. Wally was also able to install an additional vent to keep the fumes to a minimum. The new pump was designed as a fuel transfer pump with all the safety features engineered in.

Now all we had to do was conduct another test flight.

CHAPTER 24

IN THE TRAP

OR NOW WE DECIDED to concentrate on the aluminum tank and transferring fuel from it, and add the rubber bladder later. Wally removed the bladder and mounted the electric fuel pump on the front side of the aluminum tank. All of the ground tests worked fine but he wanted to test the contraption during flight.

The next morning I got a call from Bobby. He said that the Queen Air was ready and that Wally wanted me to fly it. Technically, Bobby still owned the Queen Air. He'd leased it to us as a Jamaican plane but we wanted to make some shorter-range Mexican hauls in it before sending it too far out over the water. We'd had trouble with the fuel transferring system from the start, and that's why we replaced it with the Twin Bonanza for the first Jamaica flight. The Twin Bonanza only required the single aluminum tank. That system had some bugs in it but the problems were minor and easily corrected.

While talking to Bobby on the phone I asked him if Wally was available.

"He's not here right now," said Bobby. "He left and won't be back until after lunch. Just come out and you can fly it."

"Have Wally call me when he gets back," I said, and hung up.

I'd learned a couple of things about our activity in South Texas. We had to be careful about making our flights too visible. We were engaged in serious criminal activity, and drawing any attention wasn't wise. I knew that Wally wanted to be present whenever one of his birds was out on a test flight. So I wanted to talk to him personally before making any moves in the Queen Air.

Early that afternoon Wally called. He told me that everything was ready for a test flight but there wasn't any hurry. He said that I could get it done any time during the next couple of days.

"Just take it up for about an hour and drain the tank into the wings," he said. "I want to make sure the vents are working."

"Maybe I'll come out tomorrow morning," I said.

"Whatever you'd like to do. I'll be out here around ten tomorrow. If you get here before I do, go ahead and take her up. She's all ready to go."

Later that afternoon I received another call from Bobby.

"Are you coming out?" he asked.

"I was going to be out tomorrow morning," I said.

"Well, I've been waiting here all afternoon," said Bobby. "I want to be here when you test fly it."

"Can't it wait until tomorrow?"

"I've got to go to Austin tomorrow. I think you should fly it today."

Wally had gone home but gave me the go-ahead. So, wanting to please everyone, I agreed to come out and test the system. I told Bobby that I wouldn't be able to get out there until after 5 p.m. He didn't object and told me that he'd meet me on the ramp.

When I arrived at the airport Bobby was waiting in his car. He told me that there was about twenty-five gallons of fuel in the aluminum tank and that the wings were full.

"Why don't you take me to Austin?" Bobby said. "You can drop me off and see your friend Jake."

I hadn't seen Jake since he and his girlfriend Cheri had moved there from Harlingen.

"That sounds like a good idea," I said.

By the time we got to Austin it would be dark so I figured we wouldn't draw too much attention. I figured Bobby was just looking for a free ride. I went inside the hangar office and called Jake. I told him I'd be in Austin at about 7 p.m., so we made dinner plans.

Bobby and I got into the airplane and took off. I climbed to about 6,500 feet and headed north. I'd burn off the wings all the way to Austin, and then test the system on the return flight later that evening.

About an hour and a half later we were at the Robert Mueller Municipal Airport in Austin. I parked the Queen Air in a dark corner of the parking ramp leased by Rhondelle Aviation, a small fixed base operator and flight training school. Jake and Cheri were waiting for me on the other side of the chain link fence. Bobby had a ride waiting for him; he didn't say anything, didn't thank me for the lift but just got in the car and drove off. He would have to find his own way back.

Jake knew of a good Texas steak house. He, Cheri and I had a great dinner together. We returned to the airport at 9 p.m. Jake and Cheri were eager to see the Queen Air so I lowered the door of the aircraft and escorted them up the stairs into the plane. We crouched in the back and I went forward to get a flashlight. Jake wanted to go for a quick ride. I explained to him that there was only the one extra seat next to me in the cockpit.

"That's okay," Cheri said. "I can sit back here on the floor."

I didn't think a quick flight would do any harm since we were just going to go around the patch with a brief spin over the city of Austin. I helped Jake into the copilot seat and went to the back to get Cheri situated. I closed the cabin door, crawled to the front, and flipped the battery master switch on. (I always left the switches for the rotating beacon and navigation lights in the on position so when I hit the master everything lit up inside the plane and out.)

At that point four vehicles—including two fully equipped police cars—sprang out of nowhere and surrounded the airplane. I was stunned and wondered what I'd done to prompt this surprise. I had no dope onboard and, except for flying with the unapproved fuel tank, I hadn't made any illegal trips with the Queen Air.

The officers jumped out of their patrol cars, pointed their guns at us, and demanded we exit the plane immediately. I waved my hands in the air.

"Okay!" I said. "We're coming out!"

I crawled to the back and opened the door. Two uniformed and two plainclothes officers stood at the bottom of the entry door. One of the plainclothes officers asked me to step off the plane and turn around with my hands in the air. The two uniformed officers took Jake and Cheri aside and questioned them. Meanwhile the plainclothes guys patted me down for weapons. One of them introduced himself as Bob Nesvick, a narcotics investigator with the Texas Department of Public Safety. He asked me to join him in his car. As soon as I stepped away from the plane two more plainclothes officers scurried up the air stairs into the Queen Air. They switched on their flashlights and began to search the interior of the airplane. A uniformed officer stood guarding the entry.

As I got into the passenger seat of Bob's car, I heard one of the officers in the plane shout, "We've got residue!"

"What did he mean by that?" I asked.

"He found evidence of a controlled substance," said Bob. "Now why don't you hand me your driver's license, pilot's certificate and medical certificate—and tell me just where you dropped your load."

"What?" I said. "There's no load, no way. I was just out for a test flight."

I saw Jake and Cheri being led back to the security gate, where they parted company with the officers, got in their car, and drove off. Obviously the investigators were after me and me alone. I suddenly realized I'd slipped and let my guard down and made a stupid mistake. I never should have agreed to bring Bobby here in the first place.

As Bob copied details off my identification paperwork, I saw the other officers exit the airplane. They were empty-handed. Meanwhile, Bob asked me a bunch of basic questions.

"Where've you been this evening?" he said.

"Just out with my friends having dinner," I said.

"Where were you before you landed in Austin?"

"The Cameron County airport near Port Isabel," I answered. "I live in Harlingen and was hired to test-fly the airplane."

"Why were you test-flying it?"

"They were getting ready to export the plane and wanted to make sure it would make it to the next fuel stop."

"Who owns the airplane?" said Bob.

"I really don't know," I said. "All I know is that their mechanic called me and asked if I could test-fly it for them. I do pilot services for several people around the valley. I'm just trying to build time."

"Do you know who you're working for here?"

"I'm not sure. I barely know anyone but the mechanic."

Bob nodded. "What's his name?"

"I'm sorry," I said, "but I'm nervous and can't remember it at the moment."

Bob continued to examine my licenses. The address on my driver's license was a Harlingen address, but my pilot's license listed my parents' address in the Midwest. It made for some believable confusion and lent credibility to my explanation.

Bob looked down at me as I sat in the passenger seat of his car. "Stay here," he said.

He walked to the plane and talked to the officers who had inspected the interior, along with the officers who'd questioned Jake and Cheri. I couldn't hear what they were saying but a couple of them held their hands with their palms upward as if they were confused. I began to feel better about the whole "residue" thing. Perhaps it was an attempt to coerce an incriminating statement from me. I knew there wasn't anything on the plane. I'd taken it to Mexico a few times with electronics stuffed in the back and had cleaned it out a couple of times. But marijuana was never any part of the cargo—at least not yet. If the plane had ever been used for dope smuggling it had been thoroughly swept of any residue. I never saw a speck of the stuff.

Bob returned and handed the contents of my wallet back to me. He continued to take notes on a clipboard while other officers looked over the rest of the plane. I was fairly certain they hadn't linked me to Ray or any of our recent activities. But at that moment all I wanted to do was go home. There were no FAA inspectors around, and aside from Bob and a few others from the Texas Department of Public Safety, all I saw were two highway patrol cars.

Bob got in the car with me.

"I want to talk to you," he said. "I know that you've flown for these people before but I don't think you know who these guys really are. Let me tell you a little about who it is you're involved with."

255

I was starting to think I'd successfully managed to convince Bob that I was just a fledgling pilot that worked part-time for Ray. I was hoping this would end with nothing more than a lecture from this policeman about making good choices in the future.

"A little while back," Bob said, "these guys sent a plane to Jamaica. They were dope runners trying to bring a load back in a twin-engine airplane."

Uh-oh. Somehow Bob knew about the whole Jamaica deal.

"Anyway, the guy flew to Jamaica and picked up a load of dope. But he didn't make it. He turned around and crashed back on the airstrip he'd left from. Reports are that he didn't survive."

"Have you ever been to Jamaica?" Bob said.

"Yeah, I went there on vacation once. It's a nice place."

Something told me he wasn't asking about my leisure travel. I hoped I was wrong.

"Oh yeah, what part?" said Bob. "My wife and I spent some time in Montego Bay. Have you ever been there?"

"No, only Kingston," I answered.

I wanted to get Bob off the subject. Of course I was lying. I'd been all over that country on scouting missions before my fateful flight.

"Kingston, huh?" he said. "Yeah, I've been there too. Have you ever been out to Portland Point?"

I was confused. Why were Bob and I exchanging vacation details? I'd never heard of Portland Point.

"Portland Point?" I said. "I don't know where that is."

"It's where the plane turned around," he said. "He didn't make it very far."

A car pulled up just outside the fence. Bob got out and walked through the gate and approached the passenger's side. Had I convinced him I was just an innocent victim who'd been mistaken for someone else?

Bob spent a long time talking to someone in the car. Meanwhile the activity around the airplane had subsided. Three plainclothes officers stood by the door, chatting. Bob returned to his car and got in. I was hopeful he'd say something like, "I'm sorry for the inconvenience. You're free to go."

The car on the other side of the fence backed out and drove away. Bob opened a folder and pulled out a slim laminated card. Looking at it, he began to read:

"You have the right to remain silent. Anything you say can and will be used against you in a court of law. . . ."

CHAPTER 25
ANOTHER CHANGE

I WAS ARRESTED AND HELD for questioning. I spent one night in the care of Austin City and was transferred to the County for three nights. After a preliminary court appearance I was charged with conspiracy to transport and transferred to the Federal Correctional Facility in Bastrop, Texas.

My life had changed abruptly. I called my parents and informed them of my predicament although I never completely disclosed all the details. Dad agreed to let me deal with this on my own. I had access to a phone and called Ray almost daily. He'd hired an attorney and within two weeks I was out on my own recognizance. The conditions of my release required that I not leave the county without special permission. The authorities granted me three days to return to Harlingen and gather enough clothes and personal items to last a month. I had a lot of "loose ends" back in Harlingen and had to make arrangements there for another extended period of absence.

Then there was Kara. We'd become good friends during the two and a half years we'd known each other. She knew what I'd been doing and never tried to discourage me in any way. I think she was a little intrigued to be dating someone with my lifestyle; she was attracted to the "bad boy."

Kara had gotten her private pilot's license and we shared in that common interest. We often rented a Bellanca Citabria, a tandem two-seat tailwheel airplane with aerobatic capabilities. Sometimes we'd fly over to South Padre Island and land on a secluded part of the beach to relax in the South Texas sun. We were very close and shared in many youthful joys and tragedies alike.

We had experimented with a variety of drugs. At the time I favored pot and barbiturates while Kara was attracted to cocaine. We had plenty of everything we wanted and never worried about the consequences of addiction. But addicted we would become, and ironically that was the wedge that eventually drove us apart.

Although we had so much in common, Kara was always cautious about any commitment in our relationship. I never blamed her for that. She'd moved on since my absence and had taken up residence with another man whom she'd been interested in for some time. They were eventually married but had a strange and stormy relationship that I never understood. She conquered her drug addiction and had become happy and healthy, contributing much to life. Her husband was still caught in the narcotics trap, deeply entangled in self-indulgence and dealing.

One night in a fit of rage, he beat her unconscious in their bed and set the trailer home on fire. Kara died in the blaze. It was some of the most painful news I'd ever endured. I still think of Kara and her family from time to time.

While I was in the Valley I also visited Ray. We sat on his porch talking about my arrest. When I told him that Officer Nesvick had described the flight to Jamaica in detail, Ray sat quietly staring at the floor.

"He didn't know that I was the pilot," I said, "but he did give an accurate account of when the flight landed and what time it had taken off. He even knew where I had turned around during the engine trouble. They must have been following the airplane."

"They were following you alright," Ray said. "We had a suspicion that might happen."

"How did they know?"

"We're dealing with an informant, a rat," he said. "It's probably a blessing in disguise that we got caught with an empty airplane."

"Not so great for me," I said. "There was an illegal fuel tank in that thing, you know."

"Don't worry, Bill. I'll take care of all your legal costs. Our lawyer has all the details and he's sure he can get you off on a lesser charge. They don't have any proof about the dope."

I returned to Austin a couple of days later and moved in with my friend Jake, who had a small cabin on Lake Travis. I thought about fleeing many times. I sought advice from all of my friends. No one thought that running away was a good option. Jake did have a plan to escape to Mexico and live with a friend he knew there, but he only offered it to me as a last resort.

During an appointment with my lawyer I learned that things back in the Rio Grande Valley were not going well. Whoever was tipping off the authorities was closer than we thought. Ray was arrested a few days later on possession of a controlled substance and conspiracy to transport.

"Ray had two kilos of cocaine in the trunk of his car," my lawyer told me.

"I don't know anything about cocaine," I said. "We were only into the marijuana."

"Ray wanted me to let you know that he was set up. He doesn't want you to worry about him, though. We can make a deal in your case, but Ray is another matter."

Everything I'd become accustomed to was gone. My court date was set and I was required to remain in Travis County until that time.

It was a radical change to my lifestyle. I had lost control. The calamities in Jamaica and in Mexico were clear signs that I had wandered carelessly in the wrong direction. For some reason I ignored all those warning signs. It's not that I didn't see them, but I simply refused to believe them. It was the culmination of habitual recklessness that I simply didn't understand. I felt helpless as my life crumbled before my eyes.

Everything in my past was now coming to light. I felt guilty. I was a *bandito*—a criminal—and soon I would have to answer for the choices I had made.

I spent my days alone at the cabin while Jake went to his part-time job in a video store near town. For a while I found comfort in drugs and alcohol. After I returned from Jamaica I began using cocaine regularly and would often counter its effects with barbiturates. Soon I became dependent on codeine as well. I would spend hours sitting on the front porch of the cabin overlooking Lake Travis, staring in a hyper trance at the ripples on the water. The cocaine emboldened my haughty attitude and the barbiturates sent me tumbling back into depression. I was caught in a vicious cycle of highs and lows that was ripping from me my will to live.

Having Jake around didn't help matters much. He too was a drug user and had access to pharmaceuticals anytime he wanted. His father was a doctor—an internal medicine specialist—and Jake knew how to impersonate the old man and call in his own prescriptions.

For Jake the drug use was just entertainment. For me it was a serious addiction. At first the drugs distracted me from my problems. But the more depressed I became, the more drugs I took, and the more I thought about putting an end to the raging tempest that had become my daily life.

One late afternoon while Jake was away at work, I sat on the porch with his loaded .357 Magnum in my lap. I thought about taking a stroll down to the water's edge, turning and facing the cabin, and blowing my brains out, falling backward into the lake. It seemed easy and not too messy, since my body would be washed away in the cool lake water.

I didn't have the guts to shoot myself, but I thought about it constantly. I figured that sooner or later I would find the courage.

The narcotics took a toll on my psyche as well. While battling depression I had bouts of paranoia and hallucinations. Every noise and snapping twig I heard in the woods was a narcotics agent moving in for a closer look. They were all after me. The only reason they hadn't taken me down was because I was armed with a wide assortment of pistols and semi-automatic rifles. It would have been a blood bath—mine.

But it was all in my imagination. Fantasy and reality intertwined. The constant paranoia made it difficult to distinguish between the two. I was falling and there was no one to catch me. Even Jake began to notice my detachment from reality. He cut back on his own drug use and encouraged me to do the same.

Unfortunately nothing worked. Between the alcohol, the narcotics and the fact that I was facing jail time, I was spiraling out of control. I'd failed everyone who cared about me. Everything I'd done was for selfish purposes; I never considered the pain I was causing others. I felt sick and wallowed in shame and self-pity. I'd hit bottom. Alone, sitting on the shores of Lake Travis, I truly felt I had no more reason to live.

Late one night I was awakened by a light hitting me in the eyes through my bedroom window. I didn't know whether it was the moon, a star or some planet, but it was so bright I couldn't go back to sleep. The light beamed through the pine trees outside and seemed to wash everything in my room in an eerie, bluish-gray fluorescence.

I tried covering my head with my blanket and pillow but to no avail. Even with my eyes closed and my head buried in the covers the light burned through. I lay there with my eyes wide open. I prayed the light would move on and leave me to return to my darkness, but the beam poured through my window for what felt like hours.

Eventually I was wide awake—sober and fully conscious. I thought about getting up and fixing myself a drink, but instead I continued to lie in bed staring at the light. I felt trapped and totally vulnerable.

Suddenly the hair on my neck and arms stood on end. My head felt clear; I was completely aware of what was happening.

I thought I was dead.

But how could that be? My heart raced, and I still felt the emotion and anxiety that had begun when the light burst through my window. The shadows in my room began to move ever so slowly. I couldn't tell if the light was drifting away or coming closer.

I decided that I was hallucinating. I got out of bed, walked to the window, and looked at the light head-on. I unlatched the windowpanes and swung open the double sash.

The light was still there. I reached out into the cold night sky toward it, spreading my fingers. I pulled my arm in, walked back to my bed and sat down, hanging my head. I began to cry. I was frightened. I had no idea what was happening and felt totally lost and confused.

Something was keeping me in the room because every time I considered fleeing, the thought would vanish as quickly as it came. I couldn't even bring myself to stand up again. I sat there trembling and

263

crying, wishing the light would go away or that I would awake from the nightmare.

Then I thought about all the things I had done in my life. I tried to hide my face as the shame arose in my heart. No matter how hard I tried, I could not hide from the guilt that penetrated every part of my being. With both hands I pressed hard against my face, hoping to find some relief. I could hear the voices of all the people I'd lied to and hurt. All I wanted to do was to go home. Again I prayed that the light would go away and leave me in peace.

As I prayed, something changed. I began to ask for forgiveness. I told God that I was sorry for what I'd done and asked Him to take away my shame as I couldn't bear another ounce of it. I felt remorse over what I'd done with my life, God had always watched over me but I denied His calling. Even in my fumbling, He was there protecting me for some reason. I'd broken His laws and those of man. Justice was about to lock me down until I changed. I knew He was able to show mercy but I didn't know how. I had a lot to learn and needed a teacher. I desperately needed a savior. It was Jesus.

I was shaking. I was crying. Everything that had been locked up inside of me spilled out onto that bedroom floor. It was as if I could see my emotions flowing out of me and across the cold linoleum.

I knew that my time in Texas—and everything I had done there—was over. I begged for a new start. I prayed that if God would see me through this struggle, I'd turn my life over to Him.

I lay down on my pillow and cried myself to sleep.

CHAPTER 26
PILOT FOR THE KING

R ay had been right. In court my lawyer pointed out that I was very young and a very foolish man. He expounded on my zeal for life and potential to contribute to this world in a more positive way.

The federal magistrate agreed. He said that I'd gotten involved with the wrong people. He said that although I was legally an adult, he didn't believe I was old enough or wise enough to keep myself out of trouble.

So much had happened since I'd crossed the boundary between right and wrong that the line had become blurred. The deeper I went, the more I disregarded that line and the less I was bothered by my conscience.

The judge sentenced me to two years' probation. I was required to leave Texas and not return during that period. The judge thought that I could be changed by changing my environment and that if I agreed to return to the Midwest he would rule on a lesser charge in a merciful way.

God had done His part. He orchestrated the events in such a way that I would soon find myself back home in the Midwest, living at my parents' home. He worked through my parents, who showed mercy, patience and forgiveness. Dad was a wise man and he knew I'd strayed from the path of righteousness. I was too ashamed to tell him all that I'd done, but I am certain he knew enough. His main concern was for my future, and in his understanding way he offered me the opportunity to forget my past and look ahead. His capacity for forgiveness was immense. He was one of the greatest encouragers I've ever known. I prayed that I would be a better son and that my days of disappointing him would end.

As I said, God did His part, but would I do mine? The magistrate was right: I was young and foolish. Time would eventually erase my youth, but as for my foolishness, I learned that I had a long way to go. I'd made a promise to God and so far hadn't kept my part of the bargain. Although I was changed, I didn't acknowledge in what ways. I didn't understand that I'd bargained with the creator of the universe. I was incapable of grasping the depth of what had happened. To me God was some old man sitting high in the heavens, waiting to punish anyone who didn't obey him. As far as His daily interaction with His creation I mistakenly thought that once he'd set things in motion he stepped away and became an observer, as if leaving everything to chance. I had no comprehension of His wisdom and power. Nor did I understand the immensity and depth of His love.

I was taught that God was all-powerful and all-knowing, but I never truly understood what that meant. To me eternity was the thought of reaching age forty. I was certain that on that night in the cabin on Lake Travis I'd been visited by an angel or perhaps God himself. But I didn't feel worthy enough to receive what He was offering. In my pitiful state I witnessed only a fraction of His glory. I couldn't grasp His awesome ability to change me.

Throughout my years flying out of Texas God had intervened in my life more than once, and each time I felt different. I know that He rescued me from peril but I didn't know why. I was ungrateful and remained self-centered and prideful. I continued to live as though I had more to do with my existence than the one who gave it to me in the first place.

I gave things time. I spent time with my family; I spent time with myself. Within a few months I was back on my feet, had my head screwed on straight, and vowed to keep my nose clean. It was a dramatic change!

I never questioned the existence of God. I wasn't an atheist and I didn't believe in them anyway. I only lived my life as though God was there for the final chapter and beyond. I never figured he desired to have an active role in my day-to-day existence.

I had a fairly normal childhood but a very different worldview than most. As a child I became aware that I possessed some kind of spiritual gifts. I was the recipient of at least two of these: Prophecy and Wisdom. In 1 Corinthians 12 the apostle Paul speaks of these gifts. The gift of Wisdom is an understanding of God's will and His truth as applied to everyday life. The gift of Prophecy is widely misunderstood. Many believe that its only purpose is to foretell future events. It is often misused in this context. Prophecy may in fact be a forward vision of things to come, but just as in the gift of wisdom it is a confirmation of God's written word. In the church it is exercised in the form of speaking. To prophesy is to speak something into existence. Prophecy is intended to edify Christ's church. Like many of the gifts of the Holy Spirit, prophecy and wisdom cannot be controlled by human action. The Holy Spirit will gently nudge your spirit. It is our prerogative to recognize the unction and act on such an anointing.

I must have been called as a child but I was ignorant to the purpose of His calling. I was aware of His gifting but to me these wonderful abilities were normal and I never thought too much about them. I assumed that everyone had abilities similar to mine. I could know certain things about certain situations. On occasion I could predict events before they happened. In my immaturity I didn't fully understand how using these gifts would annoy my siblings as I would fumble through my prophetic episodes.

Sometimes, while sitting around the living room watching TV I would get up and run to the phone before it started to ring. Another time, while riding in the car I began to sing a song that was popular twenty years before. The next song to be played on the car radio was that song. Normally, that wouldn't be too great of coincidence, but this particular song was popular before I was born and it had long been dropped off of many radio station playlists and rarely made the airwaves.

All through my childhood and well into my adult years little things like that would happen to me. I couldn't control it then and I still never know exactly when the Holy Spirit will reveal something to me now. To this day I am often baffled by my gifts. The most common thing is when I will mention someone's name about three seconds before the telephone rings, and find out that person is calling me.

I've never used my true giftings for pleasure or sport. I never had that kind of control over them. And my nonchalant attitude about them had caused me to take them for granted and not use them for their intended purpose either. Soon after childhood those gifts became dormant inside of me, buried beneath the growing layers of life experiences.

For the next seventeen years I continued to fly. I climbed my way up the professional ladder. I hauled cargo for a few years and eventually landed a job with a major airline. For seventeen years I ignored God and what He'd done for me. For seventeen years I buried the bad times and only talked about the funny episodes I'd had in Mexico. I still wasn't sure why God had spared me.

I settled down, and with a wife and two children I felt that maybe I'd finally found my place in the world. On the surface I was walking the line as an honorable man who kept his commitments and told the truth. I was given responsibilities in which trust was a key factor. I truly wanted to be a new man, but there was always something in me that remained unchanged. I was still wrestling with alcohol and pornography, and I slipped a couple of times and used marijuana again. The drugs and pornography were mostly occasional entertainment but the alcohol had a real hold on me. I'd safely fly my passengers to their destinations, then find the nearest hotel lounge and order a few drinks.

I was trying to fill a void that was growing, creating a gaping chasm inside of me.

The overload of booze started changing me in not-so-subtle ways. A violent streak began to grow stronger. Sure, I'd been in fights during my cargo-hauling days. But most of them were bar scuffles that saw me thrown out of the joint by the bartender, manager, bouncer, or police.

Once, however, I went too far. In a fit of rage I almost sent a man over the third-floor railing of a motel. We'd been drinking heavily and were arguing with each other. We were standing in front of my room with the door closed and my wife and first infant son sleeping inside. I don't remember what the argument was about, but the man paused and began to urinate on my motel room door. I took it as a direct assault on my wife and child . . . and I snapped. I pummeled him and smashed his head against the concrete walkway that overlooked the swimming pool. As the rage took over I seemed to gain supernatural strength. After the man slumped to the floor unconscious, I picked him up and started to throw him over the black iron railing.

Here again, God intervened. For some reason I stopped just before making the final push. I saw a vision of the man's limp body lying broken on the concrete below. The vision was so clear I thought it was real. I quickly pulled the man back over the railing and retreated to my room, leaving him to recover from his beating.

The next morning I was sitting at breakfast alone in the motel restaurant. The man I had almost killed walked in. He was badly hung over and hadn't cleaned himself up yet. His hair was heavily matted with dried blood. His cheeks, lips and forehead were black and blue, and one eye had swollen closed. He walked toward me slowly and sat down across from me in the booth. I couldn't believe that he wanted anything to do with me. Maybe he wanted to resume our argument from the night before. Maybe he was looking for revenge.

He looked at me and forced a smile through his split lip.

"Some night, huh?" he said.

This beaten man painfully sipped on a glass of ice water. He looked at me.

"Oh well, no hard feelings, okay?" he added.

I felt humbled. It was a moment of incredible grace from a fellow human being. I felt terrible for what I had done. This man knew that I'd taken my anger out on him, yet sitting there in his pain and bloody brokenness he found it in his heart to forgive me. He seemed to have a better understanding of my human faults than I did.

Unfortunately that episode still didn't change me. I still had a lot of rage inside.

I had another physical outburst when I was scolding my son, who was then about nine years old. He had teased his younger sister to the point of a major scuffle and I'd asked him to stop. When he continued

269

and the noise and crying intensified, I raced down the stairs into our basement playroom, picked him up, and threw him across the room.

Fortunately he landed on the sofa. I was lucky: I hadn't aimed at anything. I just wanted him to stop.

My son wasn't injured but he was frightened. The look on his face made me realize I'd driven a wedge between us. It was that incident that gave me a clearer picture of what I was capable of doing to other people . . . and to my own family.

It took nearly injuring my son to convince me that I had a serious problem.

Alcohol was my first enemy to conquer. I tried on my own power to give it up for thirty days. It didn't seem that difficult and I actually succeeded . . . or at least I thought I had. At the end of that period I felt that I was finally getting things under control, but I soon learned a lesson on how a worldly substance can imprison you. Soon my alcoholism came back, and with a vengeance.

I was hurting the people I loved. I was back on a path of destruction, and now I was taking others with me.

I had to do something before I hurt anyone seriously.

I love my wife and children dearly. They are my bond with a life of sanity. I viewed my family life as evidence that I was a new man. Before I married my wife I'd made a promise to myself that I would never lie to her. When we met I fell in love with her the moment I laid eyes on her. There was nothing that was going to stand in my way and I couldn't live without her. I still feel that way over twenty years later. She is my lover, my spiritual partner, my soul mate, my best friend. I know beyond a doubt that our union was arranged by God. He'd given me a vision of the two of us embracing one another. It was one of the times I used my gifts in a pleasing way to Him. In doing so we've been blessed with four beautiful children.

When I finally got my life together I was nearly forty years old. I could hardly believe I'd made it that far. I began to walk obediently and was totally delivered from alcohol and many other things that would have hindered my newfound relationship. I was changed beyond a doubt and could finally see clearly the things that mattered most in this world.

All I had to do was finally realize that I cannot walk alone and that my time here amongst all who read these words is temporary. We are all spiritual beings who are given an opportunity to live on this earth. Beyond our moral obligations to one another we have a final destiny. God wants us to come home. He wants us to love Him of our own choosing; He will not force us to. He has given us His Son as the propitiation for a sinful nature that we cannot deny or escape without Him. Of all the truths I've learned there is one verse that stands out and rings true in my spirit. It is found in the Gospel of John, chapter 14 verse 6. The New King James version says it like this: Jesus said to him, "I am the way, the truth, and the life. No one comes to the Father except through Me." Having the spiritual gift of Wisdom lays open that truth in such a way that it is not only enlightening but incredibly redeeming as well. There is incredible freedom in knowing that truth alone.

I still fly and have had many wonderful experiences in doing so. I realized that one of my God-given gifts was the skill I've been using for over thirty years. I love to fly.

God gave me a unique set of skills and I've put them to good use. Sure, I've had a few tense moments here and there, but my reckless days are long over. As a pilot I'm responsible for many lives. That requires maturity as well as skill, and I do my best to fulfill that responsibility well.

Some people might say that I've just been lucky. But those who are closest to me, and know me best, know as I do that God had his hand on the flight controls with me the whole time.

As a pilot I've served my fellow man. I hope I've had a positive spiritual influence on some of my passengers in some way. I'd like to think that my life as it is now is a testimony to what God wants and what He can do, and how much He loves us. I know I still fall short at times, but I'm still here and able to ask Him to forgive me when I fail.

The best part is that He always comes through, and I'm learning to trust Him more with each new day.

I've acknowledged and thanked Him for His presence throughout all my journeys and adventures. As I leave my past behind, I look forward to the future and the promise of something much greater and permanent. Just as it is written in the book of Revelations I can see a new horizon where there will be no more death, nor sorrow, nor crying, where God will wipe away every tear from their eyes. He also tells us that if we thirst for a deeper meaning to this life, He will give freely of the fountain of the water of life.

God desires to have a personal relationship with each of us. There is nothing we can or need to do to make ourselves acceptable to Him. He will take us just as we are.

I was speaking with a man about coming to Christ. He told me that as soon as he got his life together he would start going to church and all that stuff. I felt the Spirit move in me and explained my thoughts to him in this way:

> You have a dental appointment. Before going to the dentist you go into your bathroom and brush and floss like you've never done before. We all do it. You want the dentist to think that you are good and obedient in your oral hygiene habits. And if you're lucky the dentist will comment on how nice your teeth look and how well you care for them. But the dentist knows better. Your eyes are not placed in such a way that you can see the things the dentist can see. At least mine aren't. You are blind to the hidden scum and faults in your own mouth. It's very hard for you to believe that you couldn't know this. After all, it's your mouth. The dentist might encourage you and make you feel good, but he will finish the job you so miserably started. He'll take you anyway you are, foul breath included.

God is just like that. We shouldn't think that we can somehow make ourselves presentable to Him. That's His job. The good news is that He patiently waits until we figure that out on our own. Hopefully we all will see and understand our desperate need for Him to save us before it's too late. He will take us just as we are: dirty, miserable, deplorable, lonely, empty, wanting and broken. Even if we think we've got it together, remember the story of the dentist and how we're sometimes blind to the truth of how we really are. Remember that all the brushing and flossing in our own lives has little to no effect on what truly lies beneath our shiny surface. Yes, because He loves us unconditionally, He will take us anyway.

Someone once referred to me as a "wild seed." I never considered that a bad thing. Confident and strong willed; my youthful zeal for life hid a flippant disregard for the consequences of my actions, especially when it came to my personal safety. There was something inside of me that craved adventure. It was like a demon, taunting and tempting me to take greater and greater risks, relentlessly pushing me to go farther and do more. The craving was so intense that I easily rationalized my risky behavior. My cavalier attitude also led me to compromise many of my moral convictions, all to satisfy that lingering demon inside me.

As a youth, mortality wasn't part of my vocabulary. Like many on their journey to adulthood, I knew no boundaries when it came to death. My lack of experience and wisdom disabled my ability to recognize the warning signs of impending danger that could lead to my demise. Whether it was a case of severe over confidence or simple foolishness, my cavalier attitude nearly got me killed.

Considering the recklessness of my lifestyle I have come to the conclusion that luck had little part in my escaping destruction. I've come to realize that an omnipotent God was watching over me. I've learned to appreciate His limitless abilities, and I give Him the glory for protecting me along the way. I am undeniably the recipient of undeserving grace.

In life I've navigated through the darkest of night skies; through raging storms when fear and doubt had opportunity to take hold. Even though at times I would fall to the attacks of this world, He was always right there beside me, guiding me through, to new destinations.

Life is a gift and I am a grateful recipient. I've been gifted with the ability to learn and the freedom to pursue the skills of my calling. So I will use what He has given me according to His design. Through aviation I can bring light to those still struggling and stumbling in the dark.

Flying airplanes is what He's called me to do.

I will continue to be a pilot for the King.

—*Billy Hawklyn*

www.ingramcontent.com/pod-product-compliance
Lightning Source LLC
Chambersburg PA
CBHW020611260626
47157CB00003B/970